Advance Praise for
The Bridges We Will Build

"This book reminds us of the ways women negotiate the intersections of their lives. It is accessible even as it crosses into important complications in the lives of its main characters. Enjoy!"

Dr. amina wadud, American Muslim theologian, Professor Emeritus of Islamic Studies at Virginia Commonwealth University

"In this particular moment in history, with deep rifts as well as a growing consciousness of our interconnectedness as humans, *The Bridges We Will Build* offers us a compelling vision into the possibility of true solidarity. The author's ability to use narrative as a way to tell authentic stories and to describe the human condition, whether of struggle, pain, loss, joy, or love, makes us believe that communities can, in fact, transcend socially constructed barriers towards a recognition of our common humanity. This book is nothing short of a timely and hopeful gift to us in these uncertain times."

Shabnam Koirala Azad, Dean of School of Education at University of San Francisco, Professor of International and Multicultural Education

"*The Brides We Will Build* is a story that encourages empathy toward the refugee experience. In writing it, Kacie creates characters that bring the reader closer to becoming compassionate and understanding of refugees struggling to assimilate into a new culture. The number of forcibly displaced people living both internally and externally to their countries of origin, forced to flee their homes as a result of persecution, conflict, or generalized violence, has nearly doubled in the last 10 years. This story is a reminder that we have the power to end this hatred and that power resides in our actions to confront racism and injustice themselves."

Matilde Simas, Founder of Capture Humanity, Visual Journalist

"*The Bridges We Will Build* is an insightful, well-written book about finding friendship in a world of conflict, misunderstanding, displacement and intolerance. It is a hopeful story of unlikely friends who meet in an American city and grapple with deep questions about loss, mourning, love and how to live a meaningful life. This book renewed my faith that love and human connection can overcome even the most destructive forms of trauma and prejudice."
Christopher White, Professor of Religion, Vassar

"In the process of reading this book, I found myself at times weeping, at times smiling, and at times overwhelmed with a strong mix of emotions—trauma and pain. I was reminded of how devastating the effects of war and violence are, and who refugees are. The novel is captivating, and Kacie's description of events is real, focused and appealing. If I didn't know her personally, I would've thought she were "one-of-us"—an immigrant, a refugee too. My gratitude toward her understanding of the plight of refugees and how vividly and delicately she describes it all, is immense. The novel is a work of fiction but includes elements of real-life stories, and I appreciate Kacie's honesty describing Sherry, the character based loosely on her own lived experiences."
Theresa Samuel-Boko, Marriage and Family Therapist and former Director of Adult and Families Refugee Resettlement Program for Catholic Charities of San Jose

"Kacie takes you on a voyage full of love, friendship, bravery and acceptance. In the process, the reader is challenged to step out of their comfort zone. The characters in the novel: students, teachers and staff consisting of refugees, immigrants, and Americans representing more than forty different countries, are the people who make up the community at the Unity School.

The ideas central to the novel are reminiscent of Martin Luther King's words when he said 'Love is creative and redemptive. Love builds up and unites; hate tears down and destroys. The aftermath of the love method is reconciliation and creation of the beloved community.'"
Hibo Hassan, Teacher of French at GLOBE Academy and former educator at the International Community School, the school which inspired the fictional Unity School central to this novel

The Bridges We Will Build

Kacie LeCompte Renfro

Modern History Press

Ann Arbor, MI

ISBN 978-1-61599-657-5 paperback
ISBN 978-1-61599-658-2 hardcover
ISBN 978-1-61599-659-9 eBook

Audiobook editions from Audible.com and iTunes

Library of Congress Cataloging-in-Publication Data

Names: Renfro, Kacie LeCompte, 1981- author.
Title: The bridges we will build / Kacie LeCompte Renfro.
Description: Ann Arbor, MI : Modern History Press, [2022] | Summary: "Follows the four women of various countries of origin and drastically different life experiences, refugees and Americans, as they come together at The Unity School, a charter school for refugee and American children. Here, they rediscover the hope and inspiration that seemed lost to them before"-- Provided by publisher.
Identifiers: LCCN 2022006527 (print) | LCCN 2022006528 (ebook) | ISBN 9781615996582 (hardcover) | ISBN 9781615996575 (trade paperback) | ISBN 9781615996599 (ebook)
Subjects: LCGFT: Novels.
Classification: LCC PS3618.E5757 B75 2022 (print) | LCC PS3618.E5757 (ebook) | DDC 813/.6--dc23/eng/20220302
LC record available at https://lccn.loc.gov/2022006527
LC ebook record available at https://lccn.loc.gov/2022006528

Modern History Press   www.ModernHistoryPress.com
5145 Pontiac Trail   info@ModernHistoryPress.com
Ann Arbor, MI 48105

Tollfree 888-761-6268 (USA/CAN/PR)
Fax 734-664-6861
Distributed by Ingram (USA/CAN/AU), Bertram's Books (UK/EU)

Dedication

To my mother – my first and constant example of empathy and compassion.

❧ 1 ❧

Hanan

Death, she thinks, *this is the freedom I long for.*

Shifting her weight from right foot to left, arms drooping lifelessly at her sides, all that remains to be seen is the water, that endless expanse of life and death, sustenance and deprivation. Picturing the remnants of boat and bodies, the parts that never made it to shore, remaining forever in its depths, she doesn't shiver but stands there stoically.

Unaware of how long she has been standing there, is the silent acknowledgement that time is of no consequence. She doesn't care. The life pulsing inside of her died on that beach eleven months, thirteen days, five hours and six minutes ago. Glancing at the watch on her right wrist to confirm, knowledge of that moment being the beginning and end of whatever life remains for her to live from now on has been accepted. It is all that defines her, anchoring her, tethering her to the hell this world has become.

The car engines starts, signaling to her it is time to go. Baris had agreed to take her here one last time. He is the incarnation of his name, its meaning, *peaceful.* His mother had correctly predicted what his nature would be and labeled it accordingly. Despite all the carnage, all the bodies, the death, disease and decay; despite the hopelessness of the refugee camp where the UN has stationed him and the approaching winter, he remains hopeful, jovial. He is kind and so he humors her, pities her. They all do.

There are no waves, just the slow and consistent motion of sea meeting land. The only fracture in the silence is its soft lapping sound, water against pebble. With no shoes on, despite the rocky shore beneath her feet, it isn't painful, just smooth and hard.

The water has worn down the rocks that now make this beach, taking jagged chunks of a far-off cliff and wearing them down over time, bringing them here to their final resting place. The air is cool and dry, typical of the Mediterranean mornings she is now accustomed to.

Tomorrow she leaves for America, alone. She was notified by United Nations High Commission for Refugees of her acceptance as a refugee two weeks ago. She was ready then and she is ready now. With nothing to pack beyond the clothes she is wearing, and no one to accompany her, she is free to go anywhere, anytime. That is the word the UN officer used when he told her of her updated status, *free*.

"Hanan," Baris had said in a rushed fervor when she informed him. His Greek-accented Arabic something she still spent time interpreting. "You are free! You have been admitted to the U.S. Someday you will be a citizen. You are free!"

The irony of that word, ringing in her ears every time he used it, made her want to choke him. In that moment she nodded complacently, passively, as he stared at her incredulously. "Hanan, do you know what this means?" he implored. She looked on, at him, through him, on and on.

She accepted this freedom, along with its chains. That is all this life represents for her now. Bearing the chains that hold her to this earth, she waits for the sweet blessing of death to call her name.

Strange that she would choose to come here, rather than the cemetery. Perhaps it is because here she can at least feel something. The horror of what came to pass is the only thing that makes her feel alive, the only thought she responds to. She does not need to see the three headstones, lined in a row, one large and two small, before leaving, because the truth is she never left this beach and never will. Regardless of where she physically resides, her soul will stand here, waiting to be called by Allah to join them at last.

Baris honks the horn twice, her final call. The grey water and darkening sky confirm what is already in her mind; there is nothing left to be said or done. Trudging up the beach toward the road, she climbs into the van, and rides toward the promise of nothingness that is her life without them.

⚜ 2 ⚜

Sherry

She was born into a life of privilege and she knows this. This is why she wants to offer up her life to service: service to the poor, neglected and forgotten. It cannot be done in just any way though. It has to be achieved in an international context; she knows this too. She has known this about herself since her earliest memory. Sherry was three and living in a comfortable upper middle class home with her mother, father, and older sister in South San Francisco, California. What she was doing before and what she did after, Sherry has no recollection, but she remembers that moment when her child eyes were opened. The year was 1984 and Ethiopia was suffering from yet another famine. Growing up, parents were famous for guilt tripping their children into eating everything on their plates with, "There are starving children in Africa." Unlike most youth who rolled their eyes at yet another strategic attempt by their parents to harness compliance through the telling of over-embellished truths and cliché wisdoms, Sherry honored this, because she had seen it. The image of a little boy: black, bloated, skin dry and patchy, her age or maybe younger, staring into the camera, while flies, so many flies, tormented him, crawling into the corners of his eyes, up his nose, and into his ears. Sherry remembered this face featured on the evening news that night and carried it with her always.

She thought of that face while drunk in some club in college. She cried about her guilt for not doing something sooner to the one boy who she thought would understand, but it didn't help. All that would ease this pounding in her heart would be to go to them. She wasn't sure who "them" was yet or where they were, but she knew her destiny would remain unobtainable here, in her boujee upper middle-class life. She declared her readiness to leave it all behind in search of this one truth that was more important than all the others to anyone who would listen, and they did. They admired her: friends, family, teachers...but deep down they were scared. *What would happen to a*

3

little blonde-haired, blue-eyed girl in the heart of Africa, they thought to themselves. *Nothing good.*

In college, Sherry had friends, so many friends. She would jokingly declare that they were the popular ones, but secretly she believed it was true. Unlike high school, Sherry enjoyed college. In fact, she loved it and believed these were four of the best years of her life. She needed to experience what it meant to "belong" just once before throwing it all to the wind, loving it but letting it go in pursuit of that shining truth just within her reach.

People talked about the Peace Corps in relation to her truth and thought that it might be a good way of finding it, but Sherry wasn't sure. While she was ready to give it all up, the loneliness of potentially being the only American and Peace Corps volunteer in a given area was not what she was looking for. She wanted to meet like-minded people, build community and find her truth all at once. Her older sister recommended the Jesuit Volunteer Corps' International Program. Sherry was doubting her Catholicism, but it wasn't enough to dissuade her from looking into this further. She learned that they had both an international and domestic program. The founding principles included living in solidarity with the poor and celebrating intentional community with the other volunteers placed with you. *This is it,* she thought. *This is it.*

Satisfied with her decision and confident in her application, Sherry licked the envelope shut and mailed it in. She enthusiastically attended her interview with a JVI administrator, during which she answered all of the questions posed to her honestly and progressively. *The final step of many taken,* she thought. Now it was in God's hands. She slept well while waiting, for she knew this was her fate. She knew because she had believed with all of her might since she was three years old, and that was true conviction.

Sherry babysat for several local families to make spending money throughout the school year. During one of these stints, she missed the call. The JVI rep left a voice message, and when she sat on the curb in front of the house and returned the call, the office was closed for the day. *How will I survive the next twelve hours?* she thought. Then she remembered how sure she was. It was practically a guarantee. If she had known this to be her destiny for so long, and all she was asking to do was serve, who would deny her?

The next morning she called the rep first thing, 6:00 AM California time, 9:00 AM East Coast time.

"Yes, my name is Sherry and I received a call yesterday about my application."

"Okay, Sherry. Thanks for calling back. Let me transfer you to Andrew. He is handling all of the applications and can let you know why you were contacted."

"Thank you!" Everything that came out of her mouth was too high pitched, too energetic, too nervous. Why was she nervous? She wanted this more than anything she had ever wanted in her entire life. This was her path and it was time for her to start walking it.

"Sherry?" asked the voice on the other end.

"Yes," she replied, trying to keep it simple.

"Hi, this is Andrew and I called you yesterday about your JVI application. Thanks for getting back to me. Listen, I want you to know how much we appreciate your application and your patience with this entire process, but unfortunately we cannot offer you a spot this year."

The words fell flat, heavy to the ground, dragging Sherry along with them.

"We would like to strongly encourage you to apply to our domestic program, Sherry. I think you'd be a wonderful candidate. Please think about it." His tone was kind and gentle. Sherry knew he didn't have the capacity to fathom what he had just done to her. She thanked him for the information and hung up the phone. Click went the call and click went her self-identity, off like a light switch, with a single flick of the finger. Just like that, it was gone.

She walked from the kitchen back to her room and sat in the chair in front of her computer, facing the window. She wished she could stop thinking, stop reeling, but she couldn't. The thoughts that filled her mind were ones of doubt. What was her purpose then? What was her truth? She had been so sure that this was it, but she was wrong. The most frightening question of all berated her from the inside out, taunting her with its cynicism, torturing her with its innate cruelty. *Who am I?*

She called her mom and divulged the trauma and humiliation of her rejection. She thought of all of the other people she had told about her application and plans, all the people who would be asking her, all of the people she would have to tell.

"Well," said her mother, "you need to seriously think about what the rep said and decide if you want to apply to the domestic program." The finality of it all, that she indeed would not be serving internationally, was perfectly captured in her mother's instructions. Sherry rejected the notion, detested it. She was actually offended by her mother's suggestion. *I am not meant for domestic service*, she thought. But then she realized she was, and those words were the words of her former self, the dreamer whose dream did not come true. She pulled up the Jesuit Volunteer Corps website and looked it over. She would not have to fill out another application for the domestic program. They would simply transfer her existing one to the domestic program's administrator for review. If she wanted that to happen though, she had to decide where she wanted to go.

They split the country up into regions: Northwest, Southwest, Midwest, South and Northeast. Sherry put her head in her hands, but she didn't cry. She was too pissed for that. She had to think, to wrap her head around this seeming non-truth and figure it out. The whole point of going oversees was to be the "other," a concept she had become very familiar with in her philosophy classes. She wanted to experience being out of her comfort zone, to be the foreigner, to be the one who was different, and through it all, be recreated. She thought about where she would be able to best accomplish this while remaining within the US borders. The South. She had never been there, but what she had read and what she had heard sounded more foreign to her than any other place in the country.

When she had determined this and had her application transferred, Sherry then had to choose a volunteer site in one of the JV locations throughout the region. When she decided where she might like to volunteer, this would solidify where she would live. Any romantic impressions of the south that she had acquired were derived directly from the Anne Rice vampire chronicles, predominantly set in New Orleans. She didn't think this was naïve and saw that there was a volunteer option with a children's shelter in the city. Upon expressing her interest, she was informed that this placement had just been filled. *Whatever*, Sherry thought. A state of ambivalence threatened to set in as she was making one of the most important decisions of her life. She fought it off, and tried to stay the course. She looked over the remaining placements and found one more that sounded interesting. The volunteer position was as a teaching assistant with The Unity

School in Decatur, Georgia. *Where the hell is Decatur?* she thought, very annoyed at this point. It was right outside of Atlanta. She had at least heard of that city before, and that was where she would be living if this placement worked out. She again expressed interest for yet another volunteer opportunity. This one was open.

She scheduled a call with the school's principal to complete the process and seal the deal. When they spoke it came to light that he had also attended St. Mary's College many years prior. Their shared alumni status helped solidify her stellar first impression on the man. He sounded like a kind, older man who had just experienced his truth coming to fruition in the form of this school. *If it means so much to him, maybe it can mean something to me,* she thought. The school was a charter elementary school with the purpose of providing an excellent education for both refugee and American children. Its founding principle was celebrating diversity, and with children from more than forty countries attending, it prided itself on doing just that. The school, the principal explained, had to maintain a population ratio of fifty percent American children and fifty percent refugee children according to its charter.

She would go, Sherry decided. Her truth had betrayed her, and was thus not really her truth at all. She would go to Atlanta in search of another truth, and she would find it.

All of these memories flood her mind as she sits in a terminal waiting for her connecting flight to Houston. Memories of how she ended up here, everything culminating with this. The Jesuit Volunteer year begins with a weeklong retreat in Texas, during which the volunteers are able to meet members of their future community and learn about the JV philosophy which they will be asked to follow. *It sounds a little like a cult,* Sherry thinks, laughing to herself. She watches as a few of the volunteers chat, everyone desperate to make a friend. She drops a few questions to be social, and answers the ones posed to her, but mostly she is quiet.

Outwardly she appears to be observing everyone else, but really this is the façade of all facades. Inwardly she is terrified. A year is a very long time she suddenly realizes, now that this year has actually begun, and the clock ticks so painfully slow. Maintaining a calm appearance, and holding herself to keeping it, is the only thing that keeps her from screaming to let it all out.

* * *

Reflecting back, the JVC Orientation Retreat is all a bit of a blur. As they make their way through the streets of Atlanta, to the place they will call *home* for the next year, she recalls how wrong her preconceived notions were about some of her housemates, notions and mental images based on nothing more than a handful of e-mails exchanged by the lot over the last few months.

When the plane had landed in Texas, one week ago today, Sherry found the group of volunteers destined for the retreat, and observed them. Surrounded by people, she felt incredibly alone, but reassured herself that her soon-to-be soulmates might be in this very crowd.

They had boarded a van to take them to the retreat center, and Rebecca introduced herself. She would be one of Sherry's roommates. As the van took off and Rebecca kept talking, her volume increased, until she was about to blow out Sherry's right ear drum. Her short, curly hair had gone wild in the Houston humidity, and her overall effect felt abrasive to Sherry's cool Cali persona. *Are all northerners this intense?* she thought to herself, all the while trying to smile through it. Feeling bombarded and claustrophobic, Sherry tried to remain calm. *We,* she thought a bit judgmentally to herself, *will probably not be great friends.*

Fransheska was supposed to be chubby. All of her e-mails had been centered on the spices she was collecting from the farmer's market, and all the cooking she planned to do for the group. She was a petite Peruvian though, and had moved to Florida with her family when she was ten. Her nose was a bit large, but other than that she was actually quite pretty.

The geographic origin of the group was diverse. Sherry and May both came from California, Sherry from the Bay Area, and May from Orange County.

Sherry liked May. She was smart and seemingly chill. They agreed to be roommates, while discussing their current relationship statuses and swinging on the swings one afternoon. May's long thin legs pumped the rest of her body into the air, her long, straight brown hair flying gloriously behind her.

They had been told there were enough rooms in their house in Atlanta for some members of the group to have their own, but the thought of such isolation terrified Sherry. She found a sense of comfort and solidarity in a shared space, a place for her and May to have deep conversations when they confided in one another about past drunken escapades and dreams for the future.

Ben, Mary, and Rebecca were from the Boston area. Sherry hadn't connected with them yet, but was confident she would in time. They had an entire year to make that happen.

She had been counting down the days since she left home: one, two, three... They crawled by, one after the other, so painfully slow. *A year will take forever*, she thought, but she was committed, and so, she would make it.

In Atlanta, Sherry and her roommates would each be volunteering at a different non-profit for the year. They would live in a low-income neighborhood, observing their vows of poverty and living in solidarity with the poor, all the while celebrating a culture of intentional community with one another in their home sweet fucking home. The proverbial shit excreting from some (not all) of those words was something they were each destined to taste on their semi-refined middle to upper-middle class pallets.

"When you arrive," they were told at the retreat, "a representative from each of your non-profits will be at your house waiting for you. Usually they like to bring dinner, potluck style, just to make sure you feel welcome. They will probably make sure your fridge is stocked so you don't have to worry about grocery shopping the first few days you are there. You will have enough adjustments to make, without food being one of them."

As they rolled up in the van, driven by the rep from Rebecca's volunteer placement, they peered curiously at their house. The neighborhood didn't look as sketchy as Sherry had expected. The house was brick and the front lawn looked mowed recently enough. Once the van parked in the driveway, one by one they vacated, and made their way to the front stoop. Someone fumbled for the key while the others commented admiringly about the screened in side porch.

The key slipped into the lock, and the door slowly opened.

One by one they walked into the living room, until everyone stood crowded together, looking. The makeshift furniture had seen better days, and that was putting it nicely. A couple of couches and miscellaneous chairs awkwardly lined the perimeter. Who would be the first adventurous enough to sit down and see what critters emerged from the applied pressure?

They continued to walk through the house, step by very slow step. First was the dining room, fitted with a worn round table and chairs that didn't match. On the opposite end of the room were some bookshelves caked with a layer of dust and dirt. Then, onto the kitchen, where a marinara-stained counter and fridge had become home to a large line of ants, crawling from one end to the other, and back again. There were many comments made, gasps, and whimpering.

On the other side of the wall, separating the dining room and kitchen from the rest of the first floor, were two bedrooms. The first would be Ben's, huge and empty, with little more than a twin bed and chair. The next would be Mary's, tiny but quaint, and equipped with a very small, and dark bathroom, but her own.

Making their way to the front of the house, the group made the perilous journey up the stairs. The carpet looked like it hadn't been vacuumed in years. Lint, crumbs, random filthy debris, you name it, and it was probably there, being crunched and crumbled to an even finer version of itself, beneath seven plus pairs of shoes as they clomped their way up to see what lay in wait.

Upstairs, the smaller bedroom had a door, which was a huge plus. Two queen-size beds and a shabby desk crowded the room. With the consent of the group, Sherry and May claimed this one.

The other room was large and open, no closets, no door, and two-twin sized beds in opposite corners. This would belong to Fransheska and Rebecca.

The bathroom the four girls would share appeared to have been fitted with a piece of junkyard plywood, that when pushed hard enough, scraped to a close, offering sufficient privacy to the chump shaving her legs or taking a dump.

If the house had AC, it wasn't something currently used, and the Atlanta August heat lay in a heavy bog, coating everyone and everything on that second level.

It was getting late, and the group of volunteers looked tiredly at the "beds" they were supposed to sleep on. Motivated by sheer exhaustion, they accepted their fate for that first night and reconciled themselves to what bites and nibbles that first slumber might bring.

With sleeping arrangements finalized, the crew made their way back down the stairs. They stood in the living room, dazed, confused and hungry. *That thing about a fridge full of food*, Sherry thought, *what a load of crap*. One carton of expired milk and a crusted splatter of the same marinara sauce that coated the kitchen counter summed up its contents.

The reps from Rebecca's non-profit generously offered to go pick up pizzas and drinks. The group eagerly accepted. The reps turned to make their quick exit out the front door, and that was the first time anyone noticed that the door knob was missing. They were trapped, literally. If it wasn't for the fact that Sherry and her roommates would be living here for the next 364 days, someone might have laughed at the irony, the absurdity of it all.

Someone had the idea of putting the front door key in the lock and opening the door that way, and it worked. "At least we don't have to worry about fire hazards," Ben remarked, his sweet demeanor trying desperately to keep the mood light.

After the reps left, May slumped down onto the window sill, because no one had dared sit on the bug-infested furniture yet. Her piercing scream cracked the silence as she jumped up, stuttering belligerently, something about cockroaches emerging from the panes.

Sherry didn't see anything, but nothing would surprise her now. She was the only girl who didn't cry that night.

⸗ 3 ⸗

Aida

He is trying to tell her what to do again. School has not been in session for a week yet, and this new teacher has the nerve to wag his finger at her, someone older than himself. She looks at him, smiling, nodding while he rambles on. *What is his name again?* Aida thinks. *Something like Michael, or Mike, or Micah.* Regardless, he seems like the type who would probably never bother to actually ask her a question that required a response; he likes the sound of his own voice too much for that. *Funny how some Americans take themselves so seriously*, she thinks. In her country, someone like him would be humble; he would know his place. Aida knows her place, and that is why instead of turning her back to him and walking away, she stands there, taking it. She is a refugee, and while that grants her legal status, which she is immeasurably grateful for, it doesn't give her access to much else. Catholic Charities had provided them with rent for the first several months when she and her family arrived here, but as with all types of government assistance, it didn't last nearly long enough.

Her husband qualifies for Social Security and Medicare because of his disability, and that helps, but Aida isn't getting any younger and has a daughter with an absentee husband, two young sons and two even younger grandchildren, the oldest of whom is headed for trouble. At eleven years old she gravitates toward provocative clothing and brings home the dirty words she learns in the schoolyard.

What's-his-name finally stops his blabbing and moves on to two of the students who aren't sitting still enough while eating their lunch. One of the food containers is running low and she lifts it up out of the heating tray and replaces it with a fresh one warming in the oven. For a sixty-year-old, robust woman, Aida can move. She does her job well and prides herself knowing that. The Unity School has given her family a chance it never would have had otherwise. Principal Luna offered her a job knowing that she had no experience in a school cafeteria. "This," he told her, "is a job that requires someone who is trustworthy. It is for a person that I can count on to run this cafeteria, to feed every child in

12

need of food. This is a job for you." That was the extent of her interview. He knew her story, and that sufficed. Principal Luna knows all of their stories because he takes the time to learn them, understand them. He has compassion.

Aida takes off the oven mitts and wipes her moist hands on her apron. She looks out into the sea of faces before her. It gets so loud in here and she looks forward to lunch being over, when she can go about her duties of closing up the kitchen in peace.

As a child, Aida loved to be surrounded by people. One of two children, with more aunts, uncles and cousins than it was possible to count, this had been her comfort zone. Being alone was lonely back then, and she detested it. She intentionally sought out the company of others in her days of youth. My how things have changed...

The Bosnian war came and went, leaving nothing but death and decay in its path. She heard of others returning to the old country, willingly staring the aftermath of it all in the eye. This was not for her. Enough was enough. She had seen more than one lifetime should permit, and while the memory of it all was not one that she could forget, she wished she had that option, to shut it off when it haunted her dreams, to forget the sound of the soldier's voice whispering in her ear moments before things became irreparable.

Looking out upon the sum total of so many children in one room, what many see as chaos, Aida knows it is order. Never in her life has she seen such a multitude of diversity and kinship, color and creed, true awareness and friendship. The so-called differences that people had allowed to tear her country apart were the very same that brought these children together. Mr. Luna was not just a school principal, he was a visionary.

Aida hurries back into the kitchen to check the trays and determine if they need to be replaced. She decides there's enough food to feed the next group of children, opens the fridge and removes several trays to warm in the oven. Back and forth, back and forth, she makes her way from the fridge to the oven and back again. This repetitive motion does not bore her. She finds it comforting. In the last few years she has seen this shift in herself, the tendency to cling to the smallest piece of normalcy, as though it could escape her without a moment's notice.

When she was young, Aida saw beyond the box. She lifted herself up with her own strength and peered over its edge at the world lying in wait. She made plans and promises, all to herself. Her eyes were filled with longing and ambition, her heart was filled with fire. She knew herself to be unconquerable, until she wasn't. Like a balloon popping, she deflated, and all of those plans, the beauty of the world, were burnt to ashes.

Before she can stop it, the memory returns, flooding her person with all of its strength. The smell of the woods in the early spring, the cool morning air that made her shiver as she and a few of the other women returned to their village years after the war had ended, the village that haunted their memories of childhood. She noticed, with hyperawareness, the imprint of her shoe in the decay when they arrived. The smell of smoke still seemed to cling to the air, choking them as they were escorted to the mass grave. The ground softened as it rose up beneath them in a mound, and they realized the horror of where everyone had gone. The women fell, one by one like dominoes, the undeniable impact of one upon the other. On their knees, in the dirt, they wept like the schoolchildren they once were, as their parents and siblings, spouses and children lay beneath them, dead and buried. Aida's torch blew out and the world she dreamed of went dark.

She is called back to reality by the sounds of the children; the next group has arrived. They wait anxiously in line as the teaching assistants from each class prepare plates and distribute them. *It is an inefficient way of doing things*, she thinks. *It would be more practical to have staff solely dedicated to working in the kitchen, but the school is poor like most of the children who go here.* Mr. Luna established the system and so for now it stuck. They would make it work as they did with everything else, making do the first few years until the school proved itself worthy of more state money and funding from private grants. Because the school could not afford a separate kitchen staff, the teaching assistants for each class were assigned the duty of lunch server when it was time for their students to eat. Some arrived on time, some even early, and others not at all. Aida fills in the gaps when necessary, but truly it would be easier if she just did everything. So many people constantly in and out of the kitchen caused nothing but disorder, and this was Aida's sanctuary.

The second grade students move through the line, one by one, taking their plates, many perpetually disappointed by what they are destined to eat. White, brown, black, the faces pass by her and she can't help but smile to herself. How many Serbian generals would roll over in their graves if they could see her grandson arm in arm with his little African friend, hijab and all. The thought of this pleases her. She pulls Halim out of line and hugs him tightly. All of the dreams and hopes that left her that day returned in the form of aspirations for her descendants. The world was what it was for her, but for Halim there was possibility. Hope was not a skill she had imparted upon her daughter; survival was what she gave to her child. Halim however, was born in a distant land, untouched and unspoiled. Hope had been bottled up and stored for two generations, and now given as the greatest of gifts to her grandchildren. Halim, Aida knows, will do something with it. His dreams will be Aida's dreams and these, unlike her own, might actually one day come true.

⚡ 4 ⚡

Lydia

Lydia is plagued by nostalgia for her children's days of youth. *Where did I go wrong?* she asks herself, standing over the kitchen sink waiting for the coffee to brew. She rewinds time in her mind, stopping and playing, pausing to reflect, and rewinding more. Further and further back she goes, letting time fall away like leaves off a tree. She sees her hair grow longer, turn from grey back to blonde, the now ever-present muffin top melts off her waistline, and she is restored to her former self, her younger self. She thinks about how in the beginning she took it all for granted. That if she had only known how things would turn out, maybe she would have done it all differently. She shakes her head knowingly, brushing off such a thought, because in the end she only had so much control, and this has been one of the hardest lessons motherhood taught her.

Picking up her phone, she goes into her list of contacts and hits "Lillian." The phone rings to voicemail and she cannot help but picture her daughter looking to see who is calling, realizing it's mom, and hitting "decline" instead of "answer." Despite the infinite rational explanations she could tell herself to excuse Lillian's failure to pick up, she chooses to believe in this moment that a call from mom is discriminately screened. She sets the phone down on the table, even though what she would really like to do is throw it through the window into the yard and for it to shatter into a million pieces. Then when the "convenient call back" came that night or the next day she would not be able to answer it, and maybe Lillian would understand for just a moment what it felt like to be ignored. Instead she looks down at the touchscreen, at the stock image background of bright springtime flowers, and wishes more than anything that it would ring so she could answer and hear her daughter's voice.

"You have to move forward; stop dwelling in the past," her therapist told her at their most recent session. She wondered how old his children were. He looked young, and so most likely they still needed his help with homework and cared if he went to their games.

The age of ambivalence had not yet struck and so he was ignorant. *Give it ten years*, she thought to herself as he rambled on, something about picking up a new hobby, volunteering, bullshit.

Lydia never swears out loud, but she finds herself doing it more and more in her mind. She cussed out the barista for making her vanilla latte with whole milk instead of nonfat. She cussed out the beautician for painting her pinkie nail unevenly, but she stored up her most offensive and venomous silent response for Barbara, her next door neighbor, when she set out her sprinklers just close enough to splatter Lydia's newly washed car with droplets that then dried and left water marks all over her dark red Prius.

Someday she will say it out loud, uninhibited, like a man. She will say exactly what she thinks and enjoy the look of shock and offense that spread across their faces. Maybe she will give someone the finger when he cuts her off on the road. *The possibilities are endless*, Lydia thinks, and she will get there, someday.

That day is not today though, and so Lydia pours her coffee, adds artificial sweetener and sugar-free creamer, stirs them to a milky brown and takes a seat at the breakfast table to read the morning's news. Gary suggested "going green" a few years ago, and although recyclable, the first thing to go was the traditional morning paper. She powers on her computer and opens two windows, one for Associated Press and the other for BBC. Scanning the headlines she feels disinterested, even though the whole point of this repetitive ritual is to connect. She questions her ability to do this, connect. Things just feel so bleak now. The proverbial light at the end of the tunnel only lights up when the phone rings and the voice on the other end is one of three.

"What do you do all day Mom?" Brian had asked her the last time they spoke over the phone. This question quietly stroked a fury brewing within her. The insinuation that thirty-five years as a teacher was not enough, the not so subtle ridicule by the youngest and by far most spoiled of her children, was almost enough to cause her to hang up, but she didn't. She patiently explained to her twenty-five-year-old son the logistics of her retirement. He listened impatiently, hurrying her through the details meant to answer the question he had asked. In the end it was he who practically hung up on her, while she longed for just five more minutes on the other end of the line.

Bored with the morning's headlines and distracted by her own disenchantment, Lydia exits out of the news and goes to her photos.

Aimlessly, she wanders through happier times, moments, days, years gone by and achieves her goal of numbing herself to the present and losing herself in the past. She comes to rest on her favorite picture of thousands taken over the years. Brian is barely a year. Lillian had dressed herself that morning, and at age three proudly flaunted her fashion skills destined to one day take her far from home and settle in a place her mother detested the thought of visiting. Aimee was seven and had that far-off look in her big blue eyes, Gary's eyes. Lydia joked with her husband that she had come out of the womb with that look: longing, searching, and melancholy. The three of them were so terrifically similar and different all at the same time.

The weight of Rocky's head in her lap calls Lydia back to reality. Looking down she smiles at her old friend. She rests her hand just above his eyes that look back into hers. Smoothing his short blonde fur back she strokes him from head to tail. Unlike most of the good things in her life that required her to chase them down, Rocky found her. She was driving home late one night from a parent-teacher conference and as she pulled up in front of the house, there he was, sitting in front of her trash bin. That was ten years ago. Knowing the tendency of time to pass and the negative habit of all good things coming to an end, Lydia secretly dreads the day that she knows is soon to come.

She gets up, puts her coffee cup in the sink, opens the pantry and pulls out the leash. Pushing the house key into her jean pocket, she and Rocky head on foot to the dog park. *The neighborhood is going downhill*, she thinks to herself as they walk. The dry parched lawns are glaringly obvious. The morning is hot and humid and Lydia wipes the perspiration from the back of her neck. Unaffected and oblivious to her perpetual negativity, Rocky pulls on the leash, hurrying her along.

The gate closes with a bang, metal on metal. Reaching down, she releases Rocky and is left alone with her thoughts and a leash dangling from her palm. She makes her way to an empty bench, all the while walking with her eyes on the ground, careful not to end up with shit all over her shoes, despite the fact that a little more shit really wouldn't mean much being that she was almost fully submerged figuratively speaking.

Lost in thought, thirty minutes quickly go by, and Lydia stands up and makes her way to the gate. Rocky bounds towards her, sensing it is time to go home. She bends forward, snaps the leash on to his collar and again closes the gate behind them. Together they walk, side by side, one happily in literal chains, attached to his owner by fate of being born a dog, the other in what have begun to feel like the chains of her life, weighing her down, holding her back.

She pulls the key from her pocket and unlocks the front door. Lydia drops the leash and Rocky runs ahead to his water bowl. She makes her way up the stairs, walking past Brian's old room and the one Lillian and Aimee had shared. She stops at the end of the hall and stands in front of the last one, door closed. Her hand hovers, suspended above the knob in both time and space. Each time she tries to reach down, intending to grasp the handle and turn it, she subconsciously pulls back. This process repeats itself again and again, until finally, inhaling deeply, she succeeds and throws it open. Ten paces from the door to the bed, she knows this. She walks each one slowly, this time not looking at her feet, but instead at the soft pink bedspread covering the twin-size mattress. She sits thoughtfully, feeling her weight caught by the springs, enjoying their push back, holding her up. She takes one of the pillows and holds it to her nose, inhaling its fragrance deeply. She closes her eyes and sits like this, trying to think of nothing but this smell and the memory it contains. Wiping tears from her face, she stands up. Ten more steps to the closet; she knows this. She slides it open and stares. Little shoes, little coats, little dresses, all lined up, hanging still and undisturbed. Here they will hang forever, archived in the eighties by the fashion trends of their time. *You cannot stand here forever*, she tells herself. She slides the closet door closed, walks fifteen paces to the bedroom door and crosses over the threshold, back into the reality she would sometimes prefer to forget. She puts her hand on the knob and slowly, ever so slowly, pulls the door closed behind her.

"That room is a tomb," Gary insists. "Nothing in it has changed in more than twenty years." When she thinks of the chronology of events in her life, there is only a before and an after. Perhaps this is an explanation for the anguish she experiences regarding the remaining three. In a way, they too have died. The passing away of their youths is almost more than she can bear and now she is left with empty rooms, artifacts of the time before, before the death of her oldest and the departure of the remaining three.

Lydia lifts her hand from the knob and steps away, freeing herself from the magnetic pull of everything on the other side of that door.

The phone rings and caller ID indicates it's her therapist. She contemplates letting it ring through to voicemail but decides not to postpone the inevitable, and get the call over with. "Hello?" she says casually, as though she doesn't have a clue who is on the other end.

"Lydia, it's me, Dr. Coleman."

"Oh hello Dr. Coleman. How can I help you?"

"Lydia, I apologize, but I am going to have to reschedule tomorrow's appointment. An unforeseen scheduling conflict has come up and I have no way around it. Is that alright? We can reschedule for Friday if you are free."

"It's fine, no problem at all. Friday won't work for me so can we just plan on our regular time next Thursday?"

"That sounds perfectly fine. How are things? Are you having a decent week?"

She hates the insinuation, as though her life was such a mess that managing a "decent" week would be a miraculous feat. "Yes, things are quite fine. Is everything all right on your end?" She learned that trick from him. Avoid answering a question by asking one herself.

"Fine, fine. Thanks for asking. Before I forget, a colleague mentioned something to me the other day that made me think of you and I wanted to make sure to mention it before I forget. I know you are a retired teacher and a new school opened in Decatur. It's called The Unity School. Apparently it is some kind of social immersion charter school for American and refugee children. Anyway, it sounded interesting and I thought of you because they're looking for volunteers. Since it's a charter school they only get so much state funding and there is a teacher shortage. It may be the last thing you're looking for, volunteering in the capacity you just retired from, but it made me think of you. Here, let me give you their number in case you decide this is something you might pursue."

God, he is pushy! she declares silently. Grabbing a pen from the drawer, she takes down the number.

"Okay Lydia, well thanks for understanding. I'm calendaring you in for next Thursday."

"See you then." She replies.

Click.

Lydia isn't sure what to do next. She looks at the number. Should she call? She retired at the age of sixty-five. The golden years have yet to reveal themselves. Gary won't be retiring for at least another three to four. She found herself ironically envious while he talked about his day over dinner. Random stories, conversations, confrontations, drama. She missed that in a way, the guaranteed human interaction that comes with employment. *What the hell*, she thinks. She hits the key pad icon on the screen and dials the number.

"The Unity School, this is Margaret speaking. How can I help you?" The voice sounds formal but cheery.

"Um, yes, hello, my name is Lydia and I am calling for information regarding a request for volunteers at the school."

"Hello Lydia! Yes, yes, we are asking for volunteers for various duties. What is your background? Can you tell me a bit about yourself please?"

"Well, I'm a retired middle school teacher. I've taught primarily English and Social Studies in the public school system."

"Wonderful! Now are you interested in volunteering as a teacher? How many hours a week are you available?"

She pauses cautiously before speaking. "Is it possible for me to come in and learn more about the school and the various volunteer opportunities before making a commitment?"

The response is not immediate on the other end. Lydia wonders if she has somehow offended Margaret. "I'm sorry to keep you waiting Lydia. A student had a question. It can be a little chaotic here. Forgive me, and yes of course. Why don't you come by next Monday? Does 10:00 AM work for you?"

"Yes, that's fine," Lydia responds. "I look forward to meeting you then."

They exchange information. Lydia obtains the school address and ends the call. She stares at the pad of paper. Her mind is empty, void, thinking of nothing in particular. She feels neither excitement nor regret. She is free of expectation, for the hour, the day, the week, the year. *I just need something to look forward to*, she tells herself. Pulling the address free from the rest of the pad, she secures it to the fridge with a magnet. She stares at it again, wondering. She feels nothing, but thinks, maybe even secretly hopes for the possibility that the unknown can occasionally bring.

Hanan

Baris drops her at the entrance to the camp. "You ready?" he kindly inquires. She looks up at him, sitting in the driver's seat, smiling shamelessly, hopefully, poking at her misery, and the irony he sees in it now that she has been given the green light to join the chosen few in America. He cannot see beyond his own wish for her, into the depths of her loss and pain. She knows others who lost someone that day, but no one who lost everyone, everything. In such leveling devastation, she is again, alone.

Hanan twitches her lips upward, into the briefest, slightest, biggest fraud of a smile she can manage, for him, to shut him up. "Yes, Baris," is her reply. Hopping off, she turns back, nods at him, knowing he will see the gratitude that might exist if she cared at all, for anyone or anything. He will see beyond his nose, into the reality he pretends is not there, for her sake, so she can simply be, and he will understand. If she could feel anything anymore, she would not feel guilty, because with her he is expectation free, and for his willingness and ability to honor her as she is, she thanks him. He smiles big, honks three times, and pulls away. The van creates a dust cloud that drifts towards her. She does not bother to move out of its way. She will never see Baris, that van, these people, or this camp again. The thought floats into her mind and then out, of absolutely no consequence, similar to the thought of going to America.

Lifting her long skirt above her ankles, she tromps through the dirt roads that amble through row upon row of tents, makeshift shelters for the thousands of refugees living there. She pays little attention to what is going on around her, walking forward, with only her current destination in mind.

"Habibi! Where have you been?" The strong, matriarchal voice calls out to her from inside the tent. The sounds of it, and the familiarity of the way it speaks such words, in her own regional dialect, brings her comfort. It is the only remnant of home that remains. Hanan picks up her pace, and ducks inside. Noor sits in the center of the tent, with three children crowded on her lap and two more attempting to do her hair. She is older than Hanan by only a few years, but mothers her in the same way she mothers her own children.

Noor was the one who carried Hanan away from the beach the day she first arrived, and from that moment on, became an informal member of the family. It was not appropriate, let alone safe, for a woman to reside alone in the camp, and so she lived with Noor and her five children in their crowded tent. Her tent sits empty next door, and is used for storing the various items the family has accumulated since arriving at the camp three years ago.

Hanan kneels, hugging and kissing the children, and kissing Noor on both cheeks. "I went to say goodbye."

Noor shakes her head disapprovingly. "Going there does nothing for you. Good thing you leave tomorrow, and can't go back. They should burn that beach."

Hanan looks at her friend, comparing their plights. Noor had made the same journey, two years earlier than Hanan. She, her husband, and five children had fled Syria going south, first through Lebanon, then Egypt, and ending in Libya. As a failed state following the Arab Spring, Libya had fallen into anarchy, warring factions competing for control of the country. In the absence of effective centralized governance, chaos ensued and human smugglers set up shop along the coast, because there was no one patrolling the land or the sea.

These despicable gangs of human traffickers could charge outrageous fees, hold people in inhumane conditions until they paid, or while they waited their turn, to flee whatever conflict plagued their country of origin in pursuit of freedom on European shores.

Noor had lost her husband on the journey, and now, raising and financially supporting her five children fell solely upon her, but at least they were together, at least her children were alive.

Two years later, Hanan, her husband and two small children boarded a rickety boat, packed with other people fleeing from areas of the world Hanan had paid little mind, until then. As the smugglers insisted more and more people board, the environment went from uncomfortable to unbearable. Hanan could barely breathe. She remembers looking at her husband, who sat across from her, each of them holding one of their girls, and silently begging him to get off, but they both knew it was too late and making the journey was their only option.

Gently combing her fingers through Aya's light brown curls, she had forced herself to remain calm. Thinking of the story she heard just the other night, of a mother in a similar situation, who had fought to get off a crowded boat when water began seeping in while the boat was still tethered to the dock. She had been holding her baby, not even one year old, and as the crowd pushed back, the child slipped from her arms. It was dark, and despite the mother's frantic attempts to find her child, it wasn't until later that the boy was found at the bottom of the boat, drowned in less than a foot of water.

Hanan had gone mad hearing this, but with the worsening conditions where they currently stayed, awaiting passage from Libya to Greece, Firas assured her their trip would be different, smooth, and so she bought into the hope, his hope, because that was all her family had.

He had planned their route long before Hanan could begin to accept the reality of what was befalling their country. "We will head for Greece," Firas had said, speaking quietly while the children slept. He and Hanan huddled over the map laid out on the floor of their modest apartment in western Aleppo. "Is it really necessary?" Hanan had pushed back, not yet ready to leave everything and everyone they knew behind. Despite the walls shaking from government shelling in the distance, she remained steadfastly opposed. "It will get better, my love."

In that moment, Firas had looked at her as never before. "How can you say that, with them sleeping in the next room, and the reports of government bombs and tanks getting closer every day?" He had fire in his eyes, and Hanan acquiesced. She realized the graveness of the situation fully for the first time; she saw it on his face.

They left Syria the next day.

Almost two years later, on the eve of her next journey, Hanan is not afraid. She is not expectant, or weary, excited or moved. She is nothing. She has nothing. When the grief of her loss had subsided, and she had fully absorbed her reality, without them, this is what she was left with, numbness. *Better this than what I felt before*, she thinks. Hanan could not have comprehended the depths of despair to which a human heart could fall, until it was her own heart in a downward free fall, and feeling nothing would always be preferable to that.

⚡ 6 ⚡

Sherry

The alarm goes off and Sherry gets out of bed easily. She is a ball of nerves wondering what the school will be like. Everyone begins with their volunteer placements today and hers is the farthest away with the earliest start time.

She stands in front of the bathroom mirror, applying her make-up just as she has for the last eight years of her life. Eyeshadow, eyeliner, mascara, and since she is going to be working at a school, only a quick coat of light pink lip gloss. Lipliner and lipstick don't seem necessary. Her long curly blonde hair is worn down with plenty of gel and hairspray, slightly crunchy to the touch, to hold the curls. She packs a simple lunch consisting of a peanut butter and jelly sandwich and banana. Out the door she goes.

It is barely seven in the morning, and she has to catch the 7:15 train in order to make it to the school by 8. The air is thick with humidity, and the smell of wet grass, heavy with morning dew, is growing on her. She hustles, knowing the MARTA station is about half a mile away, but not knowing how long it will take to walk there.

The Nabisco factory that their house backs up to smells sickeningly sweet of chocolate and cookies. A shift must have just ended, because several men pass her on the street, greeting her nonchalantly. *Can't they see I'm a young woman walking alone in the dark*, Sherry thinks, annoyed. *Why are they talking to me anyway? What do they want?* She continues on, picking up the pace, head down, eyes on the ground in front of her.

As she stands on the platform waiting for the train, a juicy ball of sweat slowly slides from her hairline down her neck and then back, finally being absorbed by the fabric of her bra. She feels disgusting. This is the last day she will wear her hair down for a while.

Sherry picked the southern region for her JVC year because it was as much a "world away" from the Bay Area, CA as she could get while still being in the U.S., and she wanted a cross-cultural experience. She wanted to experience being the *other*, pushed to assimilate and acclimate as the people she longed to work with and serve have done their entire lives. The train arrives and she takes the first step aboard, never feeling as blatantly *her* as in this moment.

Her whiteness is so apparent that she feels the urge to hide it, but she knows this is part of the package, the first of many uncomfortable steps on the very long journey of transformation. The type of blending she aspires to will only be achieved when she fails to see the skin color of those surrounding her, and then in turn, her own.

After one train change downtown, she finally arrives at the Decatur station. She wanders like a fool, up and down the street the school is supposedly on, until finally noticing an obscure billboard announcing the school's presence behind a Methodist church. When she finally makes it inside the school building, again she wanders. Happening upon the main office, she is directed to the music room which is the makeshift second grade classroom until the modular building, which will house grades second and third, is completed.

Ms. Clinton, the teacher she will be assisting, greets Sherry at the door, dragging a red radio flyer wagon behind her. The wagon contains various school supplies including pencils and textbooks. Everything feels rushed and disorganized, makeshift.

She opens the door to the music room, wide enough for Sherry to walk through, and a sea of seven and eight year old faces gaze back at her as she makes her entrance. Her breath stops in her chest. Here they are, what she has been destined for all along. There are children from Laos, Sudan, Bosnia, Kurdistan (Iraq), Somalia, Afghanistan, and America, together in one room, waiting for her.

"Hi, you must be Sherry," Ms. Clinton states. "Welcome to our class. We just started math, so make yourself comfortable and settle in." Sherry takes a seat in-between two of the children, and as they struggle through the math lesson, looking blankly at Sherry as she tries to guide them. It becomes apparent that neither of them speaks English. A few others work through the lesson effortlessly. These are the American kids. Sherry likes them, but it is the refugee children she feels drawn to, called to. The next twenty minutes consist of more pointing and struggling as Sherry and her two new friends attempt to communicate.

Ms. Clinton seems stressed. She too, is challenged in delivering this lesson in a way that seems successful. She is a bit scattered, searching for the right words to explain the concepts the lesson contains. At least half the class stares at her, blank slates, which can't be helping. *This is not because she is a horrible teacher,* Sherry thinks, *it is because some of these kids don't speak a word of English.* This will be a helpful reminder that Sherry will default to, to assuage her own ego, numerous times in the near future.

The subjects switch and the morning carries on, with Sherry afloat, drifting along. She feels more like an observer and less like an assistant. Ms. Clinton is nice and enthusiastic with the kids, a huge, resounding voice coming from her very tiny body. She is a powerhouse, but she is not a good supervisor. Sherry has been left to her own devices, receiving no instruction on how she can be of use.

Thankfully someone comes to the door asking for her. As Ms. Clinton resumes her rightful place in front of the class, Sherry looks up to see who she is being summoned by. Before her stands a regal, beautiful, round black girl. She doesn't seem old enough to be called a woman, and Sherry would not refer to herself as such yet, so the mental note was not one of disrespect; it was simply an observation, a compliment of the girl's youthful beauty.

"I'm Aziza," the girl says, smiling slyly and looking Sherry up and down. She seems pleased with and accepting of Sherry, and also like she walks around with something up her sleeve.

Sherry likes her immediately. Aziza lays out the schedule for Sherry who has no idea what to expect of this first day. Every classroom assistant helps out with prepping and serving lunch for the children in her class. Together they make their way to the kitchen. They are greeted by a chubby, commanding white woman wearing a hijab. She seems to be the boss. She communicates with the girls mostly by smiling and barking out orders enthusiastically for them to go this way or that way, finally corralling them to the back of the kitchen where the empty food trays are being changed out for steaming hot ones, filled to the brim.

The kitchen boss demonstrates for Sherry how to fill a plate and serve it to each child as they pass by the open window linking the kitchen to the rest of the cafeteria. She concludes with giving Sherry an enthusiastic pat on the back and says "My name is Aida." Sherry smiles, tells Aida her name, and thanks her for the tour of the workspace. Aida informs her that lunch is ready to be served.

Aziza, already an expert in the field, stands nonchalantly in front of her food trays, ready to whip out servings of mashed potatoes upon demand. Sherry stands in front of the broccoli, which looks edible, but overcooked to a mushy consistency that hopefully the children won't mind. The sounds of the doors opening and kids entering the building travels back to the kitchen, and Aida hurriedly pours what looks like a pound of salt over each tray, gesturing wildly for Aziza and Sherry to stir vigorously.

The kids pass by the window, one by one, collecting their food trays. Some seem quite pleased with the contents, while others frown in disappointment, or turn their noses up in utter disregard. Ms. Clinton is on it. "Say thank you," booms the big voice from the tiny body, and the children adhere, muttering their unenthusiastic "thank you-s" under their dispassionate breath.

When they are finished serving, Aziza helps herself to a plate of food and signals for Sherry to follow her. They sit at a table away from the children and Sherry pulls out her peanut butter and jelly sandwich, while Aziza shakes her head. "Sorry girl, but the entire school is a peanut free zone." Sherry was unaware of this, and feels stupid. She tosses it and returns to her seat across from Aziza. "Go get a plate," Aziza commands. "That's one of the perks of working in the kitchen; we get to eat lunch for free."

"Okay," Sherry replies, heading back to the kitchen. It is strange to have someone who seems younger than her take Sherry under her wing, and equally strange that Sherry finds herself so eager to please and willing to abide by what Aziza instructs. She shrugs it off because it is of no consequence and Sherry is happy to have made a friend.

Lunch leads into recess and when that is through, Sherry guides her class back to the music room. The next couple of hours consist of Ms. Clinton giving scattered instructions and scrambling to pass out various items for each lesson, everything piled together and practically spilling out of the hopeless little red wagon.

Sherry sits, hoping as things progress, she can be of more use to Ms. Clinton. The clock reads 2:30 pm and she knows from Aziza's instructions that now she needs to go to the school office. She says goodbye to the kids and Ms. Clinton before exiting the room. The office is the first door down the hall and she takes a right into it. From there, she is directed to the After-School room, and joins several other staff members at a large square table. Apparently, the assistants make up the After-School staff and Sherry has been assigned the third grade. She will have a counterpart but is unaware of who that will be.

She sits quietly. Some of the staff are very friendly with one another, having worked at the school the year before, giving the meeting a reunion vibe of sorts. Others, such as herself, Sherry makes note, are also newcomers and smile while sitting with their hands folded formally in their laps.

Kayla, the music teacher, confidently introduces herself to Sherry. She is cool and calm, with a hip hop flare that can only be considered edgy for a white girl. As she talks with other staff, a good-looking guy makes his very intentional entrance. He seemingly flirts with Kayla, although Sherry decides later that they are just friends who share a flirtatious comradery. His eyes drift in Sherry's direction, noticing her for the first time. Sherry sees him take her in and then quickly divert his attention back to Kayla. He speaks with a thick accent, but clearly and with great confidence. He laughs a lot, which Sherry likes, but also seems to like the sound of it, which Sherry considers narcissistic and does not like.

I would probably hook up with him, Sherry thinks to herself. However, based on his boisterous voice and overconfidence, she determines that she would not date him. He is hot, but ultimately not her type.

The day continues and then it ends, and Sherry makes her way back to the MARTA station. She rides the train back to her stop, and gets called things like "snowflake" while walking back to the house. *What does that mean,* she wonders as she picks up her pace. *Was I just the victim of a racist slur?* She wears this experience like a badge of honor. It is all part of the journey she has chosen for herself.

❦ **7** ❦

Aida

The late summer heat sticks to her. She gets up from her seat on the bus, walks off, and when it has rounded the corner and she has a moment of privacy, she peels her long, thick skirt off the back of her legs. *Everything sticks to you this time of year here*, she thinks, longing for the cool mountain air of home.

She fluffs the skirt, giving her legs some air, before preparing for the long walk to the apartment. When they first resettled in Clarkston, right outside of Atlanta, Aida's daughter studied hard and got her driver's license. A very kind and empathetic donor to the resettlement agency heard about her family and wanted to help. When asked what they needed, the vote was unanimous, a car. The donor provided them with one, just like that. It amazes Aida how life can sometimes be so simple, fortune just falls into your hands, and other times, it is impossibly hard, nothing comes easy, everything—the smallest things to the biggest, are all a struggle.

That car, she thinks, *spoiled us*. They got it too soon, and began to take the ease of personal transportation for granted. It was a blessing, but too early on in their American refugee experience. It set a false precedent for the ease life would present here for them. Looking back, she wishes they had never had the car in the first place. Ignorance can be bliss, and this particular bliss would have been fine with her.

The car inevitably broke down, and even though every adult member in the house was working, and her husband was collecting disability, all the money was going toward the basics: rent, food, school, and clothing. They simply couldn't stomach the thought of the $1000.00 price tag to have it fixed, when that would buy nearly a year supply of bus passes.

At moments like this however, with the mile and a half walk ahead of her, and the Georgia sun beating down on her back, she struggles to remember why they thought getting rid of the car was the best option. She could be riding shotgun, with her daughter at the wheel, talking

30

about her day while the AC blew gloriously upon her, the heat a mere afterthought when walking from the car to their air conditioned home.

"Enough," she says to herself under her breath, commanding her mind to think different thoughts, to change the subject.

She adjusts her light-blue hijab around her forehead and under her neck, hikes up her skirt on both sides, and marches on. She learned the hard way to look at the ground while walking on this particular route. Clarkston was not known for its polished, pristine sidewalks and streets. She struggles not to trip over chunks of cement dislodged by tree roots.

She thinks about the state-tax deduction taken from her bimonthly paycheck, and how according to the government's justification, this is what that money will pay to repair. *What is it the Americans say*, she pauses, *bullshit!* She has been hobbling over that same spot for the last three years, despite several calls to the city to repair it. *If I trip one of these days*, she tells herself, *and suffer so much as a sprained ankle, I will sue. Maybe then I will finally see a return on my money that the state claims as its own.* She nods, egging herself on, quite satisfied with this self-declared ultimatum she is giving them.

She thinks about the rest of the day before her. As master of the kitchen, her shift is over at 2 pm, when every hungry mouth has been fed, and the kitchen has been cleaned. The sense of accomplishment she feels when she turns off the light and shuts the door, another day's work done well, is something she cannot deny. She enjoys the satisfaction coursing through her veins, doing something that thirty years ago, she would have considered mundane. *How the world changes us*, she thinks.

In Bosnia, she'd graduated high school at the top of her class, and received a scholarship to university. She was the first person in her family, man or woman, from their small mountain village, to go to college. She applied herself vigorously, and achieved top marks in all of her classes. Her goal was to become a teacher. She wanted to work with the little ones, to bask in the glow radiating from their small faces when a concept finally clicked, when they were still small enough to reach for her hand and hold it.

University was where the whole world fell at her feet, all of these dreams in the process of becoming reality. This was where she met her husband, so handsome and clever in his youth, always knowing exactly what to say and how to say it, ensuring she was his. And she was his, all these years later, surviving the war, and finally bringing what was left of their family here to America.

Dreams change Aida, she snidely mocks her former self's youthful naïve optimism. *It is the things we cannot control that will shape us more than the things we can.* She refused to go down the rabbit hole that presented itself to her time and time again over the years. What if the war had never happened? It is a question asked in vain, that could only take her to the dark dreary crevices of her mind, and these she preferred to avoid. *Moving on.* With a huff and a grunt, reconciling the past to itself, and trying to remain focused on the present, which will be the past all too soon, she again hikes her skirt up to her ankles to step over yet another pothole.

Aida takes a shortcut, cutting through the back of their apartment complex. *Ghetto, hood,* these are the words her oldest grandchild brings home with her from school. These are the words she uses to label their home. *Sure, it is a bit decrepit, and some of their neighbors might be a little shady*—another word she learned from her granddaughter, *but it is home nonetheless. Take it or leave it, because these are our options, as with most things in America. And "leave it" would mean being out on the streets, and Lejla,* Aida snickers to herself just trying to picture it, *would not last a day out there.*

She worries about Lejla in a way that she hopes she never has to worry about Halim. Lejla reminds her of herself at this age, and this is what concerns her. She has an edge, and when she finally decides to leap off, she can go one of two ways, up or down. The difference between Aida at her age, and Lejla as she is now, are the external influences egging inherent natures on. Aida's influences were traditional Muslim Bosnian culture: wear the hijab, know one's place, do not step out of line, but still find ways to have a bit of fun— innocent fun. She was ignorant to the ways of the world in so many ways that Lejla simply is not.

Lejla's influences are booty shorts, crop tops, and the filthy mouths of her peers who have no regard for parental authority. These are the children Lejla brings home with her, and it is the company she chooses to keep that is Aida's greatest cause for concern. Aida knows deep down, Lejla is a strong, good girl. She hopes this is just a phase. But what if it isn't?

She climbs the three flights of stairs, slips her key in the lock, gives it a couple jiggles until it releases, and opens the door. She removes her hijab first, releasing her long gray hair, and gives it a good shake. The air on her neck feels amazing. She walks into her room and places her things on the bed, making a mental note to put them in their respective places before the children come home from school.

She walks back to the kitchen to get a glass of water and stops to kiss her husband on the top of his head. He is where he always is, sitting in the recliner, television on but watching nothing in particular. She fetches her water and joins him. This is how they typically spend their afternoon, from three to four, sitting together in silence, knowing one another so well that there is no pressure to fill the quiet with this and that and such and such. They simply enjoy *being*, together.

Irsad takes his hand and reaches across the distance between them, gently placing it on hers. She looks over just in time to see the upward curving of his lips, a smile. He can still make her heart beat a little faster, and raise the temperature in the room ever so slightly. Aida smiles too. She closes her eyes, giving into the sweet oblivion of mental nothingness for a few moments before it all begins again. Four o'clock is the beginning of round two. The children get home from school, which means snack, homework and showers, dinner needs to be made, and the dishes done. Aida's daughter, Nidal, works the night shift at a nursing home, and so she is sleeping, but will leave shortly after Lejla and Halim make their appearance.

She chose that name, Nidal, for the time in which she was born. There was no more appropriate word for it than *struggle*. The name was meant to be an ever-present reminder to her daughter, where and what she had come from, what she and her family have overcome. *This struggle*, Aida thinks, *ends with greatness.*

She hears the sound of water coursing through the pipes behind their thin walls. Nidal is up. This is Aida's cue. She forces herself up. Opening the fridge, she pulls out leftovers from dinner the night before. Removing the plastic wrap, she places the plate in the microwave and waits. When the plate is done heating she places it on the table and pours a tall glass of ice water to go along with it, cutting a thin slice of juicy lemon to give it a hint of flavor, just as Nidal prefers.

She sits across from the place she just set, and waits.

Nidal comes out, wearing her prescribed uniform of white shirt, beige pants, and black tennis shoes, her wavy auburn hair with golden highlights pulled back in a ponytail. Even in such drab garb, her prettiness cannot be denied. Aida smiles to herself. *My daughter*, she thinks.

"Mom," Nidal says, rushing to tell the story in their native tongue. "The school called me today. They are suspending Lejla." She stops to take a hurried bite of the meat stuffed flakey dough and continues on.

"She got into a *fight* with another girl." She says the word *fight* with utter disdain, in complete disgust that it describes the actions of one of her offspring. "I raised her better than this. She has become someone I don't recognize, someone I am ashamed to call mine." She drops the remaining food back on the plate, and rests her forehead in her palms. "What's happening?" she says aloud, to no one in particular, but Aida, her mother, answers.

"It could be worse," Aida coos to her in soft spoken Bosnian. "In America, for an adolescent girl, it could be so much worse. It could have been drugs or pregnancy, but this we can handle, together, as a family." She strokes her daughter's hair, from the beginning of her hairline to the back of her neck. Long, firm strokes, as Nidal quietly weeps.

She does not weep for this alone, Aida understands. She weeps for everything that came before, and for fear of what might be waiting.

Aida shushes her, wrapping her grown child up in her arms, and rocks her.

"Nidal, my love," she whispers in her ear. "Eat. You'll need your strength for work tonight. I will talk to our little delinquent when she gets home. It'll all be okay."

Aida is not sure she believes herself, but hopes these words are enough to see Nidal through a long night at work.

She coaxes her daughter into eating the food that remains on her plate, and sees her out the door.

"What was that all about," Irsad asks her quietly, not sure if he really wants to know the answer. Since their two sons moved out a year ago, closer to the university with easier access to classes and jobs, he has become powerfully outnumbered. What little he contributes to the continual collective female debate is often met with blank stares, so best not to debate at all, unless directly with Aida. Here, he huffs, he still has some pull.

She fills him in on the drama. She tries to keep it light, but this news from Lejla's school fills them both with a sense of anxiety. Aida wards off the urge to launch into the "this would never happen at home" diatribe because *this*, she thinks, *is just another example of what Americans call bullshit.* The *home* her Bosnian comrades love to refer to is the romanticized version of its former self. They love to evoke this concept of *home*, especially when comparing the way things are in America to how they might have been in Bosnia.

The truth, Aida remarks silently, in the privacy of her own mind, *is that home became the land of ethnic cleansing and genocide. People such as me, Muslims, and other religious and ethnic minorities, the primary targets.* She would take suspension from school and booty shorts any day over the grave possibility of what could have been, had they remained in their former home, which overnight became her hell. She shudders, and thanks God for the reality of things. They, she knows, are infinitely blessed compared to so many others. Be thankful, she tells herself; her daily mantra when her mind goes places she wishes it wouldn't.

The struggle, Aida reflects, is the essence of life itself.

⁊ **8** ⁊

Lydia

She lies in bed, awake. Gary has already gone to work, and Lydia isn't sure what time it is, and doesn't really care. No inspiration this morning, and so she lies, the deflated version of herself, in clean sheets, that smell like Tide. She breathes in deeply. This has always been one of her favorite scents, but this morning it doesn't do it for her. Her eyes trace the ceiling, having memorized its smoothness, its evenness. She knows its slight inconsistencies, remaining water marks from leaks long ago repaired, a testament to what the house has weathered.

How many hours has she spent lying like this, over the course of the last year? One of the perks of retirement, she had been told, is being able to sleep in. But Lydia doesn't sleep, she can't. It isn't for lack of trying. One Benadryl, a swig of Zzzquil, two Benadryl, two Tylenol PM, three Advil PM, and the list goes on and on and on, night after night, as does her sleeplessness. She is good from the time she initially goes to bed, typically around 10 or 11 pm, until the first time she wakes up to use the bathroom, usually between 1 and 3 am. She wakes up to pee, the family plague of a small bladder that she was lucky enough to inherit. After that first awakening, she turns and tosses, and tosses and turns. Sometimes she thinks about the past, mistakes, wishful do-overs, the anxiety-ridden *what if I had done this or that differently*. These she can understand.

Nighttime anxiety is an internal reflection of this time in her life, her *in-between years*. The term was referenced in a psychology magazine she leafed through one afternoon while waiting for her obligatory therapy session to begin. Unlike the plethora of self-help nonsense that might as well go out with the trash typically filling such articles, this term actually resonated with her, and so she claimed it, and now it is hers. It is meant to describe a state in one's being, where the past is glorious and romanticized, but the past nonetheless, gone, vanished, unable to be re-actualized. It was a beautiful time, but it is over, and the reality of that is heart-wrenching, because the present is a void, and the future is unknown, so the question becomes, *now what?* Lydia is living her in-between years and they suck.

What she doesn't understand, and can't possibly justify robbing her of sleep, is crap like the grocery list, or things she has to do the next day. Lydia now has nothing but time, so fitting it all in is not the problem.

She throws the cover off, but continues to lie there, searching for the motivation. Then it dawns on her, the appointment at The Unity School is today. She is beginning to regret making the commitment, even if it is just to go and see the school. She has become so damn good at being noncommittal, and look how far she has come. She smirks, acutely aware of her own futile attempts to bullshit her way out of her own head. Lydia sits up, swings her legs around the side of the bed, and puts two feet flat on the floor. Something wet and squishy caresses her right ankle, and she smiles knowingly. Rocky was there, waiting for her, still in bed himself. His big black nose, attached to his big blonde head, prodded her, *get up*!

Rocky, she thinks, *is the antithesis of noncommittal.* He shows up, wholeheartedly, day after day, always there, always ready. At better times in her life, the thought of the family dog being her inspiration, the example she strives to follow, would have been frightening. Now it simply is what it is, and it gets her up.

Fifty minutes later, she feels the weight of the car key in her hand, like an anchor, sinking her into the chair. Shower—check, coffee— check, news read—check, Rocky peed—check, her excuses to stay home and linger—obliterated. Punctual to a fault, Lydia will be on time, probably early. With a dramatic sigh that only the dog will hear, she slams the front door shut and proceeds to the car.

* * *

10 am on the nose, she observes. Lydia sits there in the parking lot, looking around. She missed the school the first time, drove right by. It is located behind a church, *so they must rent the space*, she thinks. She rings the bell and announces herself and her appointment. The door buzzes and she pushes it open.

Lydia walks down the hall until it dead-ends into a closed door, separating her from a room filled with singing children. She now has the option of turning left or right. She looks both ways, as if crossing the street, and chooses to go left because there is more noise coming

37

from that direction. She pops her head through the open door, and luckily it is the main office.

A middle-aged woman is sitting at a desk, and she looks up at Lydia, smiling. "You must be the volunteer," she says. *So it has been decided, established without my consent*, Lydia thinks begrudgingly, *like so many other things in my life.*

"I'm Margaret," she says, holding her hand out, but not standing up. She casually pats the chair across from her, offering Lydia a seat.

As Lydia shakes her hand and sits, she feels Margaret studying her, curiously, as though she is privy to the snarky remarks made by the voice in her head.

"So how did you hear about us?" Margaret asks. Her voice is gentle but firm.

"My ther—, uh, oh excuse me." Lydia laughs awkwardly. "My friend, my friend." She can't believe she almost said the words "my therapist" to some stranger she is meeting for the first time. Faking composure, she forces the conversation forward. "I am a retired school teacher. I thought retirement would be more than it has proven itself to be." Lydia shrugs her shoulders, and decides to stop fronting. "Can you tell me more about your school?"

Margaret is still smiling. She looks at Lydia through her glasses, eye contact never wavering, with big, brown cow eyes. Pretty and soft, like the light gray bob framing her face. She is not chubby, nor is she firm. She is warm.

"The foundation of the school is a lifelong dream of my husband's and mine. Liam started out as a teacher and then got more involved in the administrative side of education. He is the principal," she says smilingly, softly and proudly. "I'm the school nurse and help out however else I can, wherever needed, which often feels like everywhere." She laughs lightheartedly, unburdened by the work that is her life's calling.

"What was the dream exactly?" asks Lydia, her curiosity peaking. *Don't act too interested*, she reminds herself, *you haven't committed yet!* She sits up straighter, and tries not to lean in quite so much while talking, distancing herself.

"Refugees," Margaret replies. "You know, these kids and their families come here with nothing, I mean literally. A family of five might share a single suitcase. The parents and older kids have been through it all, seen the worst things imaginable. The younger ones are born in the camps, and know nothing else. School, what is that? Some of them have never set foot inside a classroom. And then of course, there are the American kids, a lot of whom come from very poor families, and some who come from wealthier means. Together, refugee children and American children, they can build a new world, the one I think most of us wished we lived in. If they are raised to see one another's gifts and ways in which they are each unique and different, but taught to celebrate these things, instead of judging one another because of them, then we have succeeded."

Lydia looks into her big brown cow eyes, and wonders. *What is it like to be so convinced, so sure about what you are doing?* She had felt that way about her children, watching them grow up, raising them, she knew this was her purpose—them. Now they are adults, with purposes of their own, and she is left floundering.

"Does this sound like something you could get behind?" Margaret asks, a large smile spreading across her round face.

Lydia doesn't reply right away, distracted as usual, by the thoughts and memories running through her mind.

Suddenly, she is brought back by a soft sensation on her right hand. She looks down and sees two little black hands holding her large white one. She notices how dirty the little fingernails are. Lydia looks up, and finds herself startled. She didn't know skin could be that black. It is like oil, black, thick and beautiful. The whites of the two little eyes looking into her own stand in shocking contrast to the skin surrounding them.

A smile instinctively spreads across her face. Using these muscles feels strange, smiles being few and far between these days. Two rows of glorious white teeth reveal themselves when the child smiles back. The two strangers continue holding hands, saying nothing, just grinning.

"Lydia, I would like you to meet Nabora," Margaret says.

"Well, hello there, Nabora. How are you?"

The child stands there silently, unresponsive to Lydia's question, aside from the grin that remains plastered to her face.

"Nabora just arrived with her family from Sudan and doesn't speak English yet. Give it a few months and she'll be fluent," Margaret confirms, winking at the little girl.

Nabora giggles, and releases Lydia's hand. She lifts her arm to reveal a scraped elbow. Margaret coos, and turns to the cabinets behind her desk. She rummages around, surfacing with some alcohol wipes and a Band-Aid. Margaret motions for the child to come to her, but Nabora shakes her head, and nods towards Lydia.

"Oh," Margaret says, stifling her laughter. "It appears we have a special request."

Lydia smiles, slipping all too easily into the role, and tends to the wound. When all is said and done, she is thanked with a hug and the child skips away, back to where she came from.

"Well, unless you disagree, Lydia, I think it has been decided," Margaret says.

Lydia looks at her. "I'll start Monday of next week if that is okay."

"I think that should work just fine. We have a few positions open. What is your availability?"

Lydia hadn't really thought about what she would be willing to commit to, because before she arrived, she hadn't planned on committing at all. "What are the positions?"

"We have an after-care position, which would be from 2-5 pm Monday through Friday, and a classroom assistant position that would be from 8 am-2 pm Monday through Friday. Margaret pauses for a moment, weighing a possibility in her mind. "I'll be right back," she says and disappears into the office behind her desk.

Emerging a few moments later, she is followed by a tall, tired, smiling man. He holds his hand out, firmly shaking Lydia's. He is Liam, the school principal. They exchange pleasantries and a few teaching war stories. She likes him, she decides, perhaps even admires him a bit. While his humble attire of worn-out khakis, faded blue button up shirt, and scuffed brown loafers do not command immediate reverence, his whiskery white mustache, growing boisterous beard, and loud wholehearted laugh invoke an immediate sense of devotion that cannot be explained with reason. You feel it before it makes sense.

Clearly old enough to retire himself, his golden years are being spent working, but with purpose and conviction. Lydia wants to feel that again. *If I can't create my own*, she thinks to herself, *then maybe I can borrow his*.

"Well, listen Lydia, we actually have a teaching position open in the second grade. It doesn't pay what you are probably accustomed to, coming from the Atlanta public school system with twenty plus years of experience, but would you consider it?"

Mentally Lydia freezes. The possibility of teaching again, full-time, had not crossed her mind. If she is getting paid, that would mean a contract, which would mean long term commitment. She isn't quite there yet.

"I...I think I would like to start out as a volunteer, and the after-care position sounds like the amount of time I can commit to starting out. Let's see how that goes, and then we'll see."

"Okay," Liam says, shaking her hand firmly again, and then releasing it to push his simple silver rimmed glasses back up to the base of his nose. "We have a deal. I look forward to seeing you Monday."

He turns, and retreats back into his office, closing the door behind him.

"I think we'll assign you to the second-grade for after-care." Margaret determines. "That way you can get to know the children you would be teaching, should you decide to apply for the full-time position later." She makes a note of the assignment and smiles, not worrying about revealing her ultimate aim. "Things have a way of working themselves out," she says, looking up over her glasses at Lydia.

So much smiling, Lydia thinks, wondering what it must be like to live in a permanent state of bliss. She nods in response. *What am I getting myself into?*

⸗ **9** ⸗

Sherry

The Unity School had early release today and so she arrives home before everyone else, which gives her the perfect opportunity to decompress. Seeing the box on their doorstep, and Emma's name on the return address, fills Sherry with nostalgia. The birthday present from her friend reminds her that despite college feeling like a lifetime ago, it's only been four months.

She runs upstairs, throws her backpack on the bed, and pulls the box out from the closet. Opening the treasure chest, she pulls out a single clove, which makes her mouth water slightly. She longs for the slight euphoric buzz it gives her after deeply inhaling once or twice.

She and her friends liked to smoke these in college, on occasion. Sherry would never sink so low as to be considered a *smoker*, but once or twice a week, sometimes three, wasn't going to label her as such. She thought about the time that she and Rachel had hidden Emma's cigarettes, and how pissed she got. They did it out of love, because Emma was flirting with being labeled a *smoker*, and this was unacceptable.

Rachel and Sherry became friends through friends, about halfway through freshman year. Emma was busy with her older, completely unworthy boyfriend until a year later when he cheated on her while away on a study abroad trip.

With the change in relationship status, Emma was suddenly around all the time. This gave Sherry the opportunity to finally get to know the stranger she had been living with for the last six months. She thinks fondly of Emma's big debut one night at a campus party. Rachel and Sherry recognized her full potential, but also understood she needed a little help getting there. They helped Emma choose what to wear that night, a pair of tight jeans and hot little red tank top. They insisted she wear her contacts instead of glasses, and let her long thick mane of blonde-streaked hair flow freely down her back.

That was the beginning of a beautiful friendship, Sherry thinks. She and Rachel had grown apart senior year, barely talking when they moved out of their apartment; both equally frustrated with the other's self-involvement and unwillingness to acquiesce. Emma however, would come and visit her this year; she was sure.

Sherry steps outside onto the crumbling front steps, lights up the clove, and takes a long gluttonous drag. The buzz hits her slowly, pervasively, and lingers just a bit before dissipating, at which point she takes another long slow inhale.

Fall is in the air. The mornings are cooler now, which means she doesn't need to wash the sweat out of her bra on a nightly basis. Sherry can feel herself changing with the season. After that first day, she stopped wearing makeup other than mascara to work, because it would literally melt off her face by the time she got home in the evening. She has almost destroyed her sixty dollar pair of Steve Madden black loafers. The chunky two inch heels that got her around just fine on Saint Mary's campus were now worn down to about an inch in height from all the tromping around in playground tanbark and the daily hikes to and from work. The next pair of shoes she gets will be a durable one.

The house is beginning to improve. She and her roommates spend their weekends picking up donated furniture to replace the bug-infested couches and chairs they tossed in the dumpster that sits in their driveway. They finally figured out how to work the air conditioning, and slowly but surely were purifying the house by deep-cleaning each room.

Intentional community, one of the main principles dictating our lives this year, does not mean we will all be best friends, Sherry reflects. It means things like a chore wheel that rotates on a weekly basis, and the group eating dinner together once or twice a week. She admits to herself though, that she does feel a growing sense of comradery with the crew. Life, under any other circumstances, would not have brought them together, and yet, through free-will, great intentionality on each of their parts, and a deeply rooted sense of purpose, here they were. Each being cast, by choice, into the role of other, in the hopes that it would strip from them the confines of the old world order where white and wealthy reign supreme, and usher them into the new world, reborn cleansed and free of their former tendencies to make assumptions, stereotype those cast into the role of other through no choice of their own, and take for granted the world their white skin and upper-class status gives them access to. *We*, Sherry thinks, *are pioneers*, and she knows she will make a difference.

Sherry admits to herself that she too had her moment, a breakdown, where the weight of her choice to come here, felt like it was crushing her. She had looked down on her roommates that first night, when every girl but she was brought to tears. She declared herself the strong one, but really, she was just very good at compartmentalizing, until she wasn't, and it all came bubbling to the surface. Unfortunately, it happened at work. Sherry called her mom, and all it took was the sound of that voice, calling her *"sweetie"* and every vulnerability she had tried desperately to bury unearthed itself. She couldn't speak, she was crying too hard. Finally allowing herself to feel the impact the last couple of weeks had on her, and their contrast to the spoiled life she had led before, were paralyzing. Her mom became frantic on the other end of the line, because all she heard was her child sobbing, deep guttural moaning, and wheezing as she struggled for air.

Sherry had told her mom everything, because she had to. She could no longer feign indifference, that everything would be fine, because it so was not.

She sat crumpled in the grass outside the school, and confessed the entire truth to the person who usually had the ability to make all things right in the world. Sherry refused the offers to fly her home, or for her mom and stepdad to fly out. She realized suddenly that she was a world away, and so she was on her own. She had her family's support, but unless she wanted to give in and give up, this was her reality for better or for worse.

This choice, Sherry thinks to herself while taking the final drag from the dwindling clove, *is what keeps me from being able to fully submerse myself in the reality of the other I want to identify with.* She was not born into this, she chose it, and could choose something else at any time. She can fly home to her middleclass neighborhood and start researching grad school programs at a moment's notice. The other she strives to understand wears poverty like chains, held to the earth by their weight, denied time and time again the key to set oneself free.

And so she remains, one month in to what will be the longest year of her spoon-fed life.

❧ 10 ❧

Lydia

She sits on the playground bench, smoothing Martha's hair back and gathering it into a ponytail. Several of the other children stand around her, watching, chatting, insisting they are next in line for a hairstyling. Lydia laughs and encourages them to calm down, promising everyone will have a turn.

Across from her, on the other end of the playground, stands Mya, her beautiful Burmese colleague. Two of Mya's children attend Unity, and she began working there this year. She is one of the Kindergarten classroom assistants during the day, and helps Lydia with the second grade afterschool class in the afternoon.

Lydia smiles in her direction and waves. Mya smiles her bright warm smile back and returns the gesture. Lydia feels a strong connection to this woman, twenty-five years her junior. She sees in her what she sees in herself, a mother. *Mya's spoken English has come a long way in the last month,* Lydia thinks to herself, admiring her friend's steady progress. They are able to communicate with one another on a limited basis, but Lydia feels more connected to Mya than she did to former colleagues she had worked with for years.

A month, she thinks, unable to believe time has gone so quickly, reflecting back on her meeting with Mrs. Luna, and how that woman had gotten her to agree to volunteer 15 hours a week, within five minutes of meeting her. Lydia was never that quick to commit to anything. She typically needed time to ponder, think over the alternatives, but in this case she had said "yes" before even realizing the word was coming out of her mouth.

Lydia the cynic might be experiencing a conversion, she thinks, smiling to herself. Gary looks at her differently these days. He has always looked at her lovingly, but the worry is gone. *He must notice the change I feel in myself too.* This makes her happy.

She squeezes Martha's shoulders, signaling her hair is done, and it's the next child's turn. "Can I go to the bathroom Ms. Lydia?" Martha asks. Lydia says yes, knowing she wants to look at herself in the mirror. Off she runs, and Amira plops down in her place. She leans back into Lydia's legs, affectionately, this being her way of asking for a hug. Lydia wraps her arms tightly around the girl and sways back and forth a few times, before releasing her and combing her fingers through the long, dark hair.

So completely different, and so equally beautiful, Lydia thinks. She watches the children playing together. *Children from more than ten different countries, in one class.* She watches the Iraqi boy and American girl take turns pushing one another on the swing. *Mr. Luna is a visionary. This school is helping form the next generation*, and this thought makes her think the world might actually stand a chance.

* * *

Lydia pulls into the driveway. She remembers Gary is working late tonight at the office, preparing for an upcoming case, so she is on her own for dinner. She appreciates the occasional night to herself, free of the obligation to cook, content to eat frozen pizza and binge watch whatever show she is into at the moment.

Rocky greets her at the door, shoving his enormous head into her legs, whining incessantly. She drops her bag and keys on the floor, gets on her knees and hugs him.

She feels light, content.

The next few hours are spent checking e-mail, showering the day away, scarfing down an entire cheese pizza singe-handedly, and catching up on Parenthood, her current Netflix obsession.

Lydia awakens to Gary spreading a blanket over her. She must have nodded off while watching her show. Her eyes flutter open, groggily.

"Let's go to bed sweetie." Gary holds out his hand, helping her up, and together they make their way to the bedroom.

"How is prep for the case going?" Lydia inquires, asking more out of a sense of spousal obligation than authentic interest. She loves him, but his work is a bore.

"Good. We pretty much have everything ready. We are just finalizing the list of witnesses and then prepping them will be the last step before we go to trial."

"Oh that's great," Lydia says tiredly, barely getting the words out before passing out on her pillow.

She wakes up the following morning to the sun shining brightly through the window and sheer white shades that are more for decoration than actually shielding the room from the incoming light.

She looks down over the side of the bed and Rocky snores contently beside her. Gary has already left for work. *It must be around eight,* Lydia thinks.

There is still some coffee in the pot, and she pours a generous size cup. Settling down at the kitchen table, she opens her laptop and peruses BBC news. *The world is such a depressing place.* She realizes after this fleeting thought, that she does not feel the weight of it all this morning, and come to think of it, she hasn't felt the weight of it in a while. She smiles, deeply satisfied, and hopeful that this might be the beginning of a new norm, and this time, not to be attributed to an increase in her antidepressant.

She told her psychiatrist that she wanted to try going drug free. He was reticent to consider her request, but when she played the "It's my body, and I'll do whatever the hell I want with it," card, he deferred to her common sense and his assessment of Lydia's undeniable progress, and agreed to help her slowly taper off. That was two weeks ago, and despite the decrease in dose, she feels good, and this makes her happy.

Then, she notices what she had failed to see when first entering the kitchen. A note is propped up by the bananas in the fruit bowl, the upper left corner lazily flopped over, inhibiting her ability to read it.

She gets up, grabs the note, and returns to her seat. *Fuck,* she says to herself. *A note from Gary never means anything good.* He defers to this method of communication when he is scared of what her reaction will be. *I was having such a good twenty-four hours. If this messes that up, he is on his own for dinner for the rest of the week. And,* she snickers snidely to herself, *I will make him come with me to my next session with Dr. Coleman, for couple's therapy.* Satisfied with the consequences she is assigning to the potential affront, she feels empowered to go ahead and read the damn thing.

Sweetie,

I wanted to discuss this with you last night when I got home, but you were already asleep, and I need an answer by this afternoon, so the timing is what forced me into having to write you a note. I know how much you hate it when I do this, and that you think it is me trying to avoid a confrontation, but this time, I am confident in assuming that there will be a confrontation regardless of whether I talk with you in person, or bring the subject up in a letter.

Aimee called me yesterday, hysterical. She is fine, nothing life threatening, but she and Mark are separating. I think it was her decision, but she is still a total wreck, and wants to come and stay with us for a while, until they figure out next steps.

So, the silver lining is that one of the kids is coming home! Never thought that would happen, but never say never, right? The part of this that you are going to loathe me for suggesting is that I think we should make up Karen's old room for her. That is really the only space we have right now that is free, with furniture we don't really need.

I don't mean for this to sound heartless, sweetie, it's just that it has been twenty-five years now, and every time I have brought it up, you refuse to engage me. I need you to think about what it is like for me though, as the one who wants to move on, who can't go in that room, but knows it is there, a permanent fixture in the home we both live in.

It is time, and now we have an actual reason that will benefit one of our other children, so please think it over. We can talk when I get home tonight. I love you.

~Gary

Lydia sees red, and then nothing, through the tears. She cannot think, she cannot speak, she cannot hear, but she can feel. She feels like she is dying, like the inside of herself is decaying at an accelerated rate.

She struggles to sit down, and collapses on the floor. This is when she hears it, a terrifying, guttural, moaning. It goes on and on. It's not until a few moments pass that she realizes the sound is coming from her.

This terrifies her, that she can succumb to such an extent, still. She thought she was better! She thought she had moved past this. She was so wrong.

He, she thinks, *is doing this to me. How can he make me relive this again? He thinks he loves me, but he doesn't! He does not understand! He doesn't know me!*

She feels no grief for her marriage though, only rage, which gives her the strength to get up off the floor, and wipe away the tears. She tucks her despair away for another time, allowing the anger to sustain and move her. *Aimee may not be the only one getting separated.*

She turns the note over, and writes in huge all caps, "FINE, ASSHOLE". Composing herself, she uses the bananas to prop up her response, and smiles, satisfied.

Lydia takes a hot shower, and lets the scalding water cascade over her. She wants it to wash away the remnants of anguish that cling to her skin like a disease. She feels covered, stifled, suffocated by this oppressive force. It has been twenty-five years and she wants herself back. *Who is that? I don't even know what I look like, what I feel like without this.* By *this* she means the grief, the ever-present, all-consuming, oppressive force that she despises. After so much time, it still lies in wait for her, dormant, a sleeping toxin ready to seep through her pores into her blood at any moment. She is aware of its presence, the fact that it is always there, a part of her, partially defining her, and she loathes it.

In the beginning, after Karen's passing, she succumbed to it, because there was simply nothing else to do. It was not a choice, it simply was. Losing a child almost destroyed her. If she hadn't had other children she was responsible for, she would have given in, because the grief was that powerful.

Over time however, it evolved into a choice, and she chose it, time and time again. It was all that she had left, this gut-wrenching, soul crushing sadness and darkness, to acknowledge what she had lost, and she reveled in this reminder, because it made her feel close to the one who was gone.

"Dead and gone!" Gary had yelled. Lydia remembers his hands on her shoulders, shaking her, trying to bring her back to life. "She is dead and gone! I can't go on living like this, living for both of us! I need you! Our children need you! You have to choose, between your black hole of nothingness and us. I will not wait forever."

He had never yelled at her before that night. The kids were asleep in bed, she and Gary hadn't had sex in over a year, and she recoiled at his slightest touch. She achieved the bare minimum, in her marriage, as a mom, and as a teacher. It was all just a matter of time, when people decided she had been allotted enough time to get used to being the parent of a dead child, and began to lose patience with her inability to get her shit together.

She ran up the stairs to Karen's room, and lay in her bed, covering herself with the Disney princess comforter. She had stayed like that, looking at the ceiling, for hours. Eventually her heart beat returned to its normal pace and her stomach and fists unclenched. She knew he was right. Her selfishness was undeniable. She had known this for a while, but was waiting to see how long she could get away with it.

That night, staring at the ceiling in her dead daughter's bed, she chose life over death. She chose the living over the one who had passed away, and she chose her family over herself. The grief would eventually kill her, and she was actually okay with that. She felt like the walking dead anyway, but her family needed her, and so she chose them.

That was more than twenty years ago, and she can feel herself slipping back, but she no longer finds any comfort in that place, and so she resists the temptation to say "Fuck it all" and just slide. She gets her purse, slips Rocky into his harness, and together they get in the car. She takes the backroads to Peachtree Street and then takes that north to Midtown. She parks her car on the street and looks up at Aimee's third story condo.

Gary is right, she thinks, now wishing she hadn't written that reply for him to find first thing when he gets home from work. *Too late now*. She and Rocky head to the front entrance. She is going to help Aimee pack her shit and move back home.

≈ **11** ≈

Sherry

His name is Ashraf, she came to find out. He is from Afghanistan. He is loud, boisterous, overly confident, foreign in a way that is slightly disconcerting to her, and hot. He is a senior at Georgia State, studying business, came with his family to the U.S. as a refugee 6 years ago, and has asked Sherry on a date. She goes through the list of what she already knows about him, obsessively.

He had approached her last week, one day during afterschool, while they were both outside supervising their classes on the playground. He mentioned it so casually, offhand, as if it were the most natural thing in the world, the two of them having lunch. If it is, why is Sherry mulling over it, and considering retracting her "yes"?

The leaves are starting to change colors and fall from the trees, and the weather is finally bearable. She isn't dripping with sweat at 8 am when she arrives at school following her morning commute, which is a nice change.

In all fairness, Sherry knows she encouraged him. She and Aziza had been at a baby shower for a co-worker a few weekends ago. It had ended around 10pm and the night was young. Aziza mentioned dancing, and Sherry mentioned Ashraf. It was bold she knew, and Aziza gave her that look.

"Really? Giiiirl, you didn't tell me you have a thing for him!"

"I don't," Sherry had insisted defensively. Suggesting he join them had been an impulse she wished she had suppressed. She couldn't help that she was curious about him though. "I just know you guys are friends, and hang out."

"Sherry please! Let's call him and see if he can meet up."

Aziza dialed his number and explained the situation when he answered. The conversation was quick, and she hung up without Sherry understanding where they had left things.

Sherry looked at Aziza, waiting expectantly.

"So, what did he say?"

"I knew you cared! Stop trying to act like you don't! He's going to meet us there in 30 minutes."

"Where?" Sherry squealed; suddenly full of nerves and regret.

Aziza looked at her like she was dumb. "At the club."

Shit, Sherry thought to herself. *Now what?*

Good thing she had worn her tight jeans and heels. She was going to need a drink. She thought of her monthly stipend and vow of poverty. One drink would set her back at least seven bucks. She would get a Long Island Ice Tea to maximize the amount of alcohol per dollar she was spending. College drinking logic had yet to fail her.

They had spent most of the night dancing together. Other friends from Unity had met up with the group, so Aziza was entertained, but for Sherry it had been as though no one else was there. The following Monday at school it was as if Saturday night had never happened. Both of them were culpable for the over-emphasizing of nonchalance; neither of them knowing what to do next.

Then, almost two weeks later, he approached her, asked her out, and she said yes. *Weird*, was Sherry's first thought.

"Why weird?" Emma had demanded during their weekly phone update. "That is how it is supposed to go. He likes you, so he asks you out."

"It has never been this easy before," was Sherry's reply. "Think about it. Literally every guy that I liked, hooked up with, or briefly dated in college, made everything so hard and complicated. There has always been drama, angst, will he call, and if he does, will he call again, his friends tell me he likes me, but he never makes a move, he makes a move, trying to get in my pants, and then when I tell him I'm a virgin and it ain't gonna happen, he disappears." Sherry goes through the litany of frustrating dating scenarios she experienced for the last four years, all of which Emma knows from beginning to end.

"I always had to do all the work, or least the majority of it. I don't even know what a real relationship feels like." She would only admit this to Emma. To all other friends, she happily passes out dating tips and guy advice when consulted, as though she is an expert. *The only thing I am in expert on is how to handle rejection*, she thinks to herself.

"Maybe this is a new beginning," Emma encouraged her. "It's a good thing you said yes, and now you have to go on the date and see. You said he was hot, so what's the big deal? It's one hour of your life. Go and see what a real date feels like."

"I've been on a real date," Sherry said in an exasperated tone. "It's not like I don't know what that is. It's the relationship part that is mysterious to me. I mean, I know what one is supposed to look like, and I know from my experience what it isn't supposed to be like."

"Sherry," Emma said, "I'm not saying you have no experience with the opposite sex. We both know that isn't true. I'm just saying, that based on what you've told me so far, it sounds like this guy likes you. Let him pursue you, let him take you out, let him pay, let him work for it. That's all I'm trying to say. You deserve a guy who is going to put in some goddamn effort, okay?" Emma's tone reflected the frustration Sherry felt. She had been witness to the worst of it.

She had taken Emma's advice, and decided to let things play out. She would leave her "yes" as is, and let him come to her.

The last child in After-care is signed out by his mom, and Sherry collects her things. Ashraf jogs her way and Sherry's heart is suddenly in her throat. "Hey," he says, flashing his beautiful smile full of almost perfectly straight white teeth. "So, we still on for tomorrow?" he asks, his large forehead furrowing, waiting for her response. She notices how perfectly his short black curly hair is gelled in place. *He would have spiral curls if he grew it out,* she thinks, her eyes drifting from his hair, to high set cheekbones and strong jawline, finally landing on those big luscious lips.

Sherry feels relief wash over her. It is then that she realizes her angst about him retracting the invite. *That is a good sign! It means I want to go.*

"Yep. My lunch break starts at 11:30 and I have about an hour."

"I'll pick you up in front of school. See you then." He smiles again, but this time more softly, mouth closed. His eyes linger on hers a bit longer than necessary and Sherry feels the butterflies in her stomach take flight.

* * *

She gets up early to allow extra prep time for date day. The key is to pick something cute to wear that is sexy but still appropriate for school. She chooses the black tank top with pretty pastel flowers stitched in the upper left corner. It offers full coverage in the front, and dips lower in the back, but she can still wear a regular bra without it showing. She wears her grey hoodie over it, a hand me down from her younger sister.

The day is cool enough for her to be comfortable wearing the hoodie throughout the morning in class with the kids. She wears it zipped all the way up, feeling more comfortable this way, but plans to ditch it before lunch.

While assisting the kids with their lessons, Sherry's mind is elsewhere. She feels anxious and giddy, and then suddenly it's 11:15. She heads to the kitchen where Aida is waiting for her with a smile. The two have become quite friendly, a silent comradery that snuck up on them. If someone asked Sherry how they had become so buddy-buddy, she wouldn't have a clue.

Sherry is too distracted to bask in the glory of the newfound friendship, one of many she enjoys with her colleagues at Unity. She makes a mental note to intentionally appreciate it later. Standing in front of her tray, she spoons out food, plate after plate, for the children she has come to love. She is on a high she realizes. Smiling to herself, she knows it is because of Ashraf.

Making her way to the front of the school, she sees him toward the back of the parking lot, leaning against his car. It is a decent nondescript navy blue sedan. He smiles as he sees her approaching.

"Ready?" he asks warmly.

"Yep," Sherry replies coolly, having trouble holding his gaze. She nervously tries not to appear nervous and shifts her eyes from his, to the car, to the ground, and then back to him.

Ashraf makes his way to the driver's side, indicating that he is not going to be opening her door for her. Sherry swallows her disappointment. Her stepdad always does this for her mom, and she sees it as a sign of chivalry, which apparently is dead today.

Unimpressed, she gets in the passenger seat and buckles up. "So I was thinking we could go to this restaurant I used to work at. It's called Kabul. Have you ever had Afghani food?"

"No, but I'm up for trying it," Sherry says, trying to sound bright and shiny, but unable to get over him not opening the door for her.

"Okay," Ashraf says happily. "Let's go."

The car ride takes about ten minutes as they make their way toward the Emory campus. Sherry has never been on this side of Atlanta before and she reflects on how pretty it is. Lovely two-story middle class homes line the streets, different colors and personalities, all with lush green laws rolling out before them. It reminds her of home.

They pull into a strip mall and park. It is a hole in the wall with a few tables outside and more seating inside.

"Let's order," Ashraf directs her to the counter. He exchanges vibrant hellos with the cashier. They shake hands warmly. His eyes dart from Sherry to Ashraf and he cannot hide his enthusiasm. They continue to exchange friendly banter in a language Sherry does not understand, but she is able to translate the subliminal message reverberating between the two men. It feels like he is congratulating Ashraf, and this makes Sherry simultaneously feel awkward and flattered.

"Okay," Ashraf says, looking her way and smiling. "Want to sit?" He says it as more of a suggestion than a question, and takes the lead on making their way outside.

Taking a seat, Sherry places her napkin in her lap, force of habit.

"Do you think the waiter will bring a couple menus?" Sherry asks.

"I already ordered," Ashraf replies.

"You did? When?"

"When we were at the counter."

Sherry ponders how to say what she is about to say without seeming high maintenance. "The thing is, I only eat free range meat products." She folds, unfolds and folds her hands again. They are getting sweaty, the conversation starting to make her anxious. She slightly wishes she could turn off her internal code of ethics occasionally, but knows this is not an option.

"If I don't know that whatever I'm eating came from an animal that was raised that way, I can't eat it."

"I know." He says, staring directly into her eyes. "I did my homework, with Aziza's help." He smiles and gives her a little wink.

Her stomach whirls, similar to the feeling she gets at the beginning of an epic drop on a rollercoaster. She is starting to like him. His confidence, which she found annoying at first, is charming as hell.

"So tell me about yourself? How did you end up in Atlanta working at Unity? I know a little from Aziza," he says with that smile, "but honestly not very much."

"Where should I start," Sherry says, looking upward, as if searching for an answer floating above her in the atmosphere.

"I am from the Bay Area, California. I grew up in a suburb of San Francisco, about twenty minutes south of the city, called San Bruno. I went to Saint Mary's College in Moraga, which is in the East Bay, about an hour from my home. I have two sisters and I am the middle, but don't worry. I don't suffer from the middle child complex people love to talk about, because my parents were very intentional about always giving me the same amount of attention as my sisters, so if anything, I was the lucky one, because I probably got more." Sherry smiles at Ashraf, and he grins back, obviously entertained by her soliloquy.

She pauses, so as not to hoard the air in the room, and give him space to reply, but all he says is "Go on," with the same boyish, entertained smile on his lips.

Sherry likes the way he looks at her. She feels seen. She knows how rare it is to feel as though another person sees you, or is at the very least trying to see you, and she feels her heart beginning to open, but cannot define it as such quite yet.

"I always knew I wanted to work with an international underserved population, and up until a few months ago, assumed it would be overseas. I knew this about myself since I was very young. So, my senior year, when it came time to apply to various organizations, I decided to go with JVI, the international branch of the Jesuit Volunteer Corps. They ended up rejecting me, because I have very little international travel or work experience and don't speak any other languages. I speak a little Spanish and French, but am definitely not fluent.

"So when they rejected me, it was like this existential crisis, because they were telling me I could not do what I always thought I was supposed to do, but they also encouraged me to apply to the domestic Jesuit Volunteer Corps, and so once I got over the trauma of the initial rejection, I did, and was accepted."

"How did you end up here though?"

"Well, I figured if I wasn't going to be in another country, I would like to go to the place most culturally different from where I'm from, and that would be the South. So they sent me a list of potential places I could volunteer, and Unity was one of them. When I read the description, and the fact that it was a school for refugees, I knew where I was meant to go, and honestly, my first day at the school confirmed my decision. Seeing all of those children from all over the world, together in the same room, was amazing."

"You are amazing," is Ashraf's reply.

The moment is disrupted by the waiter bringing their food. A few plates piled high with steaming rice, vegetables, yogurt and bread are placed before them.

Sherry combats her anxiety of trying to eat and carry on a conversation at the same time, throughout the meal. Her nervousness diminishes her appetite, *but this is good*, she thinks, *because I will lose weight*. She refers to this process affectionately as the "In-Like Diet."

"So you are from Afghanistan," Sherry says between bites, tossing the conversation back in his court.

"Yeah," Ashraf replies, sounding flat and intentionally unaffected, as if being an Afghan refugee in America were the most normal thing in the world.

"I grew up in a village outside of Kabul, the capital. After the U.S. invasion, my family and I left. Things were always bad when the Taliban was in power, but with the war, my parents knew it was going to get worse before it got better. We escaped to Pakistan, were there for several years, but fortunately we have family in Germany, so then we went there, and when we were granted refugee status in the U.S., we came here. Atlanta is where we were originally resettled, and we've been here ever since."

"Wow," Sherry replies, cursing herself for sounding so lame.

"It sounds like you and your family went through a lot." She wants to be sympathetic, but not overly so. She doesn't want him to feel like she pities him.

"We did, but we are good now. I'm sitting here with you, aren't I?" He looks at her, unwaveringly.

Sherry feels her face get hot, and she knows she is turning red. Taking a long sip of her diet coke, she smiles from behind the straw.

They finish their meal and have the waiter pack up the leftovers. Ashraf pays the bill, which confirms for Sherry that this is indeed a date. She leans back happily into her chair, looking at Ashraf as he works out the math for the tip, and breathes in deeply. *I wonder*, is all that comes to mind.

≈ 12 ≈

Lydia

"Why are you the one moving out?"

Lydia gently questions her daughter, rolling up a framed photograph of the young couple on their wedding day, three years ago, in bubble wrap.

"I offered. I'm the reason we're at this point. Mark doesn't want to separate. He is convinced we can work everything out, and get back to where we used to be. The thing is, I'm not sure I was ever even where he 'used to be,' and that is the problem." Aimee pauses, tucking her long, straight blonde hair behind her ears, and breathing deeply. Lydia says nothing, giving her space to keep going if she wants to.

"I need time and space to clear my head. I just feel so freaking weighed down and tired. Mom! I am only thirty-two years old. I shouldn't feel this way. I need to figure my shit out, before taking things any further." She places a picture of happier times on the floor, freeing her hands to rub the exhaustion away from her hazel eyes.

"What do you mean, sweetie?"

"Well, about six months ago, Mark started talking about having a baby, a lot. He is ready to start a family. When I looked at him and tried to imagine it all, I felt like I was looking at someone I love, but am not sure I am in love with, and that terrifies me."

"Honey, all marriages have their ups and downs and times where it is hard as hell, and then light as air."

"Yeah but mom, this early on? Did we get married too soon? Did we really know each other when we said 'I do'? These are the questions that keep me up at night. I need to figure out what my answers to them are, and I need to be alone to do that."

"Well, you can stay with us as long as you like. We are making up Karen's room for you. You'll have everything you need. Bring whatever you want from here, and we can keep the rest in storage."

Aimee stares at her mother dumbfounded. "I know sweetie," Lydia knowingly replies. "It's time."

"Mom! Can you handle that? Are, are you sure?" Aimee implores, her voice wavering.

Based on her daughter's reaction, Lydia is now acutely aware of how necessary it is to move forward, for her sake, and her family's. As long as that room is there, in that house, just as it was twenty-five years ago, one of her feet remains anchored in a tortured past, a past she is ready to sail away from.

"Was it your idea, or Dad's?" Lydia looks at the floor, not wanting to make eye contact with her very intuitive daughter. "Daaaad!" Aimee says, in an accusatory tone.

Lydia knows that despite her daughter's aspiration to remain neutral in all aspects of life, she has a tendency to side with dear old mom when it comes to family discrepancies. *This will not be divisive,* Lydia tells herself, reflecting ironically on the note that awaits Gary at home.

"Listen love. Your father suggested it, and I agreed, because it's time. It was probably time a while ago. I just wasn't ready until now."

Aimee watches her mom. Lydia knows she is trying to decide if she buys what her mom is selling or determine it's a load of crap delivered to her on a hot heaping tray of attempted, but failed, familial appeasement. The truth is, this is not the first time it has come up, and created seemingly insurmountable mountains of divide between her and Gary, but this time, she actually is ready.

"Okay," is Aimee's simple reply. With that, she drops the subject and continues packing the remnants of happier times shared by her and her husband.

"This isn't how I imagined it," Aimee says, running her finger along the cover of their wedding album.

"It never is, honey. It never is."

* * *

Lydia and Rocky are heading home, and she is cursing midtown traffic. She is hopeful that she might make it there before Gary and intercept the damn note. Now that she has come to terms with things, and accepted his proposal, she just wants to move on, and not have yet another thing to have to talk through with him. If he sees that note, he will assume she is not ready, and World War III is a high likelihood.

Rocky barks in seeming agreement from the passenger seat. She looks at her friend, and thanks the heavens for his company. Unconditional love and no need to explain yourself, who could ask for more?

The Prius rounds the corner and pulls into the driveway. She pushes the garage door opener hesitantly, knowing what waits inside will determine her short-term fate. The door slowly rises, to reveal an empty garage. Lydia breathes a sigh of relief. Just as she is almost through the exhale, she hears the friendly beep of Gary's Camry behind her. "Shit!"

She throws open her door, not bothering to let Rocky out, and makes a mad dash for the kitchen. There, in all its glory, stands her snide note, leaning casually against the bananas. She grabs it, crumples it up, and tosses it in the trash on her way back out to the garage. Gary and Rocky meet her halfway.

Gary looks at her, acknowledging the oddity of her actions. "Well, that was a bit strange," he says laughingly. "Everything okay?"

Rocky stands between them, wagging his tail, pleasantly ignorant and unaware.

"Everything's fine. I just really had to use the bathroom."

"Did you get my note?" Gary asks, getting straight to the point. He hadn't always been so direct, but after years of dancing around the issues in their marriage, they both embrace the fact that there is no more time to be wasted.

"I did." Lydia resists the urge to draw her response out, letting him brew in hopeful expectancy of the answer he is looking for, combined with the fear of hearing the one he is not, but she resists. *I will not be divisive*, she commands internally.

"That's fine. I was actually just at Aimee's place, helping her pack, and process. Those kids have a long road ahead of them, whether they take it together or alone. Why does life have to be such a bitch?" She smiles at her husband, because even though she means every word of what she just said, she doesn't want things to be heavy between them. She wants to pop popcorn, cuddle together under one blanket on the couch, and watch a crappy rom-com. Is this what they usually do on a week night? Sometimes, but not frequently, and Lydia wants to be like one of those happy couples in the movie they will watch tonight, even if it isn't one hundred percent authentic and true to their current situation. *We will make it true*, she decides, sharing her suggestion with Gary.

He is game, and so they proceed. He in his threadbare slippers that Lydia would happily use to feed the first fire in the fireplace this coming winter, and Lydia in her ancient fleece nightgown that was in all honestly, probably a hand-me-down from her own mother's closet.

Sexy, Lydia laughs to herself.

No new beginnings, no promise of a happy ending. Life is not a fairytale. It is real and it can be raw, but it can also be ripe with love and blessings, and the latter is what Lydia is choosing for herself. She has spent enough time masochistically torturing herself with the former. If those kids from Unity and their families, who survived war, genocide, and god knows what else, still have enough hope to create a decent life in a foreign place, full of people who both want them and don't want them here, then she can suck it up. She can be thankful for never having to endure all of that, and recognize the grace of the life she is living.

⸗ **13** ⸗

Aida

The conversation she had with her granddaughter the night before did not go well. When Lejla arrived home, wearing something that Aida never would have let her out of the house in, she simply couldn't hold back any longer.

She scolded her, in front of her grandfather, thus publicly shaming her, and this was most likely Aida's first mistake. Such an approach worked wonders with Aida and her peers when they were children themselves, but it seems to have lost its intended effect on her granddaughter's generation.

"Twelve years old," Aida said, speaking intentionally in Bosnian. "Look at you. Parading around in something too short to be called shorts," she huffed, yanking on the jean fabric, "and what is this?"

"A top," Lejla hisses. "A top just like every other twelve year old girl in Clarkston is wearing!"

Aida points at Lejla's visible belly button. "This is not a top. It is little more than a bra. You should be ashamed!"

Lejla's big brown eyes begin to water, but she forces back the tears. Switching from Bosnian to English, she berates her grandmother for being so old and outdated, out of touch with reality and what growing up in America is really like.

Aida resists the urge to slap her across her normally pretty face. The anger she feels towards her grandmother animates Lejla's expressions in hideous ways.

"You are grounded. Give me your phone." Aida holds out her hand. Even though it's a far cry from an iPhone, it is still Lejla's social lifeline, the absence of which would sting. This is what Aida is counting on.

Lejla drops it in her hand, turns on her heel, whipping her long dirty-blonde ponytail behind her, and goes back to the room that she and her mother share.

She refuses to join them for dinner, or engage Aida any further.

When Aida checked on her later in the night, she found her granddaughter fast asleep, breathing deeply, burrowed beneath the covers. *She is just a child*, was the only thought in Aida's mind. *The filth she will attract dressed like that. Still a child but with the legs of one of those Victoria Secret models, and her bosom is beginning to grow.*

Aida knew all too well the pervasiveness of such grime in this world. She experienced more than her fair share in wartime, and after as a refugee. She would do whatever she had to, to shield Lejla from such things, even if she hated her for it.

Aida decided right then and there that she would be more present, whether she be perceived as a friend or foe, in Lejla's life. This was the time for intervening and supporting, and she would begin tomorrow.

Irsad agreed to keep a close eye on her while Aida was at work the next day, and when she returned, she would be taking her granddaughter out. All that was left to be decided, was where.

* * *

Aida arrives home from work the following day, relieved by the late October weather. It allows for a tolerable walk home. She loves seeing the leaves change colors, and the feel of crisp fall air, free of any reminder of the intolerable summer humidity. Taking a deep breath in, she enjoys the smell of wood burning nearby in someone's fireplace.

Aida had thought about it long and hard, where she would take Lejla today. It was on the bus ride home that she decided.

She enters the apartment, not bothering to take her hijab off, because the plan is to leave right away, leaving no room for objections from the snide adolescent.

There, in the living room, sits Lejla with her grandfather. It is the first time Aida has seen her appropriately dressed in a while.

They are playing a game of checkers, and despite the fact that Irsad can beat every member of the family in a few stealth moves, true to his loving nature, it is Lejla who appears to be winning.

"Deda! You're letting me win," Lejla declares laughingly. Not so oblivious to her grandfather's intentions.

"Govore Bosanski," Irsad replies, urging her to speak Bosnian.

"Ne!" Lejla says, smiling back. "I will not. The only way you will ever learn English is if you practice!"

Aida admires her granddaughter's fortitude. The truth is, after enduring the war and everything that transpired after, her husband, the perpetual academic and intellectual, is perfectly content to sit at home and enjoy his solitude. He has no aspirations of getting out into American society and assimilating. He is grateful for the security his family has living in this country, a patriot of second chances, which is what they had been given when resettled here fifteen years ago. Now he is happy to bask in the simplest of joys: recliner, TV, and loved ones.

He is not lazy or uninspired. Injuries dealt to his body during the war simply make it impossible for him to work. He rarely gets out, despite Aida's best efforts and encouragement to do so. Being surrounded by his family on a daily basis is enough. He is content.

"Idemo," Aida says, "Come on, time to go." Irsad looks her way and gives her a wink.

"Sretno."

"Luck," Aida huffs. "I don't need any luck." She winks back.

Lejla gets up from the couch and goes back into her room. She returns wearing sneakers and a dark purple cross body bag.

"Ready. Where are we going?"

"You'll see," is Aida's reply. "I am going to teach you about where and what you come from."

Lejla rolls her eyes, which Aida chooses to ignore. On any other day she would grab that little chin between her thumb and middle finger and give it a good squeeze for being so disrespectful, but today she is trying a new approach. *We'll see*, she thinks to herself, not at all convinced, but so very hopeful that it just might work.

Lejla and Aida, Aida and Lejla. Two figures make their way to the bus stop. The same Bosnian blood courses through their veins. The same bowtie lips and button noses sit upon their faces, and yet the generational gap between them lies there, exposed, like a gaping wound. Aida will stitch it up. This is her plan, and today is the great unveiling.

Lejla does not seem irritated with her grandmother, which Aida takes as a good sign. The fact that her top covers her entire torso and her jeans fit comfortably, not like a second layer of skin, Aida takes as a sign of respect, which she appreciates.

"You look nice today," she comments casually.

"Thanks," is all Lejla says. Her tone dry and slightly bitter.

Better than nothing, Aida thinks to herself. Better than nothing.

They board a bus headed southwest, and Lejla tries to act disinterested. They are headed toward Atlanta, somewhere the family rarely goes, preferring the quietude of suburbia.

Aida sits back in her seat, as if all of this is the most normal thing in the world. Baiting her granddaughter, she waits patiently for Lejla to come to her.

"Baca, where are we going?" She finally asks.

"To the Holocaust Museum."

Lejla looks at her grandmother incredulously.

"You said you were going to take me somewhere to learn about who I am and what I come from," she says, her tone accusatory, as though Aida has somehow misled her.

"There is so much you don't know," Aida shakes her head slowly back and forth, sadly. "Your mother has sheltered you for too long. It is time you know what brought us to this country. If things had worked out differently, you would have been born a Bosnian in Bosnia, but this was not an option. And so, you have spent your entire life here. Today, I will show you why."

"Fine, whatever," Lejla huffs. She sits in silence, with questions swirling in her head, refusing to ask what the Jewish Holocaust has to do with her, or Bosnia. She will not give her grandmother the satisfaction of knowing that this piques her curiosity, and so, she sits back in her seat, settling in for the long ride ahead.

Over an hour later they arrive at their destination. A brief walk takes them to the museum entrance, and Aida pulls some cash out of her pocket. She exchanges the money for two tickets at the admissions window, and Lejla mutters "Dobra, Baka," from behind her, following Aida into the building.

Aida smiles; satisfied to already see a positive effect, an acknowledgement of her efforts, from her intentionally ambivalent preteen companion.

"You are welcome."

People are gathering under a sign that reads "Tours". Aida and Lejla join them.

Aida sees her granddaughter look around, taking in the people making their way through the exhibit. Everyone with the same somber expression.

She knows Lejla is at a loss as to what she and her family have in common with Jews and the Holocaust.

"Gather round, friends," their guide calls out, standing on a chair to command the group's attention. "We are about to begin. Please don't hesitate to ask questions, but be courteous and try not to interrupt others, including me," he says with a big grin.

The guide leads their group to the beginning of the exhibit. "Let's start here," he says. "The Jewish people were oppressed and discriminated against long before World War II. Despite living in a given area for hundreds of years, many were segregated and treated as second class citizens. The War was not the beginning, or the end of this.

"There were those Jews who rose in the economic ranks of the societies they lived in, and enjoyed great wealth and privilege.

"Either way, despite wealth or poverty, beauty or beast, friend or seeming foe, Jews have historically struggled to enjoy social equality, what most of us consider a given, in most places we have resided throughout our lives."

Lejla listens intently, and Aida watches this. She sees her granddaughter absorb this information, of what it means to be cast in the role of the *other*, to be systematically oppressed and shunned, belittled and abused, berated for simply being oneself.

Lejla tunes in and tunes out while the guide speaks, telling the tale of the plight of this people, a people she is coming to see, not so different from her own.

His voice is drowned out by the images screaming at her from the walls they hang on. The photos of the Jews start out as a mixture of classes, some are poor and struggling, and others enjoy a more luxurious existence. Somber and smiling, the pre-World War II Jews stare back at her. As she makes her way through time, getting closer and closer to 1939, the dawning of World War II, the images become increasingly haunting.

Aida watches Lejla's expression as the plight of this people transforms before her from living a hard life, to barely living at all. Starved corpses littering the ground of ghettos, emaciated infants limp in their mothers' arms, ghosts, the living dead, all stare back at her, calling to her, and she can't look away.

She knows this will level her granddaughter. She is disrespectful and disobedient, but she has a beating heart, and knowing now that the world she lives in is capable of such atrocity, and is destined to repeat such behavior time and time again, will break it. *This is what is needed. She has to understand what we have survived, what is required of her given the immense privilege of the life she lives. Her conceit and arrogance will destroy her. Humility and honor will ensure she perseveres.*

From the American perspective, Aida's position might sound antiquated and harsh, but this is their truth, her people's, her family's. They are living out their second chance, and it simply cannot be squandered.

The tour ends, and Aida sees Lejla make a beeline for the bathroom. She waits for her just outside the door. Her granddaughter exits and walks past her, not noticing Aida standing there.

"Lejla," Aida calls out.

Lejla turns, directly facing her, the two are now about the same height. Lejla's face is red and puffy, her eyes tired and weary.

"Baka," she implores. "Is this what happened to us?"

How Aida wishes that the answer was no; that the global slogan "Never Again" had actually been worth something, but the truth is not so uplifting.

She takes her granddaughter's face in both hands and simply says, "Yes, but we survived."

She kisses each of Lejla's flushed cheeks, and takes her hand. Together they walk to the café. Aida guides them to a quite table in the back and taking a seat, softly commands Lejla, "Sit and I will tell you everything."

⚡ 14 ⚡

Lydia

Now that the process has begun, the only thing left to do is embrace it. She took the first of tortuous steps, by going to Aimee's apartment. She showed up, she acknowledged reality for what it is, now in the present, not twenty-five years ago, and there's no reversing that.

Sitting at the bottom of the stairs, she isn't sure how much time has gone by. She takes a sip of her coffee and looks at the stack of boxes propped against the wall. Gary brought them home from work, last night. He was intelligent enough to wait to put them there, Lydia's reminder of the task at hand, until this morning, thus allowing them to enjoy last night together. She fell asleep halfway through the movie, not really sure of the beginning or end, but very sure she and Gary had needed that time, to simply sit and be, together.

Time has brought her to today though, and today is not a rom-com. Today is real, and bittersweet. She is grateful to be forced into moving forward, into what life still has to offer, but she is fearful of where the process of moving forward, by going into that room, and packing those things in boxes, will take her.

Gary offered to do it himself. He was willing to be the one to sift through what remained, separate it into piles of "donate," "keep" and "toss," but Lydia refused. She is clinging to the remnants of a wretched past, but this is all she has left of the time before.

It is the final step of saying goodbye. A farewell long overdue, she knows this, but one that remains seemingly unbearable, undoable, until it isn't.

She forces herself to stand, looks deeply into Rocky's eyes, and picks up the stack of boxes. *No more thinking, just doing,* she decides, and begins to climb the stairs. She refuses to count the steps from the door to the bed, from the bed to the closet, as she normally would, the knowledge and familiarity of such will bring her no comfort today.

Lydia strips the bed first, pulling the light blue and pink comforter off and folding it. It is threadbare now, but she remembers it being full and plush. Corner to corner, fold, corner to corner, fold, repeat, put in box. Next are the sheets and the pillow shams, and then finally the pretty little dust ruffle. She closes the box, secures it shut with packing tape, and in black permanent ink writes the letters D O N A T E on the outside. Next is the closet.

Taking a long, deep and intentional breath, she allows herself to have a moment. She sits on the naked bed, the mattress bouncy and hard, having been made pre-pillow-top era. Bending down she breathes in its scent, and it smells like Karen, still, after all this time. It is the smell of honey, lavender, and time gone by. If Aimee didn't need a bed to sleep on, she might consider burning it, but this is not an option.

Lydia looks at the closet, a vault containing pieces of what had been stolen from her. It had snuck up on them, like a treacherous thief in the night, the diagnosis coming and going with nothing to be done, except making their child comfortable.

Leukemia, is a filthy word, Lydia thinks. *A word I refused to say aloud since the day we buried her, all ten years old of her small frail body. The coffin was thick light brown wood, and so very, very tiny.*

If there was a pill or a procedure she could undergo to remove a portion of her memory, she would have done it. There was a time when she would have willingly wiped it all away, the good, the bad, the dead and the living, just to have some peace. That time is gone, and she is better now, sometimes.

Standing up from the bed, she walks to the closet, and begins indiscriminately putting things in the remaining boxes. *It all has to go.* Dainty summer dresses, bright spring and fall leggings, a warm puffer winter coat. *No one will ever wear any of these again.* The thought alone of another body filling them, of potentially running into a family in the mall and seeing the daughter dressed in her dead child's clothes, is enough to undo her.

Lydia aggressively fits the entire closet into three boxes, shoving the clothes in them with great force. Bursting at the seams, she tapes these too, and with a vengeance writes the letters T R A S H, on each one.

One box remains, and this will be the real test. *I will survive, but have wished so many times that I could not,* she thinks. Lydia's own death seemed like the ultimate blessing many years ago. Complete freedom and peace, numbness and dark, neutrality. *I'm not there anymore though,* she reassures herself. This is all a reminder of just how far she has come, and she knows she should be proud, but having any positive feeling in relation to the passing of her child is something she cannot live with. *The guilt has always been the worst part.*

Her twenty-five year old mantra repeats itself in her head. What if I had noticed the bruises sooner? What if I had taken her to the doctor when she complained about being so tired, instead of simply putting her to bed earlier?

"What if, what if, what if! I could 'what if' the fucking world away, and it wouldn't change a god damned thing," she yells. Rocky whines and rubs up against her leg.

In the end, would seeing the doctor a month or two weeks earlier, have saved her? "No" had been the resounding answer she was given by all the doctors and nurses. It had been the beginning and the end simultaneously for her daughter. Nothing would have changed that.

The fever that refused to quit after two days, and the simultaneous nose bleeds were what prompted her and Gary to take Karen to her pediatrician. By that time, the clock had already ticked the majority of her little life away, and then she was just gone.

Keep going! You're almost done, Lydia pep talks herself through the last part of the process.

Grabbing the fourth and final box, she walks over to the shelves. Placing her hand on the delicate white box painted with pretty pink accent petals, she decides to open it. A little ballerina twirls to the tune of Too Ra Loo Ra Loo Ra. That song was their song; the same one Lydia's mother sang to her as a child. She had the jewelry box custom-made to play this specific tune, a gift for Karen's eighth birthday. Lydia watches the tiny little figure twirl around and around, and is surprised by how calm she feels. She had assumed this moment would be the clincher, the one where it all came crashing down, and she would have to crawl out of the room on her hands and knees, but it isn't.

She closes the jewelry box, silencing the song. After Karen was gone, there was a new house rule: no one could sing, hum, or play that tune on any musical device. This is the first time Lydia has heard it within these walls, in twenty-five years.

She places it in the box on the floor, along with a few framed photos of Karen with friends at school and her siblings. And then, Lydia realizes, that is it; that is everything; her daughter's life contained in four cardboard boxes.

The fourth and final box is taped and marked with the letters KEEP. Lydia stacks them outside the bedroom in the hallway, and leaves them, leaves it all, willingly, maybe even happily, behind her.

≋ 15 ≋

Sherry

Every other week, Sherry and the rest of the JVC crew are supposed to have a team building activity, and each member of the house takes a turn leading the event.

Sherry went first, and led the group in a guided meditation. Most of her roommates ended up falling asleep, but Sherry hadn't taken offense, because at the very least, she had succeeded in making the session relaxing and calming. Tonight is Mary's turn to host.

They are all exhausted, still adjusting to the full-time work schedule, and as the majority of their weekends up until now had been spent loading up the dumpster in their driveway with trash from the house, and picking up furniture donations, they had enjoyed little time to recuperate.

That was then, and this is now, Sherry thinks, as she exits the MARTA station and makes her way to the Emory campus. The dumpster was taken away last weekend, and this was followed by a deep cleaning of the entire house, in preparation both for a new beginning, but more importantly, their Halloween Extravaganza. They will be hosting their first house party, and Sherry and her roommates are ready to feel like they are in their early twenties again, the last two months having aged them significantly.

She picks up the pace, racing to meet her roommates. Someone is speaking at the Emory Student Center, but Sherry honestly does not know who. She has been preoccupied as of late. Outside of work, and the constant intentional community building at home, her free mental space is taken up by Ashraf.

Things have progressed. They had been out a couple more times since their first date, and today, following an impromptu lunch with him off campus, he kissed her, finally!

Prior to today, she had become obsessed, and could think of little else other than the fulfillment of this great longing. To feel his mouth on hers, his tongue slip between her lips, finding her own, his hands in her hair, pulling her head away ever so gently, as he trailed his tongue down her neck to taste her collar bone.

Caught up in the memory, Sherry feels the heat rise to her face, and stops to calm herself, before joining her people gathered on the steps.

"God, this place is amazing," Sherry says, greeting the group with a wave. "My college was beautiful, but this place is unreal."

"Hey Sher," Mary says in her bubbly, kindhearted way. "Any news?" Sherry wishes her friend could be a bit more discreet, but she also knows the group is excited for her. Many a detail had been divulged between her and her roommates between beers and shots on the weekends. They are all aware of her dating past, or lack thereof, and know about her new friend Ashraf as well.

"Why do you call him that?" Mary would tease her. "He has never been a friend. You are dating!"

"Until he makes our relationship official, or at least freaking kisses me, I don't know what to call him," Sherry defended herself.

Being that both had officially taken place today, she can finally use the word that to her is a personal triumph—boyfriend.

Pulling herself out of the recent past, Sherry refocuses her attention on Mary, and she can't help but smile.

"Oh my god," Mary screams, "He kissed you, didn't he?"

"Sssssssssh!!!" Sherry hisses, feeling people turning and staring at her. "Shut up!"

Mary smiles a big stupid smile. "Good! You deserve it."

Sherry feels incredibly awkward having this conversation in public and assures Mary she will fill them in later.

"Um, no you won't," Rebecca says under breath, but loud enough for Sherry to hear. She tells the rest of the group to go in and save them two seats. Pulling Sherry by the arm, to a more private space beyond the Student Center steps, she tells her, "You will tell me everything right now." Rebecca smiles deviously, waiting to be filled in.

Sherry looks at her friend, still not quite sure how the odd couple had come to be. She cannot think of any other time in her life when the two of them would have found one another. She credits Rebecca with forcing the friendship. Early on in the year she had suggested to Sherry that they take walks together, as both of the girls were aspiring runners at best.

It was on these walks that the magic happened. Sherry found Rebecca could make her laugh, arguably harder than anyone else she knew. Her offhand, blunt nature was so contrary to Sherry's calm and proper self, and she found this fantastic. Rebecca, in turn, brought out a more sarcastic and crass side of Sherry, which Sherry had grown quite fond of, temporarily liberated from the world of manners and censored speech that was her upbringing.

She looks affectionately at her friend, so thankful she is here on this journey with her. "Fine. Shut up and I will!

"So he took me to lunch again today, at the restaurant where he used to work. Instead of eating there though, he got the food to go. He's never done that before, so I figured something was up. He refused to tell me where we were going, and actually made me close my eyes on the drive there."

Rebecca rolls her eyes. "Could he be any cornier?" she says snidely.

"Whatever!" Sherry laughs. "It was so sweet, so shut the hell up if you want to hear the rest.

"So, anyway, like five minutes later, the car stops and he tells me to open my eyes. He brought me to this amazing neighborhood not far from the school, with a huge pond, and ducks, and swinging benches.

"So we walk to one of the swinging benches and sit down, eat lunch, blah, blah, blah, and then he kissed me!"

"I hope he didn't eat anything with garlic for lunch," Rebecca says, again sarcastic, but beaming.

Sherry pushes her, hard enough to make Rebecca stumble back, but the two laugh; all the jesting done in fun.

"Hurry up!" Rebecca says. "Tell me the rest. We're already late!"

"Fine, fine," Sherry squeals. "So he kissed me, but just a quick peck on the lips, while we were on the bench. You know, there were like kids and other people around. When we got back to the car though," Sherry inhales deeply.

"What!" Rebecca yells. "What happened in the car?"

"I don't kiss and tell," Sherry says, winking at her friend.

"Wait what?" Rebecca declares, obviously her mind going to places it shouldn't.

"No!" Sherry replies, annoyed. "We just kissed!"

"Okay, okay," Rebecca declares. "I knew I could get more out of you."

"Whatever," Sherry rolls her eyes. "Let's go."

Linking her arm with Rebecca's the two walk up the steps and into the Student Center. *This year,* Sherry thinks to herself, *is looking better every day.*

≈ **16** ≈

Hanan

Her flight route to "the states," as Americans like to refer to their country, had taken her from Greece, to Germany, to New York, and finally Atlanta.

Hanan had traveled abroad when she was younger, completing her primary education in England, and then returning to Syria for university, so such travels did not unnerve her, as it did many of the other refugees she came with. She could tell from their astonishment and fear that some of them had never even been on a plane.

She had smiled to reassure them, gently and confidently, hoping her calm would be contagious. They traveled in a group of ten, and the remaining nine of her group comprised of two families, one from Afghanistan and the other from the Democratic Republic of the Congo. Each had a mother, a father and children. They ultimately found comfort in one another. *I do not need comfort,* Hanan had told herself, sharply, as she felt her heart longing for something that no longer existed. She did not need purpose either, but found it nonetheless, in liaising for the group throughout the journey. Her impeccable English was of great value for the group as a whole, explaining their situation, legal status and ultimate destination as they navigated their way through airports and customs.

When they finally landed at Hartsfield-Jackson Airport, Hanan and her companions were exhausted. Exiting the plane, they were greeted by a man and a woman. The woman held a sign with Hanan's name written on it in Arabic, and others written in Farsi. The Afghani family surrounded the woman excitedly, claiming their rightful place with her according to the sign she held. The man held a sign with names written in French, and the timid but sweet family from the DRC went with him.

The woman had gently, and knowingly, approached Hanan, who intentionally hung back, for despite the relief she felt course through her veins, knowing they had found their caretakers, she had nothing to

76

contribute to the enthusiasm the rest of her companions demonstrated to their greeters.

The woman extended her hand, and Hanan took it, mustering a small smile, with nothing behind it but misery. "Hanan?" The woman asked.

"Yes," was her meek reply.

"I'm Gloria. So nice to meet you. May I take your bag?" Gloria asked, referring to the shabby navy blue carry on suitcase Hanan had brought with her.

She reached for it before Hanan had a chance to say no, and then it was too late.

Gloria lifted the empty suitcase easily with one hand, and couldn't help but let a surprised "Oh!" escape her lips. She looked questioningly at Hanan, who did not feel compelled to offer any explanation.

Hanan replied with a simple "thank you," and reached for the empty suitcase, which just like herself was a hollow container, purposeless and for show, going through the motions of presenting itself as what it was supposed to be, but the truth inside revealed that anything of substance, or purpose or value had been left on the other side of the world, washed up on a beach, and now buried in the earth.

Now, two days later, she sits in her small but sufficient room, in a small but sufficient house, in a strange city, full of even stranger people.

Gloria is her assigned caseworker and will be her guide, helping her navigate all things American for the next six months. Despite the awkwardness of their initial introduction, she found immediate comfort in the woman's soft green eyes, and kind, sincere smile.

After dropping off the Afghani family of four at an apartment complex that first night, she had driven Hanan to her new home. It was a simple house in the town of Decatur, right outside the city. As a single female, which is how Gloria had explained it, from a Middle Eastern country, she was being placed in a house with other women, because as Gloria understood, this was considered appropriate, and she was right. *Perhaps there is more to these Americans than their reality T.V. shows reveal,* Hanan had thought to herself. Gloria had been an ideal representative to send on the country's behalf.

Hanan sits on the queen-sized bed that takes up the majority of the room, and looks around at the empty walls. "I am here," she says the words aloud, with no one around to hear them.

She has an appointment with Gloria today, and she will be picking Hanan up shortly. For this, she is grateful. Aleppo had a public transit system before the war, and like all of them, it left something to be desired. The notion of taking the bus or train is not foreign to her, as she had mastered the Underground during her time in London. She would however, like a tutorial on the system prior to venturing out on it, and this is exactly what Gloria promised to give her this morning.

There are two other refugee women living in the home with Hanan, along with the elderly American homeowner and chaperone. Hanan knows they aren't really being chaperoned, but the dynamic of the house implies it. Honestly, she is grateful to the owner, for her presence and guidance. Hanan wants to be told what to do and to then simply do it. She has no aspiration of building her life anew in America. She is going through the motions, and having someone dictate to her where to go and what to do makes it that much easier to secure such an existence.

When she was younger, Hanan dreamed of what she would accomplish, the career she would have, the family she would build, the world her proverbial oyster. Now, at what feels like the ancient age of twenty-eight, she dreams of not dreaming at all.

There is a sharp knock on the door. Hanan gets up and opens it. In the hallway stands Ms. Libby, the home owner herself.

"Hanan, Gloria is here for you, my dear." She smiles sweetly, her words spoken with such gentleness. She goes to leave, hesitates, and turns back, taking Hanan's hand in both of her own, soft, wrinkled and worn, smelling of soapy perfume.

"Can I just say how nice it is to have someone else in the home I can talk to? I hope we can find time to sit and have tea. Do you like tea, dear?" Ms. Libby looks at her hopefully with pure blue eyes, her perfectly styled wavy white bob framing her old lovely face.

Hanan thinks about this for a moment. There are two other women living in the house. After meeting them though, Hanan knows what Ms. Libby is attempting to express. Hanan already speaks fluent English, and so for Ms. Libby, communicating with her is effortless. She has seen her with the others, and while there is much smiling and attempts to communicate, it is an ongoing challenge.

"You remind me of my grandmother," Hanan softly replies, smiling back. "I would love to."

"Oh, wonderful, my dear. Well, enjoy your day with Gloria, and I'll see you here at 6 sharp for dinner. We are having grilled chicken and asparagus tonight."

"See you soon," Hanan replies. This new life will possess a social component that she is now realizing cannot be avoided. *At least, thus far, I like the people I must spend time with.* She used to have an infinite curiosity about people, particularly people of different origins than herself, *but that was when I cared,* she reminds herself, *when the world still meant something to me.*

She leaves the room, shutting the door behind her. Making a quick stop in the bathroom she looks in the mirror, arranging her plain black hijab to correctly frame her face. She peers closely into the glass, and sees emptiness. Her large brown eyes are lifeless, the gleam has been gone for a while. Her skin is tightly wrapped over her cheekbones and chin, everything looks dry and stretched. She lost her desire to eat awhile back, and walks around with a slightly emaciated look these days.

There was a time when she caught people staring, on the street, in the market, at school. Her overly protective father had said her beauty could cause problems if she wasn't careful, but she was. She had always been a good girl, every parent's dream. People didn't look at her like that anymore.

Several months after they had died, while consumed with grief, Hanan longed to be as she once was, happy, but this desire quickly faded, because she realized that this is a world of opposing forces. If she could feel joy, she could also feel pain. She knew she could not survive a pain like that again, and so she asked to simply turn it all off. Months of anguish and soul crippling grief followed, until she truly thought she might simply dissolve into the dirt, ashes to ashes, returning to that from which she came, bonding with the decay her life had become. And then she went numb, the world went dark, and she finally felt free.

She heads down the stairs, and is greeted with a hug from Gloria.

"Are you ready to take Hotlanta by storm?" Gloria asks, laughing at herself.

Hanan looks at her questioningly.

"Oh, sorry, that is how the young people like to refer to the city these days."

"Oh," is Hanan's simple and polite reply.

Gloria smiles knowingly at her. "All in time, love. All in time."

They say goodbye to Ms. Libby and head for the car. Gloria buckles up, starts the engine, and they are on their way.

"So I thought we could begin the day with me giving you a tour of the resettlement office, Catholic Charities, and then we can practice taking the MARTA from there to your job. How does that sound?"

"My job?" Hanan says surprised. She knew she would have to work to pay her own way, but did not think she would be starting quite so soon.

"Well, yes sweetie. With the majority of my clients, the biggest holdup to finding work is speaking the language, and so they spend the majority of their first few months here in mandatory English classes. You already speak English, and quite beautifully I must say. I had a job lined up for you while you were flying across the Atlantic."

"Where will I be working?" Hanan asks, not sure how she feels about this yet.

"I figured a job near your house would be ideal, so you'll be working at an elementary school in Decatur. It's called The Unity School. It's a school for refugee and American kids, and the children of several of my clients go there. Everyone seems to love it."

"And what will I be doing?"

"You will be one of the Kindergarten teaching assistants. I think it will be a perfect fit. The children will love you!"

"Thank you," is Hanan's short, forced reply, accompanied by an even harder-to-force smile.

She sits in the car, watching houses and miscellaneous buildings pass by. She tries to fight it, but can feel her temperature begin to rise. She clasps her hands together so Gloria won't notice them shaking. She fights to suppress the surge of emotions from surfacing, threatening to pour out of her in an effervescent flow. The thought of being surrounded by children, not simply other people's children, but refugee children who had survived, unlike her own, was something she never considered.

Hanan sits, seemingly stoic, choking on her effort to appear normal. *It will be okay,* she soothes herself. *If this is happening, it is happening for a reason.*

She had refused to justify the course her life had taken with such romantic, empty, mystical propaganda after they died, but now, in this moment, it is all she has.

She cannot make sense of any of this, of why this world insists on continuing to torture her, to hand her test after test while she is crippled by the weight of it all.

This path however, is the only one rolling out before her. There are no other options being offered. This has been the course of her life since the war at home began, only one direction to go, and so in order to survive, she realizes in a moment of blinding clarity, that she must defer to who she was in her days of youth.

In doing so, she begins to feel the strangest of things emerge from the madness within, something she has almost forgotten, but somehow remembers its name. Hope.

≈ 17 ≈

Lydia

Lydia stands in the front doorway, watching the U-Haul pull up outside. "Never thought I'd see the day," she says to Rocky, who sits anxiously beside her, sensing change in the air.

"What can I do to help?" she calls to Aimee, as she shuts off the engine.

"Mom, seriously, your back! Every single one of these boxes surpasses the weight limit the doctor gave you for lifting."

Lydia snickers. "Every single one of the kids at Unity who love my piggyback rides does too."

Aimee rolls her eyes, and cuts open a large box toward the back of the truck. "Here" she says, handing her mom an enormous, but bearable, pile of clothes. "If you can just stick these on the bed, I'll arrange them later."

"Thank you," she yells at Lydia who struggles to see over the pile as she makes her way up the stairs.

Up and down, up and down, up and down. Lydia keeps going, until the twin mattress is completely covered.

"I don't know what we're going to do about this situation," she calls down to Aimee, who is taking a break to catch her breath and wipe the sweat from her forehead.

"What situation?"

"Your clothes. There is no way they are all going to fit in that closet."

"Can I use one of the other closets, in Brian's or my old room?"

"Sure, use the one in your old room. Brian's is filled with stuff your father has to go through, but the one in your old room is empty, I think."

"Great," Aimee says before taking a deep breath and heading back out to the truck for the next round of boxes.

Lydia quietly ducks into Brian's old room, one down the hall from where Aimee is staying. She observes the setup, trying to see it from the perspective of someone completely ignorant to the change that has

82

taken place. *It looks like the room of a neat hoarder*, she thinks to herself, *and nothing more*. Gary had offered to take the boxes labeled "trash" and "donate" to their respective new homes, having already put the one marked "keep" in the attic. Lydia had politely declined, assuring him she would, and needed to complete the process on her own, for closure.

What a croc. He would be furious if he knew the truth, she thinks to herself, while watching her daughter remove the last few boxes from the truck. The truth is that all of them, regardless of their contents, lay out in the open, amidst Gary's own boxes, scattered throughout Brian's room. *He'll never even notice*, Lydia thinks, satisfied.

She knows she is cheating, on Gary, on herself, on the process, her commitment to move on and finally let the past be in the past, but this is the best she can manage. She can sleep at night knowing all of these things, Karen's things, are still accessible should she ever need them.

My best will have to be good enough. She shuts the door and descends the stairs for the millionth time that day.

Morning becomes midday, afternoon progresses into night, and she finds herself sitting on the twin size bed in what is finally starting to look like Aimee's room. She takes her hand and runs it over the new comforter, the adult comforter, smoothing it out and admiring its tones of blues and greens with just a touch of silver threaded throughout.

"This is pretty," she says to Aimee, who is trying to decide which of her clothes should go in this closet and which should go in her childhood room.

"Thanks," Aimee says absentmindedly, still focused on her clothing dilemma. "I got it at that fair trade store in East Atlanta. I think it was made in Bangladesh. They have some really lovely stuff there. You should go check it out." She says this while attempting to squeeze one more shirt on a hanger into a space that simply doesn't exist.

"Honey, uh you might want to…" Lydia is cut off mid-sentence when the pole the clothes are hanging on, and every item hanging from it, come crashing down.

Lydia and Aimee both stare, in partial shock, at the closet. The wooden pole, as old as the house itself, literally split in two, right down the middle. It, along with the clothes Aimee spent the last few hours organizing into color coded sections, lie in an immense pile on the floor of the closet, everything everywhere.

"Honey," Lydia says, immediately trying to make light of the situation, "I never knew you were such a clothes horse."

"Why is moving always so damn hard?" Aimee pleads, crumpling to the floor.

Lydia admires her daughter's ability not to spout verbal obscenities in this moment, this moment Lydia has been waiting for, when Aimee finally surrenders, freeing herself to acknowledge the full weight of the decision she has made, to leave her husband, and allow the possibility of ending her marriage to become an actual option.

"Let's take a break," Lydia declares, jumping up from the bed. She grabs Aimee's hand before her daughter can protest, and together they make their way down the stairs.

Lydia grabs her purse on the way to the garage, still holding Aimee's hand, and leads them to the Prius.

"Get in."

The engine starts, and silently they back out, proceeding to drive aimlessly down the block.

The two women sit in the dark car. "Mom," Aimee says. "I'm fine, you know."

"I know, honey."

"This was all my choice. I made this decision, and so things are this way because I asked for them to be. I'm fine."

Lydia can feel her daughter looking at her, waiting for her reaction.

"Aimee, if you say you are fine, then I believe you. You know yourself better than anyone."

She draws in a deep breath, as though she is going to continue on, but then decides against it. *If this is what she wants to believe, then fine,* Lydia thinks to herself.

"I mean, right? I seem like myself, don't I?" Aimee asks.

"Honestly, sweetie, I've just been trying to give you your space, and not ask too many questions. This is such an enormous decision you made, and you made it without talking to me first. So, I have just been trying to respect your privacy, not ask too many questions, and just be here when you need me."

"I know, I know. This must have been such a huge shock for you and Dad. Do you want to know how I told dad? I called him one night, and just blurted it out. No forewarning. I said, 'Dad, it's me, Aimee. Mark and I are separating, and I don't know where this is all going, but is it okay if I move back home for a while, until we figure things out?' And you know what his response was? 'Of course, honey. Anything you need, we are here for you.' What kind of bullshit is this, mom? Don't you and Dad even care what is going on in my marriage?"

Lydia sits silently, processing everything that just came pouring out of her daughter. Having raised three children, all of whom went through far-from-graceful adolescents, she knows what she's dealing with here, but she also knows Aimee is not fifteen anymore, and deserves to be treated like the adult she is.

"Okay, honey. You asked for the truth, so I am going to give it to you."

Lydia had never been one to sugarcoat things with her kids. During their teenage years, when they were prone to episodes like this daily, she chose her words carefully, accepting blame for things that she knew were not her fault, in an effort to help her children navigate the complexity of emotions, relationships, and life, all of which were at a formative state during that period of their young lives. She was always careful not to say something that might make them angrier, because that would have resulted in them choosing distance from her as opposed to closeness, and all she ever wanted was to be near them. She just wanted to help them.

Nothing has changed, she acknowledges to herself silently. *I still want to hold her close, but she will not benefit from me omitting my true opinion. She is an adult, and she can handle it.*

"Your father and I love you. We love Mark too. All we want is for you to be happy. Your entire life, you have never come to me for help, deciding what to do in difficult situations. You have always made those decisions on your own. If things didn't go as you hoped, then you came to me for comfort. I am just trying to play the role you have always seemed to prefer me playing as your mom. The last thing your father and I want to do is pressure you to share things with us that you don't want to, especially about your marriage. You told me some details about how you came to this decision the night I went over to your place to help you pack your stuff. I just figured that was all you were ready to share, and the rest would come in time. Is this not what you want me to do?"

"I don't know! I don't know what I want. I'm sorry about taking this out on you. This really has nothing to do with you or dad. It has everything to do with my indecisiveness, and my fear that I started this whole process before really thinking it through. But that's my fear about my marriage in the first place; that I decided to marry Mark before I really knew him and felt sure he really knew me."

"Sweetie, I worried about you acting in haste when you were little. As a child you acted solely on impulse, but as you've gotten older, you are the exact opposite. I have no doubt that you decided to marry Mark and then to leave him, after thinking both moves to death. I can guarantee you haven't had a good night sleep in a really long time. Am I right?"

A deep exhale escapes her daughter. "I love you, mom." Aimee reaches over and squeezes her mom's hand. "Thank you. I think I am just second-guessing myself, and it's freaking me the hell out!"

"That's the whole point of separating before divorcing, honey, to give yourself time to decide what you REALLY want based on how you REALLY feel. So, use this time, and make a decision when you're sure."

Lydia stops at a red light and turns to her daughter. She wraps her arms around her, embracing her child in a hug.

"Oh, honey, life's a bitch sometimes, and that's really all there is to it."

⚡ 18 ⚡

Aida

Aida looks across the table at her granddaughter, all twelve years of her. Aida is not ignorant to the challenges she faces. She has a dual identity, one half immigrant, and one half American. One might think this is an advantage. She is bilingual, can bridge two cultures, and see herself reflected in more than one group of people. What Aida knows, however, is that despite the long-term advantages her granddaughter possesses, during adolescence these two identities feel more in conflict with one another than harmonious.

At an age when it is difficult enough to know who you are amongst your peers and society itself, what is demanded of Lejla is no small task. At home she is pressured to retain her Bosnian identity, and at school she needs to be American.

In time, with age, she will come to see the richness contained within this seeming dichotomy, but for now, what she feels is external pressure, from family and friends, to be something, someone, that is still coming to fruition. Aida is making it her mission to help her granddaughter simply celebrate herself, and understand who exactly that is.

"Baka," Lejla says, barely above a whisper, her eyes still puffy and red, "tell me."

Aida nods, knowing the time has come. Yes, twelve is young, but Lejla's ignorance will only hurt her from this point on. The time for the full truth to be revealed is now.

Speaking in Bosnian to ensure their privacy, Aida begins their story.

"Our family is originally from Eastern Bosnia. I grew up in a small village in the mountains, outside of a town called Srebrenica. Your great-grandparents, my mother and father, were born and raised there as were their parents.

"Srebrenica is a little town itself, and the villages around it are even smaller. When I was growing up, a variety of people lived there. There were Bosniak Muslims like us, Serbs, Croats and many others.

"For the most part everyone lived together in peace. Historically there has been conflict between some of the different groups, like during World War II, but for the most part, people believed in, and wanted peace.

"As a young girl, I had friends who were Christian Serbs and Croats, and we didn't know the difference between one another. I was Muslim and wore a headscarf, but that was of no consequence, simply a part of me that no one objected to. We were just children, and as with all children, we did not naturally hate each other. Finding a reason to hate something about someone else is taught, we are not born this way.

"This is the genius of your brother's school, Unity. Its mission is to combat the hate society teaches us to feel for one another, to find things that are different in people and condemn them. Your brother will spend his entire childhood in an environment where these differences are celebrated and treasured as things that make us beautiful. As Mr. Luna says, 'We are all flowers of one garden.' These differences, or things that make us individually unique, make us all the more beautiful as a whole. You understand?"

Lejla nods.

"The Jewish Holocaust took place during World War II, and when the war ended, Bosnia became part of what you now hear people refer to as the former Yugoslavia. When I was growing up, it was officially called the Socialist Federal Republic of Yugoslavia, which was a socialist state and federation. It was made up of six republics, and the one I lived in was Bosnia. These republics were multi-ethic, which means people of different ethnicities lived in them, together.

"For some time there was relative peace, at least no war, but when the Soviet Union broke up, it created a domino effect across all of socialist Europe, including former Yugoslavia.

Are you still following me?"

Lejla nods again.

"People started to become attached to their ethnic identities. The differences between the Muslim Bosniaks, the Serbs and the Croats were suddenly of the upmost importance, and each of these groups clung to their individualities. The Bosniaks and Croats felt historically oppressed by the Serbs, who had enjoyed much of the centralized power in Yugoslavia, and had advocated for their own self-interests above all else.

"The ethnic majority in several of the republics decided to pull away from the Yugoslav Federation and declared independence, as their own sovereign nations. Their success in doing so is what led to the collapse of the Socialist Federation of Yugoslavia. Their independence however, came at a great cost, and by far the greatest was paid by Bosnia."

"Baka, what does this have to do with the Holocaust, or our family?"

"I'm getting there. This is all part of the same story. I want to make sure I give you the information you need, that this all makes sense when I finish. I would rather give you too much history then too little.

"Other republics declared independence and went to war before Bosnia, but the Bosnian war lasted the longest, by far.

"It became a war primarily between the Serbs, who had held the majority of power within the Socialist Republic of Yugoslavia, and the Bosniak ethnic majority of the Republic of Bosnia, which wanted independence.

"The war lasted more than three years, and it is said that 100,000 people died as a result. Fault lies on both sides. There is no completely innocent party, but the majority of war crimes, like genocide, which is what the Holocaust was, genocide of the Jews, was committed by the Serbs against the Bosniaks and Croats living in Bosnia."

"Baka, what exactly is genocide? I know it is something horrible from the pictures of the Jews at the Holocaust Museum."

"The actual definition of genocide is the deliberate killing of a large group of people, especially those of a particular ethnic group or nation.

"That is what the next part of this story, our story, is about.

"After your grandfather and I graduated from University, we got married. We decided to stay in Sarajevo, the capital of Bosnia, because there were better job opportunities for him, and we had so many friends from University living there as well. We were young and inspired, and for me, the thought of moving back to the sleepy mountain village I came from was far from ideal.

"I worked for a few years as a school teacher, but after I found out I was pregnant with your mother, I knew I wanted to be at home, with my children. Time passed and we were very happy. There was always political and social tension, but nothing that signaled war might be a possibility. When the Soviet Union collapsed though, and nations began to declare their independence, we knew it was only a matter of time before the same wave of reform washed over Yugoslavia, and it did.

"Once Bosnia was officially at war, your father and I took your mother and your uncles back to the mountains where I was raised. We rented a small house in Srebrenica, hoping that by moving from the capital, we might avoid the worst of the war, and still manage to remain in our country. We could not have been more wrong.

"Not long after the war began, the villages surrounding the town were ransacked, forcing their inhabitants to flee to Srebrenica. My parents and brother, Tarik, joined us in our small home. The Serbian army burnt theirs to the ground. Tarik was not married, and had been living at home, looking after our aging parents until then. Without me and your grandfather, they would have been homeless, like so many others.

"The population of Srebrenica swelled with refugees entering its borders daily. In a deal brokered by the UN, the town was declared a Safe Zone, and this deal required the Muslim Bosnians to hand over their arms, and the Serbs to leave the town, and the people in it, alone. The latter part of the deal did not last long.

"On July 11, 1995, the Serbs violated the terms of the agreement. They easily overtook the small number of barely armed UN Peace Keepers, and had their way with all of us.

"That day, despite our protests, Tarik took to the hills, talking about starting a resistance. That was the last time I saw him, alive that is. The rest of us made our way several miles north to the UN base. We really believed they would protect us, that despite the Serbian army's violation of the agreement, help would be sent. We were joined by countless others, all bound and determined to save ourselves, to save our children.

"By nightfall there were thousands of us, pressed up as close to the base as possible. As the hours went by, and help never came, the reality set in that we really were on our own, unarmed, facing the greatest monster we had ever known. Terrified, we still could never have comprehended the horror of what awaited us.

"The next day, they came, descending upon us like locusts. The Serbian army began separating the men from the elderly, women and children. People became hysterical. Your grandfather and I promised ourselves we would remain calm no matter what happened next, because this was the only way to keep some control over the situation.

The army had no tolerance for dissent, and anyone objecting to their orders was made to pay for it dearly. When they took your grandfather from us, I almost bit my finger off, forcing myself not to scream. I was sure it was the last time I would ever see him.

The only comfort I found was in knowing your uncles were too little for the army to have any interest in them. I saw older boys ripped form their mother's arms, and I don't think I would have survived that.

They put those of us that remained on a bus. For two and a half hours we drove, slowly at times, the driver wanting us to see the bodies of our men scattered along the roadside. Another time we stopped and certain women were forced off the bus. Everyone else had to wait, and listen to their screams while horrible things were done to them. When it was over, they boarded the bus, and the journey resumed.

In the end, we were taken to another Muslim Bosnian safe zone and left there. Your grandfather made it back to us, but he was the anomaly, a miracle. Years later, when the world was finally ready to recognize what happened to us, and to prosecute those responsible, he testified at the International Criminal Court, against several of the Serbian Generals who ordered and partook in what happened in Srebrenica."

"But what did happen, Baka? What happened to all of those men? What happened to Tarik? Tell me! I need to know."

Aida looks at her granddaughter and realizes she is right. Despite all the details, all the dates she has spouted off over the last hour, she still has not told Lejla what it all really means. Now, seeing her granddaughter's young face, and realizing that she still does not fully comprehend the horror that defined Aida for so many years, she second guesses if this is the right call. But, it is too late now. She cannot end the story here, or it will not all make sense, it will fail to have the impact intended, to send shock waves of what this world really is, both the good and the bad, coursing through Lejla's veins, waking her up to what her story is, that she is one of the lucky ones, that her family, for the most part, survived.

"7000."

Lejla looks perplexed at her grandmother. "7000 what Baka?"

"7000 Muslim Bosnians, mostly men, were slaughtered by the Serbian army in Srebrenica. That's more than half the population of where we live now, and Tarik was one of them.

"For years, we knew." Aida pauses, struggling to stay in control.

"We knew what the Serbs did. So many families were never reunited. So many loved ones disappeared. Fathers, brothers, uncles, sons, all gone, forever."

Aida wipes the tears from her face.

"It wasn't until the war was over that the mass graves began to be uncovered, that people's remains could be identified, and we were finally able to know the fate of our loved ones. For Tarik, it was a leg, collarbone, and a few of his teeth.

"I received a call while we were living in Germany, and they asked me to go back, to where it all began. I almost didn't, but Tarik deserved a proper burial, and by this time my mother and father were simply too old to make the journey.

"So I went, alone. Your father needed to stay and look after your mother and uncles, and this was something I needed to do by myself, confront the past, to finally look it in the eye, see it stand down, and then move on.

"There were several other women from Srebrenica, who had suffered similar fates to mine on that day. We went together, the spoils of war, the survivors, the bent, broken and bruised.

"They drove us up to the site, where the digging was almost complete. It was so close to the village where I grew up. I knew those woods, the smell of the air, the birdcalls in early spring, knew it all like the back of my hand, but the war took it all from me. There was nothing left to miss, to long for, to return to.

"The grave was a massive hole of death and decay, holding our life's meaning, now reduced to little more than dust and bone, but at least we knew, at least there was closure.

"I lay there next to that hole, in the dirt, for hours. That was the closest I felt to my brother since the last time I saw him alive, strong willed and ready to fight if necessary. He would have saved us all if he could. They all would have, but the truth was they couldn't even save themselves. Instead they were dead, piles of bone and rubble brought up from the earth, only to return to it again.

"It took everything I had not to take his remains back to Germany with me. In my mind, Bosnia was the land that betrayed us, the motherland that cast out her own children. I hated her, and she did not deserve him, but he would have loved her nonetheless. It was for love of him, and respect for his undying love of that land, that I had him buried in the village cemetery, where so many gone before us, blood of our blood, were laid to rest. It brought him peace, and that was all that mattered.

⚡ **19** ⚡

Sherry

Sherry knows she is changing, much of the intended metamorphosis having already taken place. She can feel it within her, see it in the ways her new world has begun to normalize, and the old world stands next to it in such obvious contrast.

In Atlanta, the change feels positive. It has been achieved through a painful growth, one requiring sacrifice and intentionality, but the benefits of her decisions surround her, enshrining her and her sense of purpose and place in the ever growing expanse of this thing called life.

She went home for Christmas for two weeks, but when she saw her college friends, the changed Sherry felt incredibly out of place. Here, in the environment where the former Sherry had shined, this Sherry felt shabby and out of step with the people who used to be her people.

The three of them made plans to meet at Emma's apartment, all of them, except Sherry, still living post-college in the East Bay. Rachel and Emma wore spaghetti-strap satin tank tops, and Sherry made a mental note of what must be in fashion now. They went to the bar they had always gone to, countless Thursdays the last two years of college, and something felt as if it had shifted, but not in Rachel or Emma, as they remained the same.

Sherry was the one who left, who chose something else, when she could have easily remained. It was her choice, and it was she who had changed. This was the painful part, the realization that creating a new world for oneself, in which one lived in a new way with new ideals, just might mean losing one's place in the world that was, which had been wonderful but still not enough.

Sherry recognized that the change had taken place in her, and it felt like a shift of tectonic plates, ripping apart the earth that had once bonded them all together. On one side stood Sherry, and on the other, everything she had been bound and determined to shed. She had not planned for the inevitability of things shed to include many of the friendships she had longed for in adolescence and finally built with ease and success in college.

Her former self lay sprawled out in the middle, arms being torn from her body, as they reached out in opposite directions, across the divide. The right hand held desperately onto the world that was, and the left onto the world that was new. But Sherry had already made her choice, and thus with great force she took her heel and brought it down, like lightning unto a tree, dug it into the right hand of the old Sherry, and watched that part of herself fall away, away into a canyon so deep and vast that its retrieval would be impossible.

The morning commute is fantastic reflection time. She enters most days feeling as though things have been clarified, or are at least on their way to being so. This morning, however, the reminder of how much has indeed changed, and how painful parts of this process are, leaves her feeling dull and uninspired.

She missed her connecting train and is running about ten minutes behind. She walks sheepishly into her room, class having already started. She smiles guiltily at Ms. Clinton and joins the morning circle on the carpet in the center of the room.

Sherry looks around, counting the fourteen little faces that have changed her life, and counts a fifteenth.

"This," Ms. Clinton says, "is Bilan. She and her family just arrived. She's from Somalia."

Two big brown eyes stare across the room at Sherry. The tiny little being sizes Sherry up, smiling deviously. Sherry stifles a laugh, amazed at the child's uninhibitedness.

She smiles back, giving Bilan a wink. The child raises her eyebrows, surprised by such a response from a teacher, and then winks back.

What a character, Sherry thinks to herself, entertained and simultaneously preparing for some challenging behavior.

Ms. Clinton dismisses morning circle, having directed the children to their respective assignments, and pulls Sherry aside.

Mortified, Sherry is sure she is about to be scolded for being late. Today was not the first time. As Ms. Clinton launches into a completely different subject, she realizes how wrong she is. Breathing a sigh of relief, Sherry deduces from the conversation that she will be working with Bilan, who does not speak a word of English, one-on-one for the next few weeks.

While she is shocked that Ms. Clinton trusts her with the task, she happily agrees. Now all she has to figure out is what they will spend their time doing.

The objective, as Ms. Clinton explains it, is to have Bilan up to speed with the rest of the class as soon as possible. They will be working primarily on her English.

"Okay!" Sherry enthusiastically agrees to the task set before her.

"Go ahead and start working with her now. Grab whatever supplies you need, and feel free to use the vacant room down the hall," Ms. Clinton directs.

"I can do that," replies Sherry, feeling excitement accompanied by great apprehension bubbling in the pit of her stomach.

Sherry has no idea what to grab, and it seems as though Ms. Clinton doesn't either. Paper and two pencils will be a good start to the goal she has no idea how to achieve, and so armed with these, she makes her way across the room, and gently taps Bilan on her bony little shoulder.

She is built like a bird, Sherry thinks.

"You're going to come with me," Sherry says slowly, hoping Bilan might absorb some of what she is saying. This however, does not happen and the child looks back at her blankly.

Sherry decides to default to body language and motions for the girl to follow her. Bilan gets up, pushes in her chair at the little desk where she has been sitting, and follows Sherry out the door. Together, they walk down the hall, and turn into the vacant room, leaving the door propped open. The modular building was built large enough to accommodate the school growing for several more years, until it has filled grades K through Five. Currently it is only K through Three, and so many of the rooms sit unused.

The one Sherry leads them into contains a few desks and chairs, scattered, no apparent order, which drives Sherry to distraction. She arranges two desks so that they are facing one another, and places a chair at each of them. The others, she lines against the wall, orderly and out of their way, no physical distractions.

Sherry pats the chair with its back to the wall, implying this will be Bilan's seat. The child looks up at her, smiles knowingly, and sits obediently.

Sherry takes the seat facing the wall, and the two of them sit in an empty room, at empty desks, and stare expectantly at one another. Sherry looks into the eyes of the child, milky white and dark brown, Bilan's pupils dilating, taking Sherry in as well.

A deep sigh is made by Sherry, and then by Bilan. Sherry scratches her head, and so too does the child. Thus begins the game, a Simon Says of sorts, and Sherry decides she is going to use this to her advantage.

"A," says Sherry.

"A," says Bilan.

"B," says Sherry.

"B" says Bilan.

The two carry on in this manner, Sherry feeling so sly and Bilan feeling so witty and keen, until they have made their way through the alphabet several times. The game abruptly ends with the clock striking ten.

"Okay," Sherry remarks. "We are done for the day. Great job!" She holds her hand out for a high five. Bilan looks at her quizzically, and Sherry walks her through the required response.

"Tomorrow we are going to learn how to write the letters we practiced saying today, okay?"

Bilan nods her head enthusiastically, pushing her way past Sherry and running down the hall back to the classroom.

Sherry makes a mental note of the need to practice classroom etiquette during their next lesson.

Later that day, during her break prior to after-school prep, Sherry stands outside, leaning against one of the wooden pillars supporting the cafeteria. It is cold, and despite the mild winter temperatures, in Atlanta the moisture in the air always makes it feel at least ten degrees cooler than the thermostat reads, which today is fifty-five.

She watches the children play, thinking about how nothing could have prepared her for this. She entered this year with hope, but low expectations. Atlanta wasn't her first choice or how she always imagined things in her life unfolding, but it is her everything now and what was once a great mystery, things not working out how she initially thought they should, has been solved. It is all clear as day to her now.

She enjoys the momentary solitude, the profoundness of her life, that her days are filled with meaning, and she is where she is meant to be.

A soft caress against her inner left palm awakens her from the dream like state. He is standing close to her, his chest against her back, softly breathing near her left ear. Inhaling deeply, he takes in the scent of her hair which, these days, is little more than hair spray from the Dollar Store, which he seems to enjoy nonetheless.

"What are you thinking about?" he questions, gently turning her around so they stand face to face, his voice deep and husky. The wind picks up ever so slightly, and he gently brushes the blonde hair from her eyes, looking so very deeply into them.

He looks at her, into her, as if there exists nothing and no one else, but her and him, spinning on an ever so smooth axis, gravity pulling them closer and closer together, until they are almost but one entity, blazing with the fire of the sun, and everything else around them bright but distant, no distractions, nothing to detract from the reverie with its own beating heart that exists between them.

He is a head taller than her and Sherry delights in looking up into the eyes of the one who feels like he is hers. Ashraf takes a quick glance at their surroundings, before ever so softly caressing his thick lips against hers, barely a touch, but enough to awaken every cell in her body, enough to make her blood boil and the tips of her fingers and toes burn.

The sound of children playing nearby, and the intentional discretion the two exercise while on school grounds, is enough for his hands to drop her own, and the two stand seemingly innocently next to one another.

"Can I take you out on Friday after school?" he asks.

"You may," she replies, her words practically singing as they dance off her lips.

* * *

Everything in my life feels like it is pending! I seriously feel like I have done everything I can to actualize what I want my future to look like, but now it is in other people's hands. I have zero control over my own life!

Sherry knows this isn't really true. She has an enormous amount of control, and has grabbed it by the balls and pulled. She owns her life as much as anyone can, but now that she has done her part, she is subject to the will of others while she waits for them to do theirs.

She studied her ass off for the GRE, and got average scores. They measured up to her high school SAT scores, also average, and she reconciles herself yet again, to not being a stellar standardized test taker.

She wrote a kick-ass application essay for the MA program in Philosophy at Georgia State University, and secured three letters of recommendation from her most adoring undergrad professors. The MA program is in the top ten in the country, and so while she hopes she will be admitted, she is not assuming such.

"What are you going to do with an MA in Philosophy?" people love to ask her. She answers patiently and thoughtfully, in an effort to secure their belief and respect in the path she is pursuing, but the truth of the matter, is that she wants to say a big "Fuck you!" to the next person who does. People are so judgmental when they ask, their tone so condescending.

Sherry is secure enough in her ability to discern her future, the appropriate path forward, that she does not need to be able to concretely answer every question the wind blows her way. She never has. Some might say she acts in haste, but she leaves these people to themselves. Sherry prefers to think of herself as an optimist, a dreamer, and things have worked out for her quite well thus far.

"It's worked out on mom's dollar," her older sister Elisa recently cautioned her. They tried to talk about once a month, and usually the conversations went well, but this time, Sherry struggled not to simply hang up, to shut her up. "Might be harder to have such an oversimplified view of why you make the whimsical choices you do when you are $30,000.00 in debt from student loans."

Sherry remains unaffected by her sister's predictable pessimism, and everyone else's dismay. Her mom supports her decision, and Ashraf praises the idea of her obtaining a graduate degree. Her two most important champions are on board, and this is more than enough.

If she is admitted, not only will she be able to return to the subject matter that lit her heart on fire in college, but it will also secure a place for her here, in Atlanta, for two more years. She is not doing this *for* Ashraf, but he is a catalyst, prompting her in what has come to feel like her destined direction.

He told her he loved her after a few weeks of dating, and she felt hopelessly the same. It has been almost five months now, and she cannot imagine her life without him. He is her first love, and she assumes, her last. The letters she wrote in her journals growing up, to the one who was waiting for her, in some distant far-off land, had been him all along. She knew it quickly and fiercely. And yet now, their relationship has become yet another example of how she is hopelessly subject to the will of others in her own damn life, while pursuing her own damn dreams.

It had happened about a month and a half ago; they had gone to the Decatur Farmer's Market for dinner after work at Unity, before meeting up with the rest of the group at Café Istanbul. Sherry can't even remember how they got on the subject, but she and Ashraf found themselves talking about marriage.

She piled her plate high with salad, and then moved onto the goat cheese and other assorted fixings, when suddenly she heard him say he wasn't sure if he could marry her, because she was not Muslim. "Wait, what?" she had asked, sure she had misunderstood, but she most certainly had not. When he saw the hurt on her face, the realization that what he had confessed slowly sank into her deepest sense of self, he tried to delicately backpedal, but his truth was their truth and he had made the mistake of saying it out loud.

She could understand, even empathize, with him, knowing he loved her and thinking about marrying her in the distant future, without needing to seal the deal by putting a ring on her finger. What pierced her with the force of a thousand needles though, and epically pissed her off, was him wanting to marry her, but not knowing if he ultimately would because of the specific and isolated reason that she did not practice his religion. If he knew this to be his truth, and to thus be a fact that would eventually be the end of their story, she would prefer to end it sooner than later.

Her defenses are up, she knows this, because she has been put in the position of feeling like the *other*, but, she reminds herself, cursing her self-awareness, is this not precisely what she wanted to become her reality this year? To not just work with the *other*, support them in their struggles, and offer an ear to listen and a shoulder to cry on, but to become, to walk in their shoes, to see as they see, and feel as they feel.

You are pathetic, Sherry scolds herself. He is the refugee! He is the one who fled his country not long after the American invasion and fled to Pakistan. He is the one who taught his younger siblings, the ones who survived, to sell vegetables and trinkets on the streets of Islamabad. He is the one, he is the other, so stop feeling sorry for yourself! You have no right to feel animosity towards him for clinging to his traditions, to what makes him, him. You have what makes you you surrounding your spoiled self all day every day: your language, your food, your music, your culture.

She knows how she should feel. And yet, she cannot help but feel a similar piercing, a rejection of sorts, when he does not take her hand in specific places, for fear of running into someone from the local Afghan community, who might divulge the reality of their relationship to his unsuspecting parents.

"In my culture," he explained, sweetly, gently and patiently, "I cannot present a girl to my parents as someone I have romantic intentions for, unless I am presenting her as my fiancé. That is why I introduced you to them as my friend, because this way they are still able to meet you and know you, but without me disrespecting them."

Thus, the problem has now become that while Sherry wants to be respectful of, and celebrate his truth, which is what his culture, customs, and identity as an Afghan-American are, she cannot deny her own. She cannot will away the pain that returns time and time again, when their truths, their needs, collide. Her truth and her love for him are often at odds, and this is the truth she wishes she could deny above all others.

It isn't that she is opposed to becoming Muslim, in fact she had thought about the possibility long before that fateful conversation in the farmer's market.

She reflects back to her adolescence, and is still horrified by the ignorance that was hers up until this year.

It wasn't until September 11, 2001 that Sherry, or anyone she knew for that matter, really paid any attention to the words *Islam* and *Muslim*. She remembers thinking, *do Muslims believe Mohammed is God Incarnate, like Christians think of Christ?* She didn't know any Muslims, had never studied the religion in school, and so she read, as much as she could, about what she did not know, but the concepts never really came full circle, or made real sense, until she arrived here, at Unity, and found herself surrounded by Muslims, and now in love with one.

Generalizations influenced by American mainstream media gave way to the ability to discern for herself through her everyday, real world experience. Are Afghani women oppressed by the Taliban? A resounding "Yes" is her answer! Are all Muslim women oppressed? "No!" The Qur'an calls for modesty from both men and women. Sherry will clarify this to anyone willing to listen.

She not only teaches Muslim children, she works with their mothers, many of whom choose not to wear a hijab. Does this make them less Muslim than the Muslim women who do? Absolutely not. Sherry is enveloped daily by the most uplifting form of feminism she has ever experienced. Together they are all building a community that transcends borders and language, color of skin and creed. These women, these Muslim women, are powerful, and they are her people.

≈ **20** ≈

Hanan

It has been a few months since Hanan arrived in Atlanta. Much has changed in that span of time. With Gloria's assistance, she quickly mastered the Atlanta public transportation system and has come to enjoy the thirty minute commute from home to work and back again. Until now, her hours have been 8 to 3, to allow her time to acclimate and become acquainted with her new routine. Now that she knows where she is going, who she is working with, and is comfortable in her primary role as Kindergarten Teaching Assistant, her day is being extended to a full-time schedule, and she will be taking on the additional role of Second Grade After-care Instructor.

As the Principal, Mr. Luna, had explained to her during her orientation, there are currently two second grade classes at Unity School, and each class has two After-care teachers assigned to manage them. The first is managed by two other women, one of them a Kindergarten Teaching Assistant like her, and the other she has yet to meet. Hanan will be one of the teachers for the other second grade class during After-care and assumes she will meet her counterpart this afternoon during the daily prep meeting.

She remembers her first day at Unity, looking out across the small school yard, at the little children of so many races and creeds playing together, unaware of the differences that many adults sharing the same world have used as reason to hate one another, slaughter each other, and lay waste to a world that could otherwise be beautiful.

One of the little Somali girls approached her, and requested help readjusting her hijab. The Muslim children took a particular interest in her because she too wears a head cover. They saw themselves and their mothers in her. She is familiar.

The other children, white, brown and black, with their hair flying freely about, had also taken an interest in her. She is young, and despite looking "foreign," spoke perfect English. They seemed to find her curious and intriguing.

The moment when she felt a little hand reach for and settle into her own, she felt something release within her. All of the pressure steadily building within her, which she assumed would one day implode, slowly dissipated, like the controlled escape of air from a balloon that had been filled near to bursting. She looked down, and one of the little white American boys looked up, tears streaming down his face, and a small trickle of blood coming from a skinned knee. She bent down and wiped the tears from his small face and chubby cheeks, then picked him up lovingly and carried him to the office. There, Mrs. Luna applied a thick dose of loving care and comfort to his heart, along with sterilizer and a Band-Aid for his wound, and all was right in the world.

Hanan and the child returned hand-in-hand to the schoolyard, and before taking off in a sprint to join his friends and resume play, he clutched her leg in a tight embrace, nothing else needing to be said.

Hanan had thought that such an incident would undo her, unleash everything she had buried long ago, and this is what she fears the most. She knows she does not have the capacity to go back, to live in the place within herself that she left behind on that beach. But after the incident occurred, after a child needed her, and she cared for him, what she felt was far from grief, and she did not sink back into the familiar pit of helplessness and despair. Quite the contrary, and to her great relief, Hanan felt a sense of purpose, and Unity has since become her place.

It is a chilly Monday morning, and walking through the school doors, heading to her class, she catches herself smiling, unintentionally and naturally, at the people she passes in the hall.

"Did you have a good weekend?" Aziza calls out from her classroom doorway. She smiles mischievously at Hanan. "I could see that smile a mile away," she continues teasing.

Hanan looks at the Somali beauty, whose confidence and joy radiate from her, and smiles back. "Have a good day my friend," is her reply before closing the classroom door behind her. *Who knew such a place existed in the world,* she thinks to herself. *Perhaps someday such a thing will exist and persevere in my country, but that day is far from now. This school, what it models, what it actualized within these children, is what will save the world.*

The rest of the day is a blur of runny noses, ABCs, tending to hurt feelings, and playing outside. At 2 pm, Hanan ducks out of the classroom, makes her way down the hallway, past the main office, and into the general meeting room, where the After-care prep meeting is held daily from 2-3 pm. The purpose of the meeting is for the Program Director to inform the teachers what the day's activities will be and to ensure everyone is on the same page.

Hanan appears to be early, or most of the others are late. She recognizes Sherry, the volunteer Second Grade Teaching Assistant, and takes a seat next to her. "As-salāmu ʿalaykum," Sherry says, smiling at Hanan. Hanan responds, "waʿalaykumu s-salām," trying to hide her surprise. Since her arrival, she has met countless people, all of whom know she is Muslim because of her hijab, and yet Sherry is the first American to greet her with the standard Islamic greeting.

"How are things going for you so far?" inquires Sherry.

"Very well, thank you for asking," Hanan replies, again surprised by the nature of this young girl.

Then, in saunters Aziza, exuding confidence and good humor with every step. She winks and nods at Hanan, and takes a seat next to Sherry.

"Heeeey girl!" She says excitedly. The two obviously share an intimate friendship.

"Hey," Sherry replies, maintaining her ever present calm, but her words sound happy and light.

"How was your weekend?" Aziza asks. "Where did you and Ashraf take off to after Café Istanbul on Friday night?"

"We went to see a movie," Sherry replies, smiling at Aziza who seems to be fishing for more.

"Uh huh…did you actually see any of it?" Aziza pushes.

"Aziza!" Sherry exclaims, "Enough!" She says her friend's name with a perfect combination of command and humor, indicating to Aziza that this is neither the time nor the place, but that no offense has been taken.

"Fine," Aziza says with a wicked grin, "but this is not over. We will finish this conversation after school."

"Whatever," Sherry replies, officially dismissing the subject matter altogether, but the ever-present smile never leaves her lips.

Hanan continues watching the two friends, finding their dynamic incredibly curious. She is just coming to grasp the way in which Americans seem to socialize and communicate, but has seen very little cross-cultural communication, and this she finds fascinating.

Her eyes play over Sherry, this white American girl, with curly blonde hair, wearing tight jeans and a form-fitting top, and exercising such cultural respect toward co-workers and friends. Suddenly, Sherry's face turns pink, the blood rushing to her cheeks. She looks down, and then back up. Hanan shifts her gaze to see what has caught Sherry's attention and dismantled her composure. In the doorway stands a very young, very handsome man. His eyes are trained on Sherry, never drifting, controlled. He smiles at her, and it is a smile of great familiarity and affection.

Ah, Hanan think to herself. *Now I see. They are an item. So young and so in love.* Hanan looks away, feeling intrusive of this moment the two share across the table from one another.

He takes a seat at the table, and it is Aziza who speaks up. "What's up, Ashraf?"

"Hey Aziza. How goes it?" he replies coolly.

Hanan makes note of how he and Sherry acknowledge each other publicly as little as possible. He is Afghani, she realizes. Which explains their interaction, or lack thereof. They are being respectful of the Afghani elders employed at the school, and cautious about revealing their relationship. He is respectful of his parents and his culture. Public displays, or rumors of a relationship within the community would be completely inappropriate until he is ready to present her to his family as his future wife. He is traditional, and comes from a good family.

Hanan smiles. She can't help but be proud of these young people living in America, who are still able to be respectful of their traditions and cultures, while successfully assimilating with the country they now call home. *Good boy.*

Several other fellow staff members join the group, and Hanan does not recognize the final woman to join them. She is a middle-aged white woman, and this is all she is able to ascertain.

The Director of the After-care Program is an attractive woman from El Salvador. She speaks with a slight accent and appears to be in her early to mid-forties. She has an appealing personality, direct and to the point, but with a lightheartedness that typically belongs to youth.

She looks at Hanan, and extends a hand. "Hi, and welcome to the group. My name is Ana. How are things going for you so far?

Hanan shakes her hand, appreciating the firmness and confidence behind it, always impressed by strong women.

"Hello. My name is Hanan," she replies, looking from Ana to the rest of the group.

"Wonderful. Now how about we go around the table and introduce ourselves."

Everyone takes a turn saying their name, and Hanan makes a mental note of Lydia, the last person to join the group. Lydia co-manages After-care in the other second grade class, and Hanan knows she will be going to her for guidance.

Ana gives everyone instructions for the afternoon lesson per grade, and the group is dismissed.

On her way out, Ana pulls Lydia and Hanan aside. "Ladies, I want to discuss something with you. The person we hoped to hire to share the class with Hanan has taken another job, so in the meantime what I would like to do, is have you, Lydia, lead the class assigned to her so Hanan can learn the ropes. I will assist Mya with the class Lydia usually leads. I don't think this arrangement will need to last more than a couple of weeks, tops, just until we find someone to help Hanan out permanently. Okay?"

"Sure," Lydia replies.

"Not a problem," Hanan says, still too new to have an opinion on anything. She is most comfortable taking directives.

"Great! Thank you for being flexible Lydia. I look forward to hearing how the first day goes."

Ana exits the room, leaving Lydia and Hanan to themselves.

Lydia looks at her smiling. "Okay, let's go."

Hanan follows Lydia past the cafeteria to the modular building, where the second grade classrooms reside.

Lydia punches in the security code and puts her hand on the handle, but before pulling the door open, she turns to Hanan.

"I don't know what it is, but there is something about you that is so familiar." She stares at Hanan, as if trying to place her, in a context outside of the school.

"Well, we have most certainly never met before. I have only been in the U.S. for a few months."

"Maybe you remind me of a former student. Honestly, I have no idea," Lydia says laughing. "There's just something about you, my dear."

She pulls the door open, and together the two women enter the building.

After being introduced to the class, Hanan excuses herself to the bathroom. She turns on the fan to try and obstruct the sounds she is afraid she will make. She leans over the sink, gripping both sides with her hands, her clasp so hard that her knuckles turn white.

This cannot be happening, she thinks to herself. *How could she possibly recognize me? After everything I have endured, how far I have come, no one can know.*

There is a sharp knock on the door, someone else needing to use the facilities. Hanan wets a paper towel with cold water, wipes her eyes, looks in the mirror, and wills herself to finish out the day, acting as if everything is completely normal, nothing having changed.

She has survived everything thrown her way, but this, one person knowing, and then more inevitably finding out, this she cannot bear, this will be her final undoing.

⚡ **21** ⚡

Lydia

Dinner has been cooked and consumed, the dishwasher loaded, and the table and counters wiped clean. Lydia collapses on the couch, cup of steaming hot tea resting on a coaster on the table nearby, Rocky snuggling into her as close as he possibly can. *Finally*! Lydia thinks. *This is one of the ironic perks of volunteering: being tired again, and valuing my free time.*

She takes a sip of the Sweet and Spicy tea, enjoying the naturally sweet aftertaste, no sugar required. Petting her giant furry friend on the head, loving his deep, satisfied sigh, Lydia opens her laptop with no particular agenda in mind, *just perusing while I sip my delicious cup of tea, because I can,* Lydia thinks, smiling.

She hears Aimee walking around in her room upstairs, and knows Gary has already crashed, sound asleep after a solid day's work. Being surrounded, accompanied by her loved ones, is all she could have asked for. She is grateful. *It sucks that Aimee is here because her marriage might be over, but I am going to enjoy this time with her for what it's worth, and to me, it's gold.*

It is at this time of night, when Lydia finally settles down, hyper aware of the plentitude of comforts her privileged life possesses, that she thinks about her students, and even more so, their parents.

Some of the parents remind her of her and Gary when they were starting out: white, middle class, self-declared "progressives," good people set on raising good children who will be more aware of the world around them than their parents had been raised to be. Privileged people, who despite a decent sense of self-awareness, still took the majority of what life has gifted them for granted, but they try, and they care, and the world is okay with them in it.

It is the refugee families she spends the most time thinking about though. What is it like in their homes, she wonders? She has not been invited to visit with any of the families yet, and so she doesn't know with certainty, but she assumes that many of them are humbly furnished, some food in the cabinets, but perhaps not enough.

She wonders if they can set the heat to a comfortable temperature on freezing winter nights, and if they do, if they can afford to pay the bill when it arrives in the mail a few weeks later.

"Being here is enough," Mya told her one day while they watched the children on the playground. "Because it mean your family be safe, you all survive, and you together. When we first come here, three year ago, we live in a crazy place. Roaches, ants, kid selling drugs to our neighbors at night. The loud music, people fighting and yelling all the time. It scary, but better than refugee camp. When we go to sleep at night, we know we in America forever, that we safe, and finally have home. The people who want to kill us in our country can no touch us here Ms. Lydia. I never sleep so well in my life as when my family first come. We just so grateful to have place here."

Lydia had liked Mya before really even knowing her. She enjoyed watching her soft and tender way with the children, and respected the sharp but controlled tone she took with her own when they stepped out of line. She is balanced, real.

After she shared the smallest of details about her story however, Lydia found herself in awe, a semi-state of hero worship, and it helped her to not take her own life so for granted.

They all have a story, each and every parent, every single child, who wears the badge of refugee upon their shoulders. Lydia had never been so proud to know a group of people, to call them her friends, in her life. They are the unsung heroes of this world. They do not settle for surviving, but insist on thriving, because from what she could see, surviving what they fled was only half the battle. The second war they all have to fight is to begin again, somewhere new and completely foreign, where not everyone is welcoming, where they are often misunderstood and abused. *So many of them,* Lydia remarks silently, *are still smiling though, through it all their hope has not been tarnished and their perseverance remains unhindered.*

She drifts in and out of her stream of consciousness, surfing from site to site, Loft to BBC to Facebook and back again. Hearing footsteps on the stairs, she looks up to see Aimee descending them, eyes trained on her mother.

She takes a seat on the couch next to Lydia, who is now sandwiched between Rocky and her daughter. She steals some of the blanket, causing Rocky to glance back at her, determining who is disturbing the peace, and lays her head of soft blonde hair on Lydia's shoulder, while her mother gently pets her from hairline to neck, easing the stresses of the day.

"Can I get you a cup of tea, sweetie? It's that Good Earth stuff. So good!"

"I'm okay mom, but thank you. Thank you for everything."

"Are you okay love?"

"Yeah, I'm fine. I just got off the phone with Mark, and he is heartbroken that I don't have a date in mind."

"A date? For what?"

"To move back into our condo with him. He really thought it would just take a couple of weeks, that I would stay here, and miss him, miss our life, and come running back, full of realizations and clarity that I made a huge mistake. But I'm not sure I did. I still don't know. What I would give for a little clarity-shit!"

"Oh honey, I'm so sorry. This has to be so hard on you, and him, both of you."

"The worst part is," Aimee continues, "and I'm not sure if it was the anger and hurt talking, or if he actually means it, but the last thing he said before hanging up on me was that I better realize he will not wait forever, and the clock is ticking, so I better figure it out and let him know either way."

"I am sure it was the hurt talking, sweetie. You have all the power, and I am sure that has left him feeling helpless, powerless. That's pretty emasculating. I mean it's not like he cheated, or gambled your money away. You left because you are not sure you love him anymore, or maybe if you ever loved him. I am sure he feels like he is losing everything, and doesn't even have a say, despite your marriage being fifty percent him."

She had said too much, way too much, and she knew it before finishing the last sentence. Lydia has done a pretty great job about keeping her opinion to herself regarding Aimee and Mark, until now.

She peers up at her daughter. Prepared for the wrath, but what she sees on her daughter's face is far worse. Tears stream down her cheeks, and Aimee doesn't even bother to wipe them away. She has this look, of betrayal, and it's focused right on Lydia.

"Holy shit, mom. Why don't you tell me how you really feel?" Then the sobs begin, and the gasping for breath. If Lydia had a hammer, she would hit herself over the head with it.

"Oh God, honey, I'm so sorry! I really fucked up, and should not have said all of those things. It's just that, I, well I, I was just speaking to his perspective, not validating or invalidating it. I just, could imagine him thinking along those lines. I'm sorry! I'm so sorry!"

"Mom, God, stop it! Stop apologizing! Stop blaming yourself for my pathetic situation! You are right, and that's why I am upset, because that is exactly what he is thinking, and he is right too!"

"I'm such a bitch," Aimee declares, the tears continuing to flow. "How can I do this to him?"

Lydia hugs her hysterical daughter to her. She pulls her sleeve up over her hand, and wipes Aimee's face dry, silently hoping the smeared mascara will come off in the wash. She loves this sweater.

"The way I see it, you are doing this *for* him. Who wants to be married to someone who doesn't love them? That sounds like a horrible fate. You will figure your shit out, and make a decision about him, about your marriage, soon enough, and when you do, one of two things is going to happen: you will realize you do indeed love him, and will commit to making your marriage into what you both deserve it to be... or you will realize you don't love him, pursue a divorce, and set him free, so you can both find the love you want and deserve."

"Okay?"

"Okay," Aimee whimpers, head buried in her mom's lap, body still trembling ever so slightly, as the sobs slowly give way to steadier breathing.

"Okay," Lydia says, ending the discussion, but continuing to massage her daughter's scalp and temples, trying to work out some of the anxiety, so Aimee can sleep. No guarantee, but worth a try.

After a few minutes like this, Aimee lifts her puffy face from her mother's lap, and laughs mockingly at herself.

"I am such a freaking mess, mom. I need to figure my shit out."

"Cut yourself some slack. That, my dear, is what you need to do. You moved back home. You are living in your sister's childhood room. You left your husband, all so you can figure it out. You're on your way, but this type of clarity is not something you can force, it will come in time, and you and Mark will just have to be patient. If you don't want to risk making the wrong decision, and being right back here in a year or two, because you didn't really figure it out the first time, then be patient. It will be worth the effort in the end, sweetie. That, I can promise you."

Aimee goes upstairs, and once Lydia has heard the toilet flush, the water run, the door shut, and sees no light coming from underneath the bedroom door, once she is confident Aimee is in bed, at least trying to sleep, she and Rocky head off to bed themselves.

She moves covertly through the rooms, using the light of her phone to guide her, trying not to wake up Gary. Pulling back the covers, and situating the pillow just so, she eases herself into bed, turning to her right side, so she can continue perusing the internet until drifting off to sleep.

Her finger clicks on the BBC app, and swipes downward, to see if anything of interest catches her eye. She sees a feature on the one year anniversary of a family of refugees who drowned trying to make their way from Libya to Greece. She remembers this story, and is grateful to have been able to tuck it into a dark remote crevice in the back of her mind. She really wishes now, that she had just gone to bed, but she needs to know and so regardless of the potential loss of sleep this will cause, she begins to read.

Lydia looks at the haunting photo, the one that created a global outcry for the plight of migrants coming by boat in desperate search of refuge, a journey that for so many of them ended in death at the bottom of the sea. The little girl, three years old, lay face down at the water's edge, right where the sea meets the land, but those tiny little feet never set foot on that beach, alive at least, because by the time her broken body washed ashore, she had been dead for quite some time.

The next photo was another one Lydia remembered from a year ago. A Greek police officer cradled the child's limp body, carrying her away from the water, the beach, and the bodies of her older sister and father that still needed to be retrieved. She looked so small, dangling in his embrace.

The final photo was of the mother, the wife; the woman who had lost her entire world through the simple act of trying to save it. The four of them had fled the war in Syria, like so many others. They had left together, but she arrived in Greece alone. Lydia had read the family's story when the initial article appeared, but this was the first photo she ever saw featuring the mom. The woman is young, and beautiful. More than anything though, she is haunted. Her eyes do not look into the camera, but one can tell from her expression that she knows it is there, stalking her, preying on her privacy and anguish. It looks as if the photo is shot right before she turns her head. It is slightly blurry and the coloring is dark. She is on the beach, and when Lydia scrolls up to the first photo of the girl face down in the sand, and then back to the photo of the mom, she realizes the woman is standing in the exact spot where her child washed ashore one year ago.

Lydia gasps, and covers her mouth, willing herself not to give in. Her body tenses, longing to release the sobs building up in her gut, but she refuses to succumb. Gary rolls over next to her, and Lydia forces her body to relax, willing herself to remain in control.

She returns to the article, and reads that the mom, who goes unnamed, was granted Refugee status and has since relocated. Lydia breathes a small sigh of relief, of hope for this woman who has survived what should not be survivable.

Returning to the mom's photo one last time, Lydia can't escape the sense of familiarity this woman invokes in her. It is more than her story, more that the fact that they both have lost a child, it is the woman herself, her face. Lydia knows she has seen her before. Nothing particular comes to mind, other than a lingering feeling that Lydia drifts off to sleep with. It isn't until sometime during the night, that Lydia sits up in bed, dripping with sweat, and the name Hanan on her lips.

* * *

The day she had realized the awful truth, about the history Hanan carries with her, was a Friday, luckily. That gave Lydia a solid weekend to pull her shit together. Had she seen Hanan the following day, she would have broken down upon seeing her, unable to control her overflowing empathy. It would have ended with the woman who lost it all comforting the woman who had it all. *How's that for ironic. Life can be such an asshole,* she thinks.

What if Hanan saw the article too? Oh my God, the stress and anxiety that will create for her. She has been through enough. If everyone at the school finds out, if local news agencies catch wind that the story that made international headlines for days is in their own backyard, the story will define her just as much here, as it did wherever she came from.

Now that Lydia knows that they are more alike than she had ever dreamed, she feels overwhelmed with the maternal calling to protect this girl, and she will. She needs to tell someone, the weight of this

114

realization being too heavy to carry on her own, and so she will tell the most solid, able-to-bear person she knows, her husband.

"Whatever it takes, Gary. I'm serious," she says to him that evening during dinner. Aimee is out and Lydia vowed she would tell him and only him. She loves her daughter, but secrecy is not her strong suit.

"If she needs a place to hide, she can move in here. We have the space, two empty rooms upstairs. Maybe you can get her a job with the firm. Her English is impeccable and she is brilliant."

Gary gives her the look, the "I support you, but really?" look.

"Not as a lawyer for God's sake, but maybe as a secretary or assistant to one of the partners. I'm being completely serious!"

"Okay, sweetie. Before we get ahead of ourselves though, go to school on Monday, and take the pulse of the situation. We'll go from there, okay?"

"Fine," she says, acquiescing to his calm. The storm within her slowly recedes.

Sunday night, after Gary has gone to bed, and Aimee is out again with "friends," *most likely a friend named Mark*, Lydia smirks, she finds herself in the doorway of Brian's old room, eyes trained on the boxes she couldn't part with.

In her rational mind she knows that Hanan will not be moving in with them, and yet the thought of *but what if she does*, will not go away.

We will need to make room, she says to herself, and determines Brian's old room is the most sensible one to assign her. This means the boxes will have to go, and for the first time, the thought alone does not make her want to rip her eyes out.

The truth of the matter, Lydia can now admit to herself, is that yes, she lost a child. No one should ever lose a child, but she was blessed with ten remarkable years. She got to see Karen grow into a young girl, to see her experience the world in all its grandeur. She got to say goodbye.

Hanan had been blessed with none of the above. Her reality had been living through a war with her babies, fleeing an oppressive regime to perhaps even-more inhumane conditions where human traffickers called the shots, all with the hope of maybe just maybe securing freedom for her family. In the end, they died, all of them: her husband and daughters, and she was left standing alone at the edge of the water, probably wondering why she had not been granted the mercy of being taken too. Hanan's reality simply was too great a burden, for any human, woman or man, old or young, to carry.

Lydia's load feels lighter. She feels capable, for the first time in twenty-five years, of this time, not just maybe, but really, moving on. She will never forget, but she will continue.

She carries the boxes down to her car, one by one stacking them in the trunk. It's now or never. She knows this. The garage door opens, a portal to a freedom she has secretly longed for all this time, and through it she goes, her ultimate destination being the door step of Goodwill, where she piles the boxes neatly for whoever opens the store in the morning, and returns home.

❧ **22** ❧

Aida

As winter prepares to acquiesce to spring, and the days become a bit longer, Aida can't help but long for the sweet days of summer on this particular Monday morning. She knows there are still several months lying between her and her heart's desire, and so she will wait, as she has on so many occasions, for so many other things.

It has been several months since she and Lejla went to the Holocaust Museum, and Aida divulged the truth to her granddaughter. Several months since the world lost some of its luster and the twinkle temporarily went out in Lejla's eyes.

She needed to know, Aida reminds herself. *I have no regrets.* She pulls her lightweight coat tightly to her, wishing she had opted for the heavier one when leaving the house this morning. The mornings are still very chilly, but the brightly shining sun had given her brief optimism that again failed her miserably.

What's your problem, old woman? Aida scolds herself silently on the bus. *Why so glum?* She isn't sure, can't put a finger on the definitive cause of her sour demeanor, but sits in her seat, well aware of the pessimism coursing through her veins.

She thinks of her granddaughter, and the silent scolding continues. *What did you expect, a complete metamorphosis?* It isn't as if nothing has changed, since Aida told Lejla the truth about her family's past. She leaves the house fully clothed now, but this could just as easily be attributed to the cooler temperatures. Lejla does not appear to feel differently about Aida, confide in her more, and perhaps this is the rub. If Aida were to be completely honest with herself, she would admit that the ideal version of the story, as it played out in her mind several months ago, would have culminated in Lejla feeling a kindred spirit connection with her Baka, but this is not how things unfolded.

If anything, Lejla seems to avoid her more than she did before. *She does not challenge me as much, but she also doesn't look me in the eye as often.* Aida confessed to Nidal, that she had told Lejla everything, almost everything, but Lejla never mentioned the conversation to her mother. It was almost as though this new reality, what her family had endured, had morphed into a dirty secret kept between her and her grandmother, poisoning the relationship slowly but surely.

You're being too dramatic. Snap out of it and stop obsessing, Aida demands of herself. She can't help but think that her granddaughter snapping and sassing like she used to would be better than this silence that lingers between them.

I will just have to be patient. Nothing of true substance happens immediately. I will wait, and hope, and try to simply enjoy the fact that the midriff tops and booty shorts are taking a hiatus.

The bus pulls up to her stop and she gets off, walking the several remaining blocks to school. She cuts through the play-yard and into the cafeteria, making her way quietly back into the kitchen.

This is her favorite time of day, seven in the morning, the kitchen warm and silent. She stands in the doorway for a moment, looking out over her kingdom. *How little our younger selves often know of what they will become,* she thinks, neither uplifted nor depressed by this thought. Like so many other things, it is simply the truth, and there is no changing that.

Eight o'clock comes and goes, all the little mouths fed and wiped clean. Lunch is delivered, the food seasoned and put in the oven, and Aida waits for her round two to begin.

The Kindergarten Teaching Assistants arrive. Mya, bright and shiny, and full of laughter and love, arrives first. She puts on the hair net that so many other assistants balked at when it became a requirement mid-year, and the plastic gloves that make everyone's hands sweat, all the while a smile equal in size to her laughter permanently on her beautiful Burmese face.

Next, and quite overdue, arrives Aziza, sauntering in at a pace that boils Aida's blood. She scolds the girl, but is unable to stay angry for long. Aziza has a way of melting away any negativity thrown her way, and simultaneously disarming the person who throws it.

"Where is Hanan?" Aida asks. "Not like her to be late."

"I saw her earlier this morning. She was in the schoolyard with her class during recess. Do you want me to go look for her?" Aziza offers.

"No! I'll go. If I let you escape your lunchtime duty, who knows when we will see you again," Aida says, with humor in her voice, but meaning every word she says.

Mya nudges Aziza with her hip, the two standing side by side as they serve the children their lunch trays. Her laughter is contagious and although slightly offended, Aziza can't help but laugh herself. They all know what Aida has said, is true. Aziza, the social butterfly, the one who knows everyone, cannot and will not be tamed.

Aida takes off her apron, smooths out her shirt, and walks outside from the cafeteria to the main building. The children pass by her in their neat, orderly lines, eager for the meal awaiting them. The sun is shining brightly and she stops for just a moment, closes her eyes and feels its light and warmth playing upon her face. Taking a deep breath in, Aida smells the damp, freshly cut grass, and listens affectionately to the children's sweet whispery chatter.

She walks through the hall to the Kindergarten classroom where Hanan is posted, and peers through the glass window imbedded in the door. The room is empty. She tries the door, and it is unlocked. Walking into the room, she stands in the center, and listens. There are sounds coming from the bathroom, and Aida gently knocks on the door several times.

"Oh," calls out the surprised voice. "I'll be right out."

Hanan exits the bathroom a few minutes later, smiling at Aida, eyes trained on the floor self-consciously.

"I'm so sorry I am late for lunch," she begins, but Aida shushes her.

She looks at the young girl, beautiful and slight, not weighing more than one hundred pounds soaking wet. What Aida notices above all else though, are the red puffy eyes. Even a hijab cannot cover those.

She gets the sense that Hanan doesn't want to talk. The poor girl is putting forth such great effort to act as if nothing is out of the ordinary. Aida respects this.

Instead of filling the silence with awkward conversation that is unwanted and unnecessary, Aida envelops the girl in a hug. At first Hanan is rigid, and this gives way to simply stiff. Aida holds her tightly, and Hanan doesn't protest. She puts her small head on Aida's thick shoulder, as this is what it was made for, and quietly continues crying.

She may be Syrian and I Bosnian, Aida thinks. *Our stories are unique and different, but war and love remain the same, regardless of where and between whom they occur.* She and Hanan are the same. Aida doesn't know her story, what she lost on her way here, and she doesn't need to. She understands regardless of the details.

She holds Hanan tightly to her, the girl young enough to be her daughter, now in the U.S. all alone.

"We are the same, you and I. Refugees. We are the same, and you are not alone. I am here, and I understand."

In three sentences Aida has said it all, everything and anything needing to be said in this moment. Brown hijab and black hijab stand in an unending embrace, dancing around the word refugee for eternity.

⚡ 23 ⚡

Hanan

She may have just given herself away. All the effort, all the secrecy, to ensure the past stays in the past where it belongs, literally dead and buried, may have all been for nothing. *Why did I give in?* She berates herself. Masochistically, she hits the replay button in her mind, over and over, again and again. *Why cry? Why cry here, at my place of employment? Why lose composure with a coworker? Now Aida will know something is amiss, and in an effort to help, she will tell someone else, who will tell someone else, until the process culminates in Lydia realizing who I am, what I survived, who I lost, and the secret will not be so secret anymore. It will become commonplace knowledge, circulating amongst the people I spend all day, every day with.*

She will no longer have the luxury of pretending things are okay, living in others' ignorance, their unawareness, and this she clings to, for it is her only escape. If they know her story, she will not be able to pretend she has a different one, and will have to relive the one she is desperate to forget every time their eyes meet hers, because they will know, and she will know they know, and they will know she knows they know, and it will all quietly unravel, this delicate existence she has built.

Hanan had arrived at school this Monday morning, eyes wide open, expectant of what would greet her at the front doors. On the MARTA, just in case Lydia had pieced Hanan's puzzle together and told others over the weekend, she prepared herself for her coworkers looking at her differently, knowingly, to expect that even those wise enough to say nothing at all would find her gaze and hold it, asserting the fact that they knew, and finding a deluded comfort in thinking their stare meant comradery to her. She hates that look; the *I get you because I have been there* look. She had yet to meet another individual who truly understands, who has stared the depths of a loss like hers in the face, and not succumbed, but survived, as she has. People flatter themselves with the overinflated sense of their loss in this earthly realm. The truth is, most people would have walked into the sea, forcing it, not asking

121

it, to take them too. So few, if any, know what the burden is to continue on, with the loss of this life bearing down upon them every step of the way, as they stumble in some direction, any direction, because life is an aimless pursuit now, with no light or love to guide the way.

Hanan is beyond that though, and refuses to go back. She has made the slightest bit of progress, and it feels like conquering a mountain. Being here, in this country and this school, working with these people, is helping. She can feel it in her bones, in her ability to sleep more than an hour at a time at night. If people find out, however, it will not be her choice to go back to the way things were before, it will be inevitable, and then what? What of the hope that has just begun to bubble up again?

She is not ready to feel it go, slipping away as if it were never really there at all, and its absence sending her back into the abyss where nothing is everything and the concept of *everything*, a decent life, is an unobtainable delusion. Hope has brought her a fragile peace, maybe only momentary fleeting peace, but peace nonetheless. And to this, her lifeline, she desperately clutches.

But no one did anything, in the slightest, out of the ordinary. A few people, like Aziza, asked her if she was okay, because of how she looked at them across the hall, searching their faces for a sign that they knew, but they didn't, none of them; they knew nothing at all.

Hanan had struggled to fake calm and ease in the classroom, with the children, the entire morning. And then, when she simply could not keep it in any longer, the class was dismissed to lunch. She shirked her cafeteria duty, explaining to the lead teacher she was not feeling well, and deciding to make up something on a whim should Aida come looking for her.

The class departed, and when the last little pair of feet stepped out of the building and into the sun, she shut the door behind them and retreated to the bathroom. The Kindergarten classrooms each had a bathroom of their own, to ensure quick and easy access for the little people who used them. In this moment, such privacy, being in a place where she was almost guaranteed no one would come looking for her, was a godsend. She let herself go, just for a moment, watching her reflection in the mirror as tears fell from her eyes. Crying was something she had not allowed herself to do for as long as she could remember, for even though it was a relief, a release of pent up emotions, it was also an acknowledgment of a reality that she only wanted to forget.

With her tears came the rush of memories she knew was unavoidable, and then tears became sobs, so strong and true that her body shook with the grief they dispensed. And then there was a knock.

It had been Aida, and the way she looked at Hanan, understanding her grief, without knowing its source, was more than she had the power to resist. She fell into the embrace of that soft and kind woman, old enough to be her mother, and for just that moment, Hanan pretended she was. She permitted herself to put the full weight of her entire self, both physical and emotional, into the embrace surrounding her, and there she found it again, that beautiful liberating fleeting peace.

She knew Aida did not know, yet, and now it is the *yet*, that plagues her. She would have to wait, until Lydia arrived, to determine how to proceed.

The rest of the day goes by at a snail's pace. All she wants is to see Lydia, talk to her, and figure out where things stand, until then, anything she does, feels like wading through wet cement, exhausting, in vain, and nothing is concrete, just wet, heavy and burdensome.

Finally, it is time. She excuses herself to the daily After-care meeting, getting there early enough to secure a seat facing the door, so she can see, and more importantly, read Lydia's face upon arrival.

The meeting begins, and she is late, now more than ten minutes, and Lydia is never late. *This cannot be a good sign*, Hanan decides, panicking on the inside. She keeps her hands under the table, balled in fists from the stress of it all. Her knuckles are turning white and she is losing feeling. Just as her hands, from the tips of her fingers all the way up to her wrists begin to go numb, in hurries Lydia.

"I'm so sorry I'm late!" she says to the group. "My apologies. There was a horrible accident on the highway and it created massive amounts of traffic. I'm just glad I got here before school gets out."

Everyone smiles and nods, no one is annoyed or perturbed, as Lydia seems to have thought they might be. Hanan watches her closely as she settles in her seat. She is flushed, probably from running from her car in the parking lot to this room. Lydia gains her composure, takes a deep breath, and looks up, staring right into Hanan's fixated stare. She smiles casually, shakes her head in disbelief at being so late, and shifts her attention to Aziza, who is explaining the art project the teachers will be leading with the kids this afternoon.

The group breaks and people begin heading to their respective classes. Hanan and Lydia meet up for the short walk to their second graders.

"How was your weekend?" Lydia inquires.

"Good, good. Thank you for asking," Hanan replies, barely above a whisper.

"Did you go anywhere, do anything fun?"

"Yes. I actually went to Piedmont Park for the first time. It was chilly, but really lovely. The pond is beautiful."

"That's fantastic!" Lydia declares, with borderline too much enthusiasm, and then she goes on. "Oh, before I forget," now sounding more casual and nonchalant, "I figured it out, over the weekend."

Upon hearing these words, Hanan's heart skips a beat and then begins to beat faster than it ever has before.

"You look familiar, because you remind me of someone. My roommate in college was from Lebanon, and your look and way remind me SO much of her, it is uncanny really."

Hanan continues to watch her, listening to her vocal inflections and watching her mannerisms closely, until she is finally convinced of the authenticity of Lydia's statement.

Breathing an inconspicuous sigh of relief, Hanan smiles sweetly, acknowledging Lydia's comments. She says nothing though, afraid of what might come out. Lydia punches in the code, opens the door, and together they walk in.

≈ **24** ≈

Lydia

Early Monday morning, while lying in bed and listening to Rocky's deep, methodical snores, Lydia had contrived her plan. She would need two: one plan for what to do if people had seen the article featuring Hanan, and knew and another plan for if no one but she had noticed, and what she would tell Hanan to explain her idiotic comment on Friday about her looking familiar.

The first plan was simple. If people already knew, she would keep quiet. She would fake surprise, and then avoid the topic. She did not want to be a part of anything that could make Hanan uncomfortable, although, if everyone knew, her discomfort was a given. She decided her focus would be to support Hanan however she needed to. If she didn't want to talk, they wouldn't, if she did, they would. Lydia had a room ready for her if she wanted to move in, so literally, whatever Hanan needed from her, she would receive.

The second plan was trickier. How would she explain to Hanan why she looking familiar if no one had noticed the article? She stared at the ceiling, willing her mind to come up with something, anything, and then it came to her. Before working at Unity, Lydia's social circle had been homogenous, something she was not necessarily proud of, but the truth. Her friends were primarily other white, middle class women. She had, however, known a girl in college, and although she could no longer remember her name, she remembered the most important detail as related to Hanan. The girl was from Lebanon.

Syria and Lebanon are two different countries, Lydia tells herself, *with two distinct cultures, but close enough.* If Lydia claimed Hanan reminded her of this college acquaintance, she would buy it, hopefully.

She left early, so she would have time to prepare for either scenario in the privacy of her car parked in the school lot. The more time Lydia had to be in character, the more convincing she would be, and then there was an accident.

"Fuck!" Lydia screamed, to herself in the car. She hoped whoever was involved was okay, that went without saying, but she was going to

125

be late now. No way around it though, her only option being to wait, just like every other shmuck in their car.

She was ten minutes overdue, which was not that bad compared to some of her co-workers, but she ran nonetheless, from her car to the After-care meeting, stopping in the doorway, to take a quick look around at everyone, putting her finger on the pulse of the situation, and then sat down.

She could feel Hanan looking at her, practically burning a hole through her face. Lydia knew she was watching her, reading her, assessing if Lydia knew, whether she had put the pieces of this horrible puzzle together. That was when Lydia realized no one else had, and this was why Lydia knowing or not knowing was of such importance to Hanan. Lydia looked around, casually, while apologizing for being late. It appeared that, for everyone present aside from Hanan and herself, everything was exactly as it had been on Friday afternoon. They didn't know, not a single one of them.

Lydia shifted her gaze to Hanan, knowing plan number two was now in full effect. She smiled, rolled her eyes at the complication of being late, and then focused on Aziza who was presenting that day's lesson for the children.

When the meeting adjourned, and she and Hanan walked to their second grade class together, she seized the moment.

"You look familiar, because you remind me of someone. My roommate in college was from Lebanon, and your look and way remind me SO much of her, it is uncanny really," she declared, as casually and authentically as possible.

And she bought it. Hanan believed her. Mission accomplished. Breathing a deep sigh of relief, and slyly turning her head to wipe the beads of sweat from her brow, Lydia held the door open for Hanan, and the two went about the rest of their day as they normally would have.

When Lydia gets home that night, she tells Gary how it went, that disaster was averted, and no one but she knows. Hanan's secret is safe, and whatever story she decides to tell people will be her story.

"Are you sure she doesn't want anyone to know?" he asks, innocently, but setting himself up for a wicked verbal blow from his wife who is still reeling from the whole thing.

"What do you mean?" Lydia asks through clenched teeth.

"Well, I mean, having to keep something like that to yourself, having no one to talk to about it; that seems like it could be really difficult, and isolating."

"I'll keep an eye on her," Lydia says, teeth still clenched. "I spend three hours with her every day, and I will notice if she needs or wants something. If she does, I'll be there."

Consumed by his undermining comments, and the fact that he might be right, she decides dinner is over. As Gary raises the fork to his mouth, she swipes his plate, with its remaining mashed potatoes and quinoa, sets it atop of her own, and puts them in the sink under running water.

Wisely, Gary says nothing, except a quiet and gracious thank you for the meal, before excusing himself and exiting the room.

Lydia gets it. She knows what she wishes all American white middle class women and men understood. That they are the privileged few, and despite how convinced they might be that their perspective is the right one, the truth the world deserves to know and should abide by, it is not always a universally shared or respected one. Often, the privileged perspective is a steaming load of bullshit on a gold leaf china plate that they ignorantly but not so innocently expect everyone else to not only eat, but to enjoy while doing so.

She goes to town on the dishes. Dishwasher loaded and running, the disgusting glass pan used to bake chicken looks pristine after some serious elbow grease is applied, and Lydia's right arm feels like it might fall off. Turning off the warm water, she takes a deep breath, feeling better. Working out has never really been her thing, so she has had to find other ways of blowing off steam over the years, and dishes are always a good alternative.

What if I went about this all wrong, she asks herself, collapsing onto her side of the bed. It is a possibility, but it's too late to backtrack now. Better to be wrong about acting like I don't know, than wrong about how she would react to me knowing. I can't un-know something, but I can always learn something "new" should she choose to tell me about her past.

Content with her assessment of the situation, her eyes grow heavy and she drifts to sleep, waking an hour or so later to the sounds of Gary getting ready for bed.

"I'm sorry for how I reacted at dinner," she mutters sheepishly into her puffy white pillow, just loud enough for him to hear.

"It's okay, sweetie. I probably should have just kept my mouth shut."

"Yes, you probably should have, but the only reason your comment unnerved me is because you might be right, but I still think it should be her choice to tell me, not me imposing my knowledge of her past on her, because you could also be wrong."

"I think you handled it exactly the way you should have. This way, you can keep an eye on her and be there for her however she needs you to be, without potentially overstepping, or robbing her of what she might need more than anything else right now, her privacy."

No response from Lydia's side of the bed.

"Sweetie, did you hear what I said?"

She did, but Lydia has decided the conversation is over, being that there is still time for one of them to say something to exacerbate the situation and so again, no response.

"I love you," Gary says, with the slightest of chuckles, to his sleeping wife in the dark of their room. He leans over and kisses her ever so gently on the forehead, and a smile that he cannot see spreads across the face of his beloved.

⚡ 25 ⚡

Sherry

Ashraf had begun driving her home a couple evenings a week back in November when the time changed and it started getting dark at five. Now, in early April, the time has changed again, and the days are getting longer, the sunlight pervasive into the later evening hours. Despite the fact that she can now get from Unity to home before it gets dark, he still insists on driving her. *No one taught him to open the car door for a lady, but he is so chivalrous in other ways,* she thinks fondly to herself, tracing the veins on his right hand that she holds the entire ride to her house.

As they near her neighborhood, she can feel herself tensing up. Things at home, with her roommates, are becoming increasingly challenging, and that is putting it nicely. She knows what it is, why things soured and the phrase "intentional community" now sounds like a dirty word. It was how they began together, in that decrepit house. The first two months took everything out of them. Those months sucked them dry of the optimism and patience that they would need to sustain them throughout the year, and so by April, they are each spent in their own ways.

Having little or nothing left to give, while the house continues to literally and figuratively fall apart, and so much is still needed and expected from them, the remaining months of their time of service stretch out before them, a seemingly unconquerable and endless expanse. And still they remain together, but so very much apart.

He squeezes her hand, pulling Sherry out of the downward spiral of her own dark thoughts. Leaning her head back against the headrest, she looks at him and smiles. It begins as a fake one, meant to reassure him, a front that she can make it, see the year through, in that horrible house. It slowly fades to the expression of reconciliation. She will make it, because she made a commitment, a promise. She will finish the year, but the thought of what it will take from her is exhausting.

She remembers at the beginning of the year, when it was just the house that was the challenge, and wishing she could live at the school.

If everything this year had oriented around Unity, it would have been fine. There still would have been challenges, but nothing like what the JVC had dumped on her.

They all entered into the year aware of how a challenge that might not even arise could affect them. The world of hypotheticals is very different from the world of realities, and this was perhaps the hardest lesson learned by them thus far. The fact still remains, personalities and inherent differences aside, this is not their fault. It is the fault of the administrators who failed them, who sent them to that house, and then left them there when they explained the situation upon their arrival. They had been screwed from day one, but in the end they also know that they have each been tested to a far greater extent than most other volunteers, and they are still here.

If this realization is supposed to make them feel good, powerful, or strong, however, it doesn't. It makes Sherry feel abandoned and bitter. She can't wait for this year to be over. If it wasn't for Rebecca, she knows she may have already left. It is their friendship, and the trust Sherry has in her, that ties her to the sloping floor that they call home. They had confirmed it the other night, by rolling a ball from one end of the kitchen to the other by simply letting it go.

Ashraf lets her hand go to take the wheel with both of his, and maneuvers the car into a small spot in front of the house. Sherry takes a deep, deep, deep breath, sigh, deep, deep breath, and then the tears come.

"I don't want to go in."

Ashraf wipes the tears from her cheeks and whispers softly in her ear, "Someday very soon, you won't have to."

Sherry pushes his hands away and turns her face from him.

"What? Did I do something?"

"Those words don't help! They don't bring me any comfort! I don't care what happens months from now Ashraf. Today—I don't want to go in there today!"

He looks at her, somewhat alarmed by her reaction.

"I am just trying to help. I don't know what else to do. I don't have my own place that I can take you to. If I did, you would just stay with me, but that is not our situation, even if we wish it was."

"I know, I know. I'm sorry. It's not you, it's this house. I hate this house. It brings out the worst in all of us. Sometimes I wonder what our year together would have been like if we had been living somewhere else in the city all this time, somewhere sufficient, that wasn't literally falling apart around us."

"Sherry," Ashraf says, commanding her full attention. "It is almost over. You will never have to see them again, talk to them again, if you don't want to. A few more months might seem like forever, but it's not. You can do this. I know you can. I know what might help. What if we start looking at apartments for you this weekend? We can get an idea of what is out there, and then the future will feel more real, more obtainable."

"I love you," she says, looking deeply into his eyes, into his soul, the soul that's the missing half of her own. "I feel whole when I'm with you."

"You are my heart," is his reply. "Now go." Ashraf leans forward and plants his big, beautiful lips on her pink bowtie ones, and when they part Sherry feels like she is being torn in half.

She gets out of the car, shuts the door, and doesn't look back. Pulling her key from her pocket, she opens the front door, and closes it behind her, again not looking back. Seeing his beautiful brown face watching her from the car, and not running back will take more restraint than she has in this moment. She knows herself well enough to know that.

Sweet Ben looks up from the couch where he is perched, and smiles widely at his housemate. Of all the people Sherry would choose to open the door of this hellhole to, it is him.

"Hi Sherry. How was your day? You're getting home late."

"Hi buddy. I know. Ashraf and I grabbed something to eat on the way home."

"May is up in your room, but other than us, no else is home. I think Mary, Rebecca and Fransheska went out for beers after work today."

Sherry hides behind the gentle smile she gives Ben, feeling a slight pinch that Rebecca didn't mention the outing to her. Despite their closeness, she can't deny the fact that there is a growing distance between them as of late, and she hates it. They used to have their walks, but those ended when it began getting dark earlier, and they hadn't resumed. Sherry knows it is mostly her doing, creating this distance that she despises.

Ashraf consumes most of her free time, and while she hates to admit it, she has become the friend she hated in college, who pretty much disappeared when she got a boyfriend. Rachel and Emma had been guilty of this and it drove her to distraction. It had been easy to point the finger, claiming she would never be like that in a relationship when she wasn't in one, but now that she is, she understands.

It isn't just that though. Ashraf also provides her with an escape from the prison that is this house. She has an easy out, and she takes it often. She also happened to be volunteering somewhere with a lot of other young people, who are now her friends. Aziza makes her laugh, hard, and this helps her forget the challenges of the year that she can't escape. When she is at home, even with Rebecca by her side, it's all there, in her face, and there is nowhere to hide.

Bunking with May had come with a variety of challenges, but this would be true of any roommate. They had it out a time or two, but in the end figured out how to share a very small living space without killing each other. Ben and Mary are great, but she still hasn't really gotten close with either of them. It is the manipulative, power hungry, domineering Fransheska who makes her blood boil at times.

While most of their altercations have been passive aggressive, Sherry knows Fransheska has it out for her, because she refuses to acquiesce. *She assumed I would*, she thinks. In the beginning Sherry had been the calm, quiet and reserved one. She was accommodating and patient, until she wasn't. At a certain point, she firmly put her foot down, and in her own subliminal way, made it known to Frasheska that her way was not the only way. Sherry has been walking around with a target on her back ever since.

One night, not too long ago, when they were having one of their obligatory intentional community dinners, Fransheska hit that target, bullseye. They sat around the table in their dining room, praising the dinner she had made.

Sherry's roommates had been extremely accommodating of her self-imposed dietary restrictions. She had discovered, through a colleague at Unity that the chicken sold in the Decatur's Farmer Market was free-range, and this was the chicken they all agreed to be conscientious consumers of.

That night, Fransheska had baked the chicken to a golden, ever so slightly crisp, perfectly seasoned perfection. Accompanying the bird was a colorful array of deliciously grilled vegetables. The hint of olive oil and rosemary, enough to make a mouth water, and they did, all of them.

"Oh-my-god Fransheska!" they collectively praised her. "This is amazing!"

"I think this seriously might be the best chicken I've ever had. Like really." Sherry declared.

The praise and compliments continued to flow freely like the wine they all wished they were drinking too. The group quieted down, everyone more focused on devouring its contents than anything else, and that was when Fransheska voiced her very odd suggestion.

"Okay guys, I have an idea. Why don't we go around the table and each say one thing we have not been completely honest or forthcoming about?"

The others looked at her, slightly surprised by the seemingly random request of this evening's chef.

"Come on! It'll be fun. I'll start," she offered.

Still somewhat confused about where this was all going, Sherry sat next to her, curious as to what would come out of her mouth next. As a fork full of the incomparable vegetable medley entered her eager mouth, Fransheska dropped the bomb.

"Well, you know how we all assumed the chicken at the farmer's market is free range? Turns out, it's not."

Silence.

Sherry looked at her plate, littered with scattered chicken bones, the flesh of which now tossed and turned, slowly broken down by the acidity of her stomach.

"How long have you known this?" Sherry calmly inquired

"Awhile," Fransheska replied. "You see, Sherry, I researched it. That's what I do. I research the things I care about."

The assault on Sherry's character and morality was swift. She sat there stunned. In her mind, her left hand dropped the fork it was still holding, raised with lightning speed, and bitch slapped Fransheska across her tart little face.

In reality however, she simply sat there, saying nothing and doing nothing. The rest of the group sat in an equally stunned silence, no one quite able to grasp the reality of what had just transpired, at what had begun as a lovely dinner, everyone but Fransheska that is. She sat quietly, taking in the success of her ambush with great pleasure. She had already said everything she needed to say.

Now that the horrible night had come and gone, Sherry is happy she didn't react. That is what Fransheska ultimately wanted, and instead, the only outcome that would be noticeable to her, is that Sherry will no longer be eating any meat served in their house.

She smiles to herself, pleased with refusing to succumb to the self-proclaimed monarch of the house. She is not afraid, weary maybe, but not afraid. She now simply proceeds with caution, and the two are surface level civil. *A few more months,* Sherry thinks to herself, *a few more months.*

Sherry smiles again at Ben, excusing herself to her room to put her stuff away and settle in. Walking up the stairs, she makes a mental note of thanks at how much cleaner the house is now compared to when they first moved in. Once they had gotten rid of the bug-infested furniture, and hoarder crap from years past, the first thing they did was create a chore wheel. Everyone knew what they were responsible for each week, and they held one another accountable. No slacking; the house couldn't withstand it.

Making her way to the top of the stairs, Sherry takes a sharp left into her room. Sitting cross-legged on her own bed is May, hair disheveled, glasses on, deep in thought regarding whatever she is reading.

"Hey," Sherry greets her casually.

"Hey," May mumbles, without looking up. She continues reading as Sherry takes her shoes off and lies across her bed, staring up at the ceiling fan. They had made a room rule not long after moving in to never turn it on, because the one time they did, it almost flew off its hinge.

"Oh, oh my god Sherry! I almost forgot to tell you. Sorry, I'm reading something about Harvard's law school. It came! Something from Georgia State! I put it on the desk for you."

May jumps up and grabs the manila envelope set beneath their shared cinnamon-scented candle.

She hands it to Sherry who feels like she is having an out of body experience.

"What if they didn't accept my application? What if I didn't get in?" she asks. She looks at May dumbfounded.

"Feel it! It's heavy. You got in," May encourages her.

In this moment, Sherry feels such an overwhelming love for her roommate who has driven her mad in the not so distant past.

She rips it open and pulls out a letter, the letter of acceptance or denial. "I can't read it," she squeals, handing it to May. You do it!"

"Okay, okay! Here it goes. It says congratulations!"

Sherry screams at the top of her lungs, and Ben comes flying up the stairs. He walks in to see Sherry and May jumping up and down on their beds.

"I got in!" Sherry screams.

"She got in!" May yells.

And in this moment, Sherry realizes she was never on pause, pending, in-between what she had done in the past and seeks to do in the future. She is exactly where she has been all along, during every benchmark life-affirming moment, and every seeming setback that forced her to reset and begin anew, she is and always will be, becoming.

⸕ **26** ⸕

Aida

The weather is getting warmer, and Aida has been watching. Every morning, as she sees Lejla off to the school bus, she does a quick and inconspicuous inventory check. What is she wearing, what is she carrying with her, and what is her mood. The purpose of monitoring what she is wearing is obvious. Aida told her about their family's history so that she would know, know what they had suffered, endured, and what they had survived. She wants her eldest grandchild to feel the sense of self-respect, honor and purpose that Aida does, coursing through her veins. She wants Lejla to be aware, aware of the fact that everything she does, everything she says, is a reflection not just of her, but of her lineage.

By American standards this is a lot of pressure for someone so young, but for a second generation Muslim Bosnian-American, it is necessary. She must know that she carries them with her, all of them: the dead, the living, the yet to be born. They are all a part of her, the parts of her story already written and those that have yet to take place. She carries them with her, and the world will form an opinion, not just about her, but where she is from, based on the character she chooses to animate her actions, the voice she allows to narrate her story.

Thus far, the *what is she wearing* checks have gone smoothly. Her style of dress has been completely appropriate. It is warm, but will get even warmer, as the days of spring are drowned by the humidity of the southern summer. The real test will be when school is out for two months, when the days are long and oppressively hot, the flames of summer fun and freedom licking at her granddaughter's heels. *How will she dress then?* Aida asks herself. Time will reveal the answer to this question soon enough.

The purpose of the *what is she carrying with her* check is to assess if she presents one side of herself when leaving the house, only to change into another once at school. Aida surveys the contents of her backpack each morning when placing her lunch inside, and has seen no evidence of a change of clothes. This is a good sign.

Finally, the *what is her mood check* is perhaps the most important of them all, for it is this element that dictates the success of the other two factors. If she despises Aida, she will rebel, and do so by going straight for the jugular, that of course being her attire, for this is what Aida chose to focus on many months ago, what she chose to criticize, and so if things sour between them, back come the booty shorts. Things do not seem to have soured though, there is no stink that Aida's nose can pick up. It is quiet right now, between them, almost as if Lejla is still digesting, processing the full scope of reality Aida unloaded on her several months prior, and that is fine. *Take all the time you need girl,* Aida says to herself, *say as little as you care to say, so long as when you speak you speak kindly, and when you leave the apartment you are fully clothed.*

This morning is like any other. Up at 5, shower and dress, make breakfast for herself and Lejla, plenty remaining for those still asleep. Lunch for Lejla placed in her backpack, inventory of its contents taken, nothing to be concerned about. Long pants, shorts sleeve shirt underneath a long sleeve hoodie, Lejla gets on the bus, and Aida, who can't help but smile a deeply satisfied smile, heads out for hers. Halim, who takes a later bus to Unity, will be sent off by his mother.

The air is crisp, just the way she likes it, cool but not cold, fresh but not freezing. Her mind drifts from thoughts of her family to school, how fortunate she feels that her problems are her problems. *Compared to what we faced twenty years ago, life now, as we know it, is a cakewalk.* This is when her mind shifts to thoughts of Hanan.

How strange our encounter was a few weeks ago, she thinks to herself. *I don't know what I walked in on, but when she came out of that bathroom she was a mess.* Aida knows she had done what she could in that moment, when Hanan had clung to her as she wept. So many tears she shed, that when she finally let go, Aida's blouse was soaked through on the right shoulder. She had asked to be left alone after that, and Aida, of course, had agreed. When she saw Hanan later that day, ushering the kids back to class from the play yard, she had given Aida a small, weak smile, and since then, it was as if that moment shared between them had never taken place at all.

Aida does not need to know the details, and she is confident Hanan knows she can turn to her if ever needed. What she had said to her is true, they are the same; all refugees are in one way or another. They are survivors, and they are carriers, bringing with them all the hope and despair that a human being is capable of shouldering. She is a staunch believer in degrees of suffering. *My pain and my burden is far more but also far less than others, regardless; we have survived atrocities that cannot be erased from the mind's eye, despite how much we might wish we could. We carry them with us, but comingled with such despair is a hope unlike any other, because not only did we survive, but we have been given the opportunity of beginning anew. We are builders, of a future, of a life, not of our choosing, but a life nonetheless.*

She does not know Hanan's story, and she does not need to. What Aida does know is that they are cut from the same cloth, the same razor-sharp scissors of war and the makings of wicked men sliced away at each of their previous lives, taking with it people, places, things, but they had survived, they are here, and they bear witness.

Hours later, after breakfast has been served and the kitchen cleaned, Aida uses her small window of time before lunch is delivered to quickly check on Hanan. She hustles to the main building and lets herself in. Peeking into the Kindergarten room through the window imbedded into the classroom door, she watches, and she waits. Hanan is not there. *Maybe she is in the bathroom,* she thinks. And so she waits, and watches, the clock ticking incessantly away. Five minutes, ten minutes, no Hanan.

Not wanting to disturb the teacher, who is trying to corral all twenty five-year-olds solo, she walks across the hall to Aziza's room. Three hard knocks on the door, and Aziza looks up. She signals to the teacher that she is stepping out for a minute, and slides out to talk to Aida.

"Where is Hanan? Have you seen her this morning?"

"No," Aziza reports with a sly smile turning her lips up. "Why, is she in trouble with you?"

"Oh please Aziza," Aida says, acting annoyed but really appreciative of Aziza's ability to keep it light, real, but light. "I need to ask her something before lunch is delivered, but it doesn't look like she is here."

"Check in the office to see if she called in sick," Aziza recommends.

"Good idea. Now get back to work," she commands Aziza, who snorts in reply.

Aida makes her way to the main office, past Mrs. Luna who waves from her desk as she walks by. The school secretary confirms no call from Hanan thus far.

Peeking her head into Mr. Luna's office on her way out, she looks admiringly at the man as he sits hunkered down at his desk, stooped over both in age and deep thought. *This man who started it all, the builder of builders, is unequalled in his ability to see a beautiful future for humankind, but is wise enough to start out small and humble, here in this school and these children. These are the people,* Aida thinks to herself, *who make me willing to wake up to this world.*

He doesn't look up, and she does not need him to. She just wants to enjoy a moment of watching a hopeful world, a good world, at work. She feels blessed to spend her days here, and really, she feels blessed to have days on this earth at all. Her day in and day out, in her kitchen, roaming these halls, feeding these children, teachers and staff, are days of peace, days of unity, days of healing, for all of them.

Stepping quietly from the doorway, she passes Sherry in the hall. The two share a big hug, a simple hello and yet so much more. The gesture possesses a mutual comradery that neither can explain with words, for it simply is. They break and continue on their separate but together ways. *This ten minute window is a reminder,* Aida thinks, *of all that I have and all that we are.* Time is up and so she hustles, back to the kitchen, back to her place amongst all the moving pieces that are this school, and knowing who she is, what she is, both here and everywhere, Aida for the first time in a long time, feels full.

≠ 27 ≠

Hanan

A morning, just like any other since she arrived here in the States, up at six, dressed and breakfast eaten by seven. Out the door and waiting for the MARTA by 7:15. On the train bound for Unity, she takes a seat by the window, and watches the world wiz by. The plastic bucket seat holds her nicely, comfortably. She rests her head on the warming glass of the window for just a moment, before feeling a tap on her shoulder, gentle but firm.

"Excuse me ma'am," she hears the young masculine voice say to her. "Can I ask you a question?"

Hanan turns, a bit startled, but still calm, to see a young face, white skin, blue eyes, short light brown hair. A face no older than her own, and no younger than twenty she decides. She smiles shyly and says, "Yes, how can I help you?"

"Are you Muslim?" He continues, looking innocently curious.

"Yes, yes I am," she replies, hesitantly, but unabashed.

The young man smiles, satisfied perhaps that his assessment is correct, or perhaps for another reason. She is not sure.

"Where are you from?" He continues. "I really like your accent."

Hanan has had limited interaction with men outside of the school up until now, but knows that men and women converse freely and openly in this country, unhindered by cultural norms more common in her region of the world. She urges herself not to be taken aback, to progress in feeling comfortable in the cultural expressions of her new home, and this conversation seems like a good place to begin. Perhaps she can even share the positive pieces of her religion with this stranger who seems so eager to learn more.

"I am from Syria," she answers, "I lived in Aleppo most of my life."

"But your accent sounds English," the young man says, seeming to be confused by this.

"I attended school in London," Hanan explains, smiling at his bewilderment.

140

"Oh, okay. That makes sense." He smiles, and the conversation seems to come to an end.

Hanan turns around and settles back into her seat. Her stop is coming soon. And then she feels another tap on her shoulder. Turning back around to who she expects will be the same man as before, she sees he has been joined by a friend, equal in age, but brown eyes instead of blue.

"Are you a member of ISIS?" The man with the brown eyes asks her, his tone not as gentle and friendly as his friend's.

"Excuse me," she asks, sure she misunderstood the question.

"ISIS," he says, his expression hardened, accusing. "Do you support them?"

That is when she feels it, the instinctive gut reaction to remove herself from this situation. She looks from the face of her accuser, to the face with the blue eyes, and sees that his face has darkened, no longer seemingly sweet and unassuming.

Hanan stands up quickly, surveying her surroundings. The car is almost empty, aside from her and the two men. One other woman is sitting at the back of the train, ear buds in, swaying to the beat of whatever song she is listening to, eyes cast downward, focusing on what she is reading. This is when Hanan realizes the danger she is really in.

"Answer him," the blue eyes demand, the tone of his once kind voice, now sharp and very much on edge.

The train jolts and Hanan braces herself against the seat and then walks toward the doors, poised to jump off as soon as they open. Her stop is next. She watches as they get up too, also surveying their surroundings. She sees them look at each other, brown eyes and blue eyes lock, interconnected and ready, for whatever they have planned.

It is broad daylight, she thinks, desperately trying to reassure herself that things are okay. *If they were going to do something to someone, it would be at night, with no one around to see.* But she knows this is a lie, and the terror she feels in her stomach begins to spread throughout her entire body, shaking her to the core.

And then the train stops, the doors open, salvation. She jumps off the train, but they follow her. Her walk becomes a run, and just as the internal terror begins to rise up from her belly into her throat, allowing her to unleash a scream for help, she feels a sharp pull on her hijab from behind. *No one to see,* she thinks desperately, *no one to hear. How can this be happening? This cannot be real.*

The stairs are so close, the stairs that will carry her to ground level, where others will surely be, where they will see her, help her, but she is not strong enough. The pull on her hijab becomes harder, forcing her to the ground, the cement rushing up to meet her makes contact with the right side of her face, a sharp cracking sound resounds in both of her ears. She feels the pain of the fall course through her cheek bone, and her head feels suddenly warm. She looks up at them, the brown eyes and the blue, filled with certainty about something, filled with hate.

"We've been watching you, bitch," the brown eyes say. He seems to be frothing at the mouth, his distaste for Hanan and the idea of what he will do to her causing him to salivate.

"You are a loner," the blue eyes calmly state. "You make this easy, because no one will want to help an ISIS sympathizer, or any shitty Muslim. You're all terrorists, but we won't let you destroy our country." He bends down, and whispers in her ear, "We're going to send a message, and you'll be how it's delivered."

She puts her hand to her head, where it feels warm, and feels something thick and wet. Pulling her hand away she sees red, blood, and things begin to look a bit blurry. The brown eyes smile at her as she tells them to stop, pleads.

"Please," Hanan can hear herself say. "I am a refugee. I have no affiliation with," but that is where the talking ends. She cannot continue through the pain. Blow after blow from feet and fists rain upon her, first to her stomach, then her legs, shoes crushing her fingers, hands ripping the hijab from her head.

Full sentences are beyond comprehension, but she can hear words, words like "Filthy Muslim, terrorist, ISIS whore," hatred dripping, oozing from them.

"Please," she hears herself beg, blood spitting up with her words as they gurgle up and out of her mouth, through shattered teeth and broken jaw, "Stop." And just before the world goes dark, she feels them on her, hands around her wrists, hands around her ankles, lifting her, carrying her, swinging her back and forth, and then she is flying.

≈ **28** ≈

Lydia

She had patiently waited her turn, along with all the others who had caravanned over from Unity, when word of what happened reached the school. "In the spirit of solidarity," Mr. Luna had directed, "We are her people now."

They were all there at the hospital, waiting. Mr. and Mrs. Luna, Sherry and Ashraf, Aziza, Mya, Aida, and so many more, waiting. For someone who came to the country alone, who had no one listed as an emergency contact, Hanan was well represented, loved. It is the spirit of who she is, what she is, refugee, Muslim, survivor, builder, that they all understand. They need not know her story, for regardless they know *her*.

Hours she had sat there, sipping stale coffee in the waiting room, like everyone else, pretending not to know what they all already knew. She is going to die. She already had once. When Lydia's initial turn came to visit the broken, bruised, swollen form in the bed that people were calling Hanan, she had been shoved aside, asked to leave when the beeping began. Her heart had stopped. They were able to resuscitate her, but she had died, right there in that bed, already, and now it is machines helping her to breathe, machines monitoring her fragile heart that already gave out once.

"They threw her onto the tracks. After they beat her nearly to death, they left her there, for the next train to finish her off. The irony," Mr. Luna said, words spoken softly from a broken heart while weeping, "that they almost killed her because they fear terrorism, and fail to see that they are in fact the terrorists themselves. An inconvenient truth, for some people," he continued, "that acts of domestic terrorism committed by white supremacists and other disgruntled people are far more rampant, and claim so many more victims in this country, then the people committing acts of terror in the so called name of radical Islam. When will people see it? When will they understand, that almost all of us have the blood of immigrants, refugees, flowing through our veins." His voice begins to shake and

143

Mrs. Luna takes his hand, gently guiding him down the hall, a brief walk to calm the nerves.

The waiting is over now, signaled by the doctor, and Lydia walks toward the room. She is with her now, hands resting on the bed beside her, unrecognizable Hanan. She would hold it if she could, the bruised and broken hand that rests beside the bruised and broken body in the hospital bed. Beauty and youth have left her face, now covered with gauze and injected with tubes providing this and that to the decimated body.

"I'm with you. I'm here, love." Lydia does not think about what to say before saying it. Words do not typically come easily to her in difficult situations, but they flow freely from her now. "I just want you to know, that you are not alone. I am here, we are all here."

"I want you to know," Lydia continues, through the tears that spill annoyingly from her eyes, blurring her vision, distracting her from what she is trying to get out, "that I know your story. I know what you have survived. I want you to know that this end, their end, that God-forsaken beach is not your family's story. Syria, and what people have done and continue to do to each other, that is not your story either. It is part of it, but not all of it. Your story is one of love, one of willingness to do whatever it took to keep your family safe. You did everything right, but you lived, and they died. My oldest child died too, and for so long I made that my story, so much so that I almost lost everything else in the process. You however, you Hanan, kept going. You carry them with you, their beginning and their end, in your bones, inescapable, but you did not let their death become your own. You kept going, which makes you the bravest one of all."

⚡ **29** ⚡

Aida

This could have just as easily been me, she thinks to herself. The only difference between me and Hanan that made her more of a potential target is her brown skin. I too wear a hijab, I too am a Muslim. If anything, I would be the easier target. I'm an old, feeble woman. She pictures herself hobbling around the streets of Clarkston, and wonders, why not her, but she has already accurately answered her own question.

Her saving grace is her white skin. The assumption, based on her color, is that she is not from the Middle East, or an Asian country with terrorist activity. Hanan's beautiful brown skin is what made her their victim. *Even in America,* Aida thinks to herself. Her heart is broken.

She tightens the navy blue hijab around her face and neck, securing it in place. Events like these make her that much more adamant about her right to wear it, and its beautiful ability to proclaim to the world what her religion is.

If they thought that by doing this, they would make me afraid, force me to take off my hijab, and bury my faith in the ground, they couldn't have been more wrong. It is my right to believe what I believe and to worship as I want to worship. This is America afterall!

She has lived through this herself, being terrorized because of her religion and almost dying as a result. The irony is that the people who did this to Hanan called her a terrorist. What do they think they are? Are they so shortsighted that they cannot see what their actions make them? They are the ones inciting terror. This was their ultimate aim, to make people like me so afraid that we either hide away at home, or take off our hijabs and submit, out of fear, but I am not afraid!

She had looked it up, late one night after visiting Hanan in the hospital, which she has done every night since the incident occurred. The definition of terrorist is "a person who uses unlawful violence and intimidation, especially against civilians, in pursuit of political aims." *The people who did this to Hanan are the terrorists, not her!*

145

"Aida? Aida?" The voice calling her name snaps her back into reality. She looks up to see Lydia standing over her.

"Are you okay?" she questions, looking at Aida with a furrowed brow, concerned.

"I'm sorry. Yes, yes, I'm fine. I was stuck in my head thinking about Hanan. It's all so disturbing." Aida tries to reassure her, but Lydia does not look convinced.

"It's getting late. I'm sorry if you've been out here waiting long. I just wanted to make sure Hanan spends as little time alone as possible. I didn't know anyone else was here to see her."

"The more people the better," Aida says smiling up at her. "We are her family now."

Lydia nods in agreement, her eyes drifting off and her mind going to some far off place. "Listen, I was just about to go to the cafeteria to get a quick bite." She glances at her watch and takes a sharp inhale. "Oh God, I had no idea how late it is. Have you had dinner yet?"

"No, but I packed some snacks just in case," Aida replies. "Would you like some?"

"No, no, I couldn't," Lydia says, feeling guilty about how long Aida must have been waiting. "Bring them with you and we can eat together. Then you can come and see Hanan for as long as you like and after I'll drive you home."

Aida makes note of the ever-so-hopeful expression on the woman's face. The clock on the wall reads 9 pm, which is very late to take the bus, whose dependability decreases the later it gets.

"Okay," she agrees. "Thank you." In her younger years she would have refused, but with age she has come to see life is too short, and it is okay to accept help when needed. The two women make their way down the hall, away from the cold, bland waiting room.

"This place could afford to upgrade a bit," Lydia says in a snarky sarcastic tone, pointing at the pastel still-life portraits adorning the walls and worn fabric furniture. Aida couldn't care less about the décor, but laughs at the attention her co-worker pays to it.

"So, I realize you and I have never really had the chance to talk," Lydia says. Since she is an After-care volunteer, she doesn't come to the kitchen while Aida is working. The two, up until now, have been like ships passing in the night, both with a similar purpose at Unity, but simply not crossing paths until something tragic became the catalyst for bringing them together.

Aida looks Lydia up and down. The woman is dressed nicely, fitted khakis, white sweater, and a light blue scarf draped loosely around her neck. Her gray hair is cut a little shorter than shoulder length, and her shoes look like ordinary black flats. Nothing too pretentious about her, but she seems very confident of her place in this world, her world.

They are probably about the same age, but Aida looks at her the way she looks at her daughter, maternally. This has nothing to do with Lydia necessarily, for Aida looks at Mrs. Luna this way as well, and she is older than Aida by at least ten years.

The life she has lived has aged her heart. It has aged her soul. She possesses more wisdom than most of her peers and elders, for she has seen and survived far more than most. She does not put on airs, or act superior, nor does she talk down to the people around her, thus forcing them into the role of submitting to her will. She merely reacts to the way in which they interact with her, and more often than not, it is the way they would interact with a teacher when they were children.

She looks older than her age, and she knows it. Her humble awareness of this fact brings a smile to her lips. It does not bother her that this is probably the real reason why most people act in such a way around her, waiting for her opinion and following her lead, because they see her as an elder. *I'll use the influence such an assumption grants me,* she thinks to herself with a grin.

But the further they walk, and the more they talk, Aida begins to realize she is wrong. Lydia does not see her as a teacher or an elder, but in fact as a peer. There is something refreshing about the unguarded way this American middle-aged woman speaks, so freely and unapologetically. It is the way Aida speaks to herself, in the safety of her own mind, where others cannot hear. It is how she would speak out loud if she were in her country, if life had transpired completely differently. Regardless, Aida can't really remember the last time she felt like she was talking with a peer, maybe even a friend.

"So you are from Bosnia?" Lydia asks, already knowing the answer, but trying to be conversational

"Yes," Aida says. "And you are from America?"

Lydia looks at Aida, taking note of the humorous and slightly sarcastic response to her question. Smiling and laughing just a little, she replies, "Yes."

"Do you have any children?" Aida asks, keeping the conversation flowing, and wanting to know more about this American woman who makes her so curious.

"I do," Lydia says smiling to herself. Aida recognizes this smile. It is the same one that can't help but spread across her face when she thinks or talks about her own. "I have fou... I mean three." Lydia stops herself midsentence to make the correction, even though it is probably too late. She is not in the mood to talk about Karen tonight, or to think about her. Sometimes it is easier to just pretend as though things worked out differently than they really did.

Aida looks at her, very aware of what just happened, but equally aware of the fact that there is a particular place Lydia does not want their conversation to go. If anyone gets that, it's her.

Aida smiles, meeting Lydia's eyes, and says, "Me too, three. It is a very good number."

She sees the relief wash over Lydia's face, and wonders what her story, the tragedy she carries with her, might be. *No need,* she self-corrects. *Such stories are for another time.*

"I know your grandson," Lydia says. "Not well, because I work with the second graders, but I have seen him around the school. He's a beautiful little thing."

"Thank you," Aida replies. His glimmering brown eyes, full of delight and mischief, run through her mind.

"Do you have any grandchildren?" she asks Lydia.

"Not yet. Hopefully someday, but I don't think anytime soon. One of my daughters, Aimee, is married, but she is separated from her husband. She would have been the one closest to that point in her life, but now, who knows. The other two are off living their self-centered lives. They are nowhere near ready for the selflessness it requires to have a family, a couple of little narcissists." She shakes her head in reconciliation, and Aida loves it.

"My oldest gave me my two grandchildren. Her ex-husband is a loser. She is better off with him gone. When he was here it was much harder for her, for all of us. I know she is lonely, that she worries about her children not having a strong father figure, but my husband can be both—father and grandfather. He loves them plenty."

Lydia laughs, looking down at Aida, who is slowly becoming clearer to her, her edges and shape becoming more defined as they walk and talk. She can't get enough of the thick Bosnian accent that adds spice and command to everything Aida says. They carry on about this and that, sharing some of the ins and outs of their lives, silently deciding to trust one another. *Who would have thought,* they each think about the other.

Rounding yet another corner, into another hallway, they finally see a sign before them that reads *Cafeteria.*

"I didn't think we were going to have to hike to the cafeteria," Lydia says, a hint of annoyance in her tone. "I had no idea how huge this hospital is."

"Well, we made it," Aida says. "You go get your food and I'll find us a table."

Lydia walks towards the food counter, and Aida towards the tables. The cafeteria is like a deserted island this time of night. A few people are seated here and there, but for the most part, the room is theirs.

Aida picks a table in the center of the room, decorated with a fake red flower poking out of a plastic vase.

Lydia returns with a sad little salad. The lettuce is wilted and the cherry tomatoes have started to prune. "That looks tasty," Aida says, poking fun at her new friend's dinner.

"I know," Lydia says looking helplessly at the food before her. "It's literally all they had left. Luckily," she continues, with a gleam in her eye, "they also had this." She pulls out a Milky Way, opens the wrapper and breaks the candy bar in two, holding out half for Aida to take.

"Dobra," Aida says with a wink, graciously accepting the offer. "Tonight will be your first lesson in Bosnian. That is how we say thank you."

"Dobra," Lydia repeats.

"Very good, but next time more emphasis on the D!" Aida commands.

"What did you bring to eat?" Lydia asks curiously, gazing at the plastic Kroger bag resting on the table beside Aida.

Aida pulls out a bag of Flamin Hot Cheetos and Lydia lets out a small gasp.

"What?" Aida asks. "You were expecting some Bosnian delicacies? Sorry to disappoint. These chips," she pauses to slowly put one in her mouth, savoring the taste before biting down and enjoying the crunch, "are one of the best things about this country." She smiles deviously at Lydia and eats another.

Lydia lets out a cackle. She lets herself go, not caring what she looks or sounds like. The cackle turns into a belly laugh, and at this point she is having difficulty breathing. When she is finally done, she wipes a few tears from her eyes, and takes a deep inhale.

"Whew! I honestly don't know the last time I laughed that hard. Thank you."

"Anytime," Aida says, enjoying the freedom to be sassy and boisterous. Her freedom to be so is extremely limited these days, with her always needing to be the strong one, the organized one, steering the ship, at work and home. All of this leaves her little time for antics and fun.

"Alright, that's good, but enough for now. I feel guilty enjoying my time here, with Hanan in that bed, beaten and bruised," Aida says. It is the truth for both women. They found a moment of refuge from the horrific week in the splendor that only exists in the making of a new friend, something that sincerely surprised them both.

"I know. Me too." Lydia agrees, and they both settle into a more somber mood between them.

"Do you know her prognosis?" Lydia asks.

"I don't know the details, just that when she first got here, it appeared very bad, and she still hasn't woken up."

"Well, I basically interrogated one of the doctors tonight while I was in her room, and what she told me is that when Hanan arrived, her brain had so much swelling that they induced the coma. She had two broken ribs, a broken jaw, a fractured skull, and her teeth..." Lydia pauses, choking on a piece of lettuce while trying not to sob. "Oh my god, I'm sorry," she says. "When I say it all out loud it just sounds impossible, but then I know it's real, and it's Hanan." She doesn't look up, but repeatedly wipes her fingers under her lower row of eyelashes, trying to keep mascara from running down her face.

"There's more," she says, looking up at Aida, who gazes back at her knowingly. "But you get the gist. It's bad, couldn't have been much worse and still survivable, is what the doctor said. Now they are just waiting, to see if she wakes up, and if she does, what her condition will be."

"Condition?" Aida repeats, questioningly.

"Well, when there is that much swelling of the brain they just don't know. She could wake up herself, the Hanan we know and love, or she could wake up with little to no cognitive function, unable to do anything for herself. The expectation, I gathered from the doctor, is that she won't wake up at all though."

This, all of this, Aida already knows. "Hope for the best, but expect the worst," her mother used to tell her, and so she did, still. But to hear Lydia say it, out loud and forthright, made it real, tangible, something that she will have to prepare for, but she doesn't want to.

Aida looks down at the table, at her fingers covered in Flamin Hot Cheetos, and shakes her head. "You know," she says, still looking at her hands, "I think that people assume once we get here, refugees, to our new home, that everything is okay, and for some of us it's true. There are others though, and for them, this is the hardest part."

* * *

Aida stands in the doorway, and looks out across the room. The space is completely overstimulating with the incessant beeping sounds and flashing lights coming from various machines monitoring this and that. All of this is in an effort to keep Hanan alive, which she is, barely.

Aida shudders, and pulls her long, thick sweater tight around her waist. Outside the air is warm, scented with the sweet floral accents of various flowers popping up in their spring time glory. But in the hospital, the AC is set to what feels like a permanent sixty degrees, freezing.

She lingers, not really sure why. Aida has been here every evening since the attack, keeping vigil over her friend. Even when she returns home the vigil goes on. The house is typically dark and quiet except for the T.V., which although set to mute, continues to emit a soft hum of white noise accompanied by the low, content snoring of Irsad, who insists of staying up until she gets home. Each night for the last week, before turning the lamp on her bedside table off, together they have lit a candle that continues to burn until the dawn, to ensure their vigil for Hanan is not broken.

We still fall asleep every night holding hands, Aida thinks. When they were younger, and the need to cuddle wore off, when security in their marriage was found in other things like the unconscious reliance on one another to simply get it all done, and the belief that the other would always follow through, they drifted to their separate sides of the bed. After Srebrenica, on their first night in a filthy little German motel, with the children tucked in-between them, all five of them sharing the same queen size bed, he had taken her hand in the dark,

151

and both of them made a silent promise to never take it all for granted again.

"Who did you lose, sweet girl?" Aida's question fills the room as she walks across it. Sitting in a worn chair by the bed, she reaches over and holds Hanan's cold, bony, broken hand in both of her own, warming it with her own body heat.

"I don't really need to know, but I think I can guess. I know, that regardless of who they were: mother, father, sister, brother, husband, child, best friend, you lost everyone. And with them, you lost everything. I can see it in your eyes, the way you refuse to let yourself be happy for more than just a moment. The children make that hard though, don't they? I have seen you when you are with them, caught up in the moment, forgetting yourself and your terrible past. I have seen that you can still experience true happiness, the most real kind, until you remember. I have seen you in that moment too, when it all comes rushing back, never having really left, but tucked away just long enough to give you a moment's peace. And when it does return, that beautiful light in your eyes goes dim, and then dull, because no matter how good your life here might be, it is not a life you are living with *them*. She touches her aging hand to Hanan's cold cheek, sharing her warmth and tenderness in the simplest of gestures, but it not enough. She longs to embrace her friend, young enough to be her daughter, to rock her and tell her all will be alright. But Aida knows this is the lie of all lies. Everything will not be alright. There is too much hatred in people's hearts, too much fear in their ignorant and easily persuaded minds that motivates things going so very wrong each and every day. So, she sits there, unable to hold Hanan's broken body to her own, knowing for now her hand to Hanan's cheek will have to suffice for it is all there is.

"I don't pretend to know the depth of your despair, love, but I know it runs deep. I know it has carved a permanent canyon into your soul. At its greatest heights, the view from this creation is stunning, with sunrises and sunsets like no others. Despair, like joy, can be breathtaking. At its bottom though, there is only darkness and cold. No other living thing can reach you there, and this is where you spend most of your time, wishing and waiting, for *them*. As I said, I do not know the depth of your canyon, but I want you to know I have one too.

"I don't know where you are right now, if you are here in this room and can hear me, or if you are stumbling around down there, at the bottom of that dark place inside you. But I want to tell you that I know where you are going. If you return here, we will be waiting. If you go, they are already there. Both places are good, both have love. No matter where you go from here, you will be loved."

Aida doesn't cry. She has no tears to shed this evening. Raising the limp hand to her lips, she gives it a soft kiss and then places it back on the bed beside Hanan's body. "Love," she whispers into the air. "You are loved."

❧ **30** ❧

Sherry

"The doctors are saying she could be in a coma permanently. Even with the swelling down, it's impossible to know exactly what her brain function is, or what she will be like if she does wake up. It's an awful waiting game. Nobody knows, and that's the most infuriating part of this whole thing." Aziza pauses to take a long sip of her sweet tea.

Sherry looks across the table at her friend. She has no words. As of late, Sherry has found herself speechless, a semi-permanent state that she drifts in and out of on an as-needed basis. If Ms. Clinton needs something from her during the school day, she speaks. If Aida asks her a question during lunch duty in the cafeteria, she will answer, because she has to. Ashraf and her roommates know better though. They know not to ask much of her that requires a response these days, and not to take her silence personally. It's not them; it's her. She is in her head, thinking, thinking, thinking. What she is thinking about is still a mystery to those on the outside looking in, but they know she needs time after what happened, and so they give it to her.

"No," Ashraf says, perhaps a bit too forcefully for the given audience, but he cannot help himself. "That is not the most infuriating part of this situation," he says, his words possessing vehement passion, not directed at Aziza, but spoken in response to her nonetheless. "The most infuriating part, is that they still have not found the two bastards who did this to her. There were witnesses for fuck's sake! People literally saw them throw her onto the tracks, but it's like they disappeared into thin air after that. Bullshit!"

"Okay, okay, I see your point," Aziza says coolly. Her intention is not to get him riled up again. "It sounds like the Atlanta PD is doing everything they can to find them. That's what the detectives said when they came to Unity a few weeks ago to interview everyone. They pretty much interrogated me," Aziza says with an awkward laugh. "Seemed like they were pretty serious."

"It's because you're black," Sherry says, shattering her silence with words of brute force. Ashraf and Aziza both turn and look at her, an incredulous expression on each of their faces. "It *was* an interrogation because you are black, and they haven't found Hanan's attackers yet because she is brown and Muslim. Your worth is measured by the color of your skin mostly, and then by your religious orientation. Let's be honest. Every single one of those white police officers and detectives has considered it at one point or another during the investigation."

"Considered what?" Ashraf asks.

"That maybe those men knew something no one else did. Maybe she is a terrorist, an ISIS sympathizer; maybe those two men did us all a favor."

Aziza looks at her stunned. "I can't believe I just heard those words come out of your mouth. Ms. 'I believe in the inherent goodness of all people,' and 'world peace is possible.' When did you become so dark?" she asks, shaking her head, the ever-present smile fading from her face.

"When my friend was almost killed by two men committing an act of domestic terrorism, when being brown and Muslim suddenly means you are walking around with a target on your back. When the man I love, and my closest friends, became perceived of as societal threats, bad enough to kill, and when I realized I can't take either of your safety just walking down the street for granted. That's when!" Sherry is not staring at anyone when she finishes her rant, she is staring into the air; her look is icy and hard.

Ashraf cups his hand over hers which are folded together on the table. Both of them fit under his one. He looks at her, deeply, imploring her to talk to him. She can feel the heat of his stare, but refuses to make eye contact. She can't look at him right now.

The table has become silent, and the poor waiter picks just the wrong moment to wander over casually, requesting their order. All three of them look up at him. Silence. His realization that he just walked in on something he really wishes he hadn't dawns on him and with a small smile, he turns quickly on his heel and hurries away.

Café Istanbul is quiet. The Friday evening crowd not yet having arrived allows the group of three to smoke their hookah uninterrupted. In another hour or so, the café will fill beyond capacity and the Kurdish music will be turned up. The word "habibi" will be shouted from one end of the restaurant to the other as the patrons greet one another jovially, because it is Friday and the weekend has just begun.

Typically, there is no other place Sherry prefers to be. She loves their Friday night ritual of gathering together at the same place time and time again. She loves knowing that whether they discuss going beforehand or not, she can count on everyone being there, because this is their place. What she loves is the consistency, the dependability, and the slight buzz and euphoric feeling the hookah ever so graciously gives her.

Today they came early. It was a minimum day, originally scheduled to allot the afternoon to staff development, but Mr. Luna wisely canceled the event and let the staff go after lunch when the children were sent home. The children and staff all feel it, the month of April closing her doors, and summer cannot come soon enough.

Sherry is looking down at her lap, thoughts swirling in her mind. She has always been a thinker, a lover of the written and debated word. This is why she majored in Philosophy. To spend her days reading the insights of the greatest thinkers the world gave birth to, and based on their postulations on various subjects, being able to spend countless hours defining and refining her own world view is how she would like to spend the rest of her life. But, she must have the ability to do something with her thoughts. She cannot ignore the innate call to put them into action. It is this very conundrum, of not knowing exactly what she thinks, and thus not knowing what to do, that is causing her such inner conflict, making her hyper aware of the world's nefarious chaos, from which she cannot look away.

"I still think those things," she says, but barely above a whisper. "Or at least, I want to. It's just that," she pauses, trying to steady her shaking voice and suppress the tears that are fighting their way out. "I have never been afraid before. It's like, I have always known the world of humanity is capable of horrible things, but it has never touched me personally, until now. I have never been afraid for the people I love. What a beautiful fucking bubble my life has been."

With these words the seal is broken, but the tears come in a slow stream, not the torrential downpour of salt water and snot she had feared. She looks up at her friends, and smiles weakly. "I love you both, and I hate the part of the world that hates the most beautiful parts of you. But I don't know what to do. I feel completely helpless, and this feeling is infuriating. I should know what to do, and I should be doing it!"

Aziza takes her hand and puts it over Ashraf's, which is still lying over both of Sherry's. "Girl, you are doing something. Just by sitting at this table with black and brown people, by loving Ashraf the way you do, hell Sherry, you gave up your privileged white life to come here and volunteer. You know your skin is white, you know mine is black, and your man's is brown, but you really believe we are equal and the same. We have had different experiences, and face different challenges in the world, and you know this, you acknowledge it every day in the life you are leading. You are doing something. If you can do more, do more, but don't undervalue the action you've already taken. Find that hope within yourself, cause the world ain't giving it away for free these days."

"Okay?" Ashraf asks Sherry, imploring her to come out from the confines of her mind and join them.

"Okay," Sherry replies. What Aziza said rings loud and true, and she remembers what brought her to this strange place to begin with. This year has taught her that she can never truly be the *other*, for in America her white skin simply grants her too much privilege for that, but she does understand what it is like for them, to live in this world as the oppressed. She walks hand in hand with them, day after day, and this is good. It is not enough, and she can do more, but it is a good place to be looking forward from. It's a start.

* * *

Time has gone by, simultaneously slow and at warp speed, but how can this be? How can this month have felt like the longest one thus far, and the last day of school being today still come as a surprise?

Either way, it is the fifteenth of May and Sherry looks to the summer with neither excitement nor discontent. It simply is. With school out, her volunteer assignment will be teaching a second-third grade combination class for Unity's summer school, which will be for refugee children K-sixth grade. Children from the surrounding public schools will also be attending, and thus she won't only be working with ones she already knows.

Summer school doesn't start until May 31st though, and tomorrow she is leaving to visit home for one of the weeks she has off. After that, she won't be back to California until Thanksgiving, having accepted a spot with Georgia State's Philosophy MA program, and that will be the longest stretch of time without seeing her family yet. She needs this coming week, to be home, to see her family and friends, and to have just a taste of what her normal used to be, blessed and cursed by seemingly blissful white middle-class ignorance to what the struggles of

157

most of the world consist of. Just a week to pretend the bubble is real, and lounge about within it.

The kids are bouncing off the walls. They can sense the imminent summer. Regardless of what they will spend their time doing, the longer hours of sunlight, and time off, seem to speak to them of infinite adventure and promise. When lunch has been served to all the hungry little mouths, backpacks zipped and shoes tied for the last time this school year, Sherry leads them from their classroom to the main building to wait for the bus.

She watches the sunlight dance across their faces. These faces of every color and creed have become her faces, ones that have left a permanent mark, and changed her forever. Bringing up the rear is Bilan, her little Somali companion. The child, dripping with sweat, struggles to put on her hijab. Since the weather has gotten warmer, it has become a daily ritual for her to remove it during morning recess and to leave it off the rest of the day, but she never fails to remember to put it back on before taking the bus home, her parents none the wiser. *Good luck to them,* Sherry thinks, giving her little friend a wink. The wink is returned and Sherry chuckles. *If ever there was a rebel, it's this one. Only seven years old and already so slick.*

She lines them up against the wall, pointer finger raised to her lips, encouraging their silence. She looks at them again, these children, her children. When she is with them, it all effortlessly makes sense. Each one is given a hug, an embrace containing the sum total of her being. Those little hands that reached for hers, countless times over the last ten months, are ones she will miss. Next year, they will be replaced by new little hands, and while Sherry knows these too will reach for hers, she cannot imagine loving them as much as the ones standing before her.

The bus pulls up, and she sees them off, one by one. They blow her kisses from their seats, barely able to contain their excitement for the summer that is just beginning. And when the bus disappears down the drive, and the sound of the children's chatter and laughter is replaced by silence, Sherry makes her way to the music room that was once her classroom, the place where it all began, where she first saw their faces, and found her true purpose in this messy beautiful world.

All the others are there. She is the last one to take a seat. Mr. Luna has requested the staff's attendance from 2-3 pm, one last chance to gather together before dispersing until the next school year. Sherry takes the empty seat next to Aida, who put her arm around her shoulders, squeezing Sherry to her soft and cozy form. Sherry puts her head on Aida's shoulder, and the two sit together, taking in the past year, its successes and heartache, equally moved by both.

"Any updates on Hanan?" Sherry asks, lifting her head to look Aida straight in the eye. She and Ashraf had been to visit her several times over the last two months, and every visit was the same. Ashraf would recite passages from the Qur'an and Sherry would hold Hanan's limp cold hand between her two warm ones. There was never a change in her condition, despite all the hope and all the prayers. Her coma dragged on, and the doctors never knew anything more than they had the last time they were there.

"No, my love," Aida replies. "I was with her last night, and cornered the doctor when she came to check on her. No change. But listen, there is something else I want to talk to you about. My grandson, Halim, will be in your class for summer school. This makes me happy, because I know you, I trust you. He will be in good hands."

"My granddaughter, Lejla, is going into seventh grade, and so she is too old to attend, but I am wondering if she can be your assistant."

Aida pauses and looks at Sherry, an undeniably hopeful smile spreads across her face.

"Well," Sherry responds, slowly and thoughtfully, trying to account for all the ways this could go horribly wrong if she says yes. She had heard about Lejla, heard the other Bosnian women whispering in the hallway, things about inappropriate clothing and a filthy mouth; not necessarily what Sherry wants to expose her class to this summer. Her first attempt at an easy way out, without having to actually say no is, "I'm not really in charge of staffing. I think you would have to ask Mr. Luna."

"Done," Aida says, the smile still sheepishly sprawled across her wrinkly endearing face.

"Oh!" Sherry cannot hide her surprise. "Uh, what did he say?"

"He said it is up to you. It is your class, so it is your decision."

Shit, Sherry thinks. *I can't say no, but I am so afraid to say yes.* She looks at her friend helplessly. "How about this, let's try it out for a week, and if everything goes smoothly, she is welcome to continue on as my assistant."

"Thank you my friend," Aida says joyfully. She takes both of Sherry's hands, and individually presses them to her lips. "I am sure you have heard people talking, and I am sure the things they have said about my granddaughter are not all that nice. I won't say those things aren't true, because they are, or they were. She is better now though, so much better, but summer can change all of that. I want her to be occupied, and you will be a good influence. Thank you! You are saving me, and her!" Aida ends her passionate speech by hugging Sherry tightly to her and kissing her hard on each cheek.

Sherry hugs her back, laughing at the display of affection. Other staff members are looking their way, curious about what just happened.

"I'll keep my eye on her," Sherry whispers. "It will be okay."

Mr. Luna, clears his throat, signaling he is ready to begin. The hum of consistent conversation comes to an end. Sherry looks around. They are seated in a circle, always egalitarian. Mrs. Luna is sitting to his left, upright and attentive. Her husband has a lot of fans, but without a doubt, she is the biggest.

Sherry will miss these faces over the next two months, some more than others. Aziza is sitting to her right, Aida to her left, and Mya, Ashraf and Lydia are peppered in with the rest of the group. He must have requested the After-care staff to come too, Sherry thinks to herself. She loves that they are as much a part of the team as full-time staff, but alas this is all part of Mr. Luna's consistent rollout of his vision.

He takes Mrs. Luna's hand, which Sherry makes vague note of, but this is not what alerts her. It is when he raises his right hand to wipe something from his eye, that she suddenly realizes, before the words can leave his mouth, why they are all gathered here.

"She's dead," Sherry blurts out, covering her mouth with both hands seconds too late.

People are gasping, shouting "No, no!" But his silence confirms it.

"Yes." Mr. Luna says gently. "Early this morning, her heart stopped. They tried to resuscitate her, but this time, her heart refused. It was too weak, she was too weak. I'm so sorry."

The room erupts, she can see it, so many tears, looks of utter confusion and denial. Ashraf is in front of her, crouched down, hands on her knees. His lips are moving, but no sound is coming out. She sees Lydia grab her bag and exit the room. Aziza and Aida sit crumpled in their chairs on either side of her, completely consumed by their grief.

But Sherry feels nothing. She makes eye contact with Mr. Luna from across the room and his tired old eyes have lost their light.

Ashraf takes her hand and leads her outside to his car, and now they are driving. She can finally hear him talking, but nothing he says is making sense. She leans her head back against the seat, closes her eyes and lets the world around her go blank.

≉ **31** ≉

Lydia

It can't be true, she thinks. *He is wrong! When I get there, she will be in her room, lifeless, but alive. She's not dead!*

Lydia doesn't know the speed limit, but she knows she is going around 80 mph. Her eyes dart from the road in front of her to the rearview mirror. She is trying to keep an eye out for cops. This is a residential neighborhood, and so the speed limit is most likely 25 mph, but she doesn't care. She has to get to the hospital.

Almost there! she thinks, right before the car ahead of her suddenly stops at a red light. Lydia slams on her breaks, tires squealing. Looking into the rearview mirror again she sees dark black skid marks. Evidence she had been there.

"Hurry up! Hurry up!" she screams at everyone and no one. Beating her fists against the steering wheel and honking the horn, she wishes inanimate objects could be affected by her fury, but the car in front of her does not move, its driver as stoic as the hunk of metal and plastic itself, and the red light refuses to turn green.

"Fucking go!" she yells at the top of her lungs. She catches a glimpse of herself in the mirror, and gasps. The reflection that greets her is that of a maniacal lunatic, but she doesn't care. Her appearance is her last priority. Hanan is her first, Hanan and only Hanan. She simply has to get to the hospital, confirm she is still alive, and then everything will be fine.

The light turns green, and she is off. Pressing on the gas, she is setting a new acceleration record for the Prius. She swerves to the right, and cuts off the heartless driver that was in front of her. She rolls the window down just far enough to give him the finger, before pressing even harder on the gas and making note of the smell of burning rubber that follows her.

After what seems like forever, the hospital is on her right, and she takes a sharp turn into the parking lot. She squeezes in-between two mammoth SUVs in a slot designated *Visitor*. Slamming the car door behind her she takes off in a sprint. *Did I lock the door?* she thinks,

162

but again, it doesn't matter. If she hadn't, she wouldn't stop to go back.

Running, running, running, brief stop to catch breath, running, running, running. And then she is there, right outside the doorway of the room she had spent so many evenings in, reading to Hanan, holding her hand, baring her soul. Right there, at the edge of the mountain, where just beyond the precipice lies the truth, but she can't move forward.

Move! she screams at herself. *Move!* But she can't, because somewhere between the school and here, she realized he was right. *Mr. Luna was right, and she is dead.*

This is the truth, whether she is ready for it, wants it, can stand it or carry it. It is the truth, and she feels it in her bones. Lydia shakes, the chill of this realization causing her blood to feel as if it is freezing in her veins.

She wills herself beyond the threshold and through the doorway. All that stands before her is an empty bed. The room is vacant, clean, sterilized, waiting for its next resident. Unaware of time, Lydia is not sure how long she has been standing there when she feels a gentle hand on her back.

"Hello," a soft voice says. There is emotion emitted from the words, but it is controlled. "I was Hanan's Case Manager with Catholic Charities."

Past tense, Lydia thinks. *She is already using the past tense to talk about her.* It all feels so suddenly final, despite the fact that she knew this was the most likely outcome for her friend. Everyone did. For months, they had known that this moment was coming, so why does it come as such a surprise?

She turns to acknowledge the voice. The woman drops her hand from Lydia's back and smiles. Lydia finds her gentle green eyes comforting.

"My name is Gloria," she begins. "I can't believe it's true. My boss told me this morning when I got to work, but for whatever reason, I didn't believe her. I had to come here to see for myself."

Lydia steps aside, so that Hanan's room is visible to her.

"Oh my," Gloria says, barely above a whisper. The heartbreak in her words is palpable.

Lydia reaches out for her hand, and holds it in her own. Two strangers, united in their sense of loss and bewilderment at a future denied to someone young enough to be their daughter.

"I'm Lydia," she says with a weak smile. "I worked at Unity with Hanan." She catches herself doing it too. Past tense is a terrifying thing. There were times in her life when she had wished more than anything that a particular situation was only able to be discussed in the past tense. Situations she wished could be pushed from the present to the past, because having them be her day to day reality had almost been enough to undo her, but this is not one of those times. She would give anything to hear herself speaking about her friend in present tense, and know it wasn't merely wishful thinking.

"Oh, yes," Gloria says, releasing a deep exhale. "She loved it there. I think those kids are the only reason she kept going."

"Probably," Lydia agrees. If those children were all that got her out of bed some mornings, then for Hanan they must have been a lifeline.

I wonder if she knows, Lydia thinks to herself. *How much of Hanan's story is this woman aware of?* It doesn't really matter, she decides. She will not be discussing it with anyone either way. Alive or dead, Hanan's secret would remain hers.

"Do you know where they took her?" Lydia asks.

"Yes. They took her to an Islamic morgue, to prepare her body as her faith requires. Catholic Charities will be making funeral arrangements. I'll make sure to call the school to let everyone there know when it is."

"Thank you," Lydia says.

"Would you like to grab a cup of coffee?" Gloria asks kindly.

But Lydia does not have it in her right now. She needs to go home.

"No, but thank you for the offer." She almost continues to thank Gloria for bringing Hanan to the US in the first place, and for making sure she had a home and help once she arrived, but she stops herself; because after all, despite that fact that Gloria played no part in how things unfolded, coming to the US was what killed Hanan in the end. She would thank no one for that.

* * *

Back in the car, she sends Gary a text. *She's gone. Hanan died this morning.* That is all it says. He tries calling her several times on the drive home, but she doesn't answer. When the garage door opens she sees his car parked inside. He is already home, waiting for her.

She isn't sure if she wants to see him or not, but she doesn't want to be alone either. The ambivalence is setting in. She knows food will soon lose its taste, and many a day will be spent in bed. Call it her process, her personalized stages of grief. She has been there before, and she dreads going there again, but it feels inevitable.

She parks the car, closes the garage door behind her, and walks through the door leading to the rest of the house. Passing through the laundry room, she stops first in their bedroom to take off her shoes and place them on one of the shelves in their walk-in closet. She puts her slipper socks on, settling in for the night, and walks toward the kitchen.

He is sitting there, with one cup of steaming tea in his hands, and another placed at the seat across from him, her seat. He is looking up expectantly, having heard her come in, and the soft smile on his face is one of compassion and tenderness. Above it, his brow is furrowed both in concern and thought. Their eyes meet and he pats the placemat across from his, signaling for her to take a seat.

She sits, with the full weight of this new reality weighing her down, chaining her to this earth, to this cruel and unrelenting world that she wishes was so different from how it really is.

"Here, sweetie," Gary says, pushing the mug toward her. "It's your favorite, Sweet and Sour. It should be cool enough to drink now."

She puts her hands around it, feeling its warmth, and he places his hands around hers. "I love you," is all he says. It is all he needs to say. Knowledge of everything else is held between him and her, for he has been here too. He knows where she is going, and simply wants her to know she is not alone.

"I feel numb," Lydia says, surprised by the sound of her own voice. "I don't want to go there again, Gary," she whispers, eyes downcast. When she lifts them to meet his, they are brimming with tears, about to spill over.

"What do I do?" she pleads, but still barely above a whisper.

"Think of what you will say," is his response.

"Where?"

"At her funeral."

"What do you mean?" she asks, his ambiguity frustrating her.

"Think of what you will say to honor her, when everyone gathers to say goodbye."

"Why should I be the one to speak on her behalf?" Lydia questions, not sure if it is the right thing to pursue.

"Because," Gary says confidently, "whether you choose to share everything you know about her or not, you know it, and it will shape the way you speak about her. You are the best person to acknowledge her life, because as far as we know, you have the deepest understanding of what Hanan went through. Maybe other people know, too, but we don't know that. I think addressing everyone she knows, speaking to the life she led, and saying the final goodbye, will give you purpose, and hopefully closure. It will help you actually say goodbye and I think the last time you were in this place, you didn't do that, and so the pain and guilt along with all the other awful things that plagued you lingered. This might help you move on."

Lydia sits quietly, staring into her cup of tea, lost in thought. "I decided I wouldn't reveal her secret, when I was at the hospital. She died before even talking about it with me, and so what right do I have to tell the world, now that she is gone and has no say in the matter?"

"I am not suggesting that you should tell everyone. That is up to you. One thing that you do need to think about though, is that if they find the men who attacked her, now that she has passed away, it's murder. Knowing her full story, and what she went through before coming here, will be vital to the decision the jury makes."

"Can you please stop talking like a lawyer, and just be my husband!" Lydia demands. She had not thought of this until now, but she knows he is right. If Hanan's case goes to trial, which it will if they find the two men who killed her, she will have to tell the world. *They will find them,* Lydia tells herself. Living in a world in which people can do this kind of thing to an innocent person and simply go about their lives, possibly doing it again to someone else, is more that Lydia can bear.

"You're right," she says, looking Gary straight in the eye. If there is a story the world needs to know now more than ever, it is hers. If I can play any part in fighting the hatred that men like them create, I will."

"Okay," Gary says, reaching across the table and taking her hands in his. He squeezes them, and looks deeply into her eyes, letting her know what she has always known, but so often chosen to ignore. He is with her, and always has been. She is not alone.

⚡ **32** ⚡

Aida

She awoke early, dressing quietly before stepping outside into the warm morning air. Springtime in Georgia is her favorite season. The pervasive scent is floral, and the humidity has not yet struck. She wears her typical lightweight long skirt, long sleeved lightweight shirt and light blue hijab. On her feet are her favorite pair of ornate, black and gold sandals. She even took the time to paint her toenails last night, the color a cool mint green that Lejla had offered to her, apparently the hottest color of the season, as her granddaughter explained. Aida looks down at her feet, wiggling her toes. The freedom she feels with exposed feet is indescribable.

Today is not a joyous day. It is not one that brings her any happiness, although it does invoke a deeply rooted sense of gratitude for the wellbeing of her kin. Beyond that, all she is looking for is a sense of peace, and to carry that with her this morning through the night, in the name of Hanan.

Catholic Charities Refugee Resettlement had made arrangements for her body to be prepared and buried at Al-Farooq Masjid in the city. Aida, along with a few of the female Muslim Case Managers, had assisted with bathing and wrapping the body. Physically handling her friend's remains was something that brought her great honor. She stood there in place of Hanan's mother, whom she knew nothing of, and yet was connected to. She stood there in place of every female relative who would have performed ghusl had Hanan's life transpired differently, had she passed away an old woman in Syria, surrounded by those who had known her since childhood, her children and grandchildren. Aida helped wrap her body in the Kafan in their place as well. She was not there as herself, but as a vessel for those whose rightful place was by Hanan's side to pass through.

She would however, not be attending the burial. Burying her brother in Bosnia after seeing the mass grave from which his remains were resurrected, and feeling that cursed soil in her hands, was the last

167

time she would bury anyone. This small accommodation is something she allows herself unapologetically.

And so, instead of being there this morning, to participate in giving the body back to the earth from which it came, she walks, she likes to think, with Hanan by her side.

Aida smiles, raising her face to the sun, and feeling its warmth settling upon her. She has spent so much of her life grieving, perhaps more intensely this last week than any other time, and she is done. This is her life, and she refuses to live any more of it in fear, fear of what has happened, and what could happen. She refuses to grant the men who murdered Hanan such satisfaction. She has instead decided to take back the power they think they have, the power the Serbian Army wielded over her fallen loved ones. They will have no more of her. She is reclaiming what is left of her time on this earth, be it a week or thirty years. The days left between now and her inevitable end, are hers.

* * *

Unity's cafeteria is full, practically bursting at the seams with people who have come to say goodbye as a community to Hanan. Aida casually makes her way back to the kitchen, to make sure the caterers aren't disrupting her things. Everything appears to be in its rightful place. Despite school being out for the summer, she still regards the kitchen as hers.

She had offered to cook for the gathering, but Mr. Luna had insisted she attend as a guest, not an employee. Making her way back out to the main room, and seeing the hundred plus people in attendance, reaffirms his decision as the right one. If he had agreed to her initial proposal, she and Hanan would have missed their walk this morning, and this walk is a new beginning, for both of them.

For a reason that eludes her, Lydia will be addressing the group today, saying words on Hanan's behalf to the people who have come to say goodbye. She knows the two of them worked together with one of the second grade After-care classes, and must have grown close in the process. Beyond this, she cannot reason why Lydia would be the one to speak today.

While Aida does not know the details of her life, she feels as though she understands Hanan's soul. She knows the chains that shackled her, whether in Syria or America. She has a sense though, that Hanan's chains were more burdensome than her own, for Aida had come to this

168

country with most of her family intact, and Hanan began and completed her journey here, alone.

Mr. Luna steps up to the mic, tapping it with two practiced fingers to ensure it is on, and in his gentle and kindhearted away, asks people to take a seat.

"Friends," he says, "family, today we are here to honor a fallen comrade. We have all come with love in our hearts to support one another as we grieve this tremendous loss, and try to begin the process of saying goodbye. Unity has been Hanan's family since she arrived in the U.S. Speaking on her behalf today is Lydia." He pauses, looking at the woman standing next to him, and smiles.

"The two women worked together for many months with one of our After-care classes, and in the process, became good friends. Thank you, Lydia, for being willing to share what you came to know of her, with us today."

With that, he steps aside, offering the mic to her.

Aida watches Lydia as she clasps and unclasps her hands tightly together. She shifts her weight from the left foot to the right foot, unable to find a comfortable position. *She is so nervous*, Aida thinks. Looking around at the crowd, she sees that all the seats are taken. Everyone else stands, lining the perimeter of the entire room. The number of people present must have doubled since the last time Aida checked. *No wonder she is struggling*, she sympathizes.

She watches as Lydia continues to stand there in front of the mic, looking out into the crowd, a blank expression on her face. The silence is beginning to feel awkward and Aida can hear the crowd starting to whisper amongst themselves, unsure of what is happening.

Quickly standing up, Aida walks to Lydia's side and gives her hand a squeeze, to let her know she is not alone. Lydia looks at her friend, the one with whom she unexpectedly bonded over Flamin Hot Cheetos, and smiles. Aida smiles back and continues standing there. With that, Lydia begins.

"Um, hello everyone," she says, her voice a bit shaky. "I'm not accustomed to speaking in front of such a large crowd, so please bear with me as I try to say what deserves to be said today."

"Hanan is someone who was special to all of us, whether we knew her well or not. She was a member of this amazing community, and she was our friend. She took care of our children, and loved them with a gentle kindness that is unrivaled."

Aida notices the change taking place in her friend as she continues speaking. As she finds the words, Lydia is finding herself. She can now stand on her own. Aida discreetly backs away and walks back to her seat, now one of the multitudes staring up at Lydia as she addresses them all.

"I worked with Hanan for many months in our second grade After-care class. We spoke a great deal about Unity and the children, but never much about Hanan herself. She was always quiet, perhaps even guarded about her past, and while I assumed it was because she had suffered tremendous loss on the journey that ultimately brought her here, it wasn't until I was reading the BBC news online one day that I connected the dots."

"I never mentioned any of it to Hanan, because it was so apparent that she didn't want people to know. In an effort to forge any kind of life for herself here, she didn't want people associating her with the tragedy that is part of her story." Lydia pauses, and takes a deep breath.

Aida looks around the room. She looks at Mr. Luna, to see if he seems to know what comes next, but he along with everyone else looks at Lydia expectantly, fearfully, for to add any more hurt to the story of Hanan's that they already know, might simply be too much to hold in their tender hearts.

"We all know Hanan came here alone," Lydia continues, her voice steady and direct. "And there is a reason for that. I don't know what became of her extended family, whether they remained in Syria after Hanan left, or if they made separate journeys, but I do know that when Hanan left her home in Aleppo, she did so with her husband and two little girls. They traveled from Syria to Libya, and then took a boat from there to Greece, but Hanan is the only one who completed the journey alive."

Aida is frozen. She hears the words Lydia is speaking, and is registering the horror of it all, but she cannot physically react. While everyone near her is gasping and looking around at one another, she sits silently and perfectly still, a prisoner in her own body.

"I think many of us remember the photo that was released more than a year ago. It was a picture of the body of a toddler that washed ashore one of the Greek islands, after a boat carrying hundreds of refugees capsized. That toddler was Hanan's youngest child. They never released photos of her five year old sister and father, but they were on that beach too, lying face down in the sand, while the sea that drowned them lapped at their heels."

"This is why Hanan came here alone, because her entire family died on their journey in search of nothing more than safety from the war-torn country they used to call home." Lydia pauses to wipe away the tears that slide down her flushed cheeks, and it is when she does this that Aida becomes aware of the cascade of her own, but she doesn't bother to try and dry them.

"Hanan lost everyone, she saw her husband and children die, and she had to go on living. Having lost a child myself, I don't know where she found the strength, but I do know that Hanan is the strongest person I have ever known. The fact that she had anything left to give makes her a hero, my hero.

"Let her life be a testament to the strength that we all carry within us. She survived what I know would have killed me. And the horrible truth of the matter is that she is not the only one. So many refugees have lost their husbands, wives, children, mothers, fathers, sisters and brothers on that same journey. We just happen to know her. What about them? What about their suffering?

"I watch and I listen to the rhetoric circling around the word *refugee*. I see rich western countries, like our own, electing leaders who promise to strengthen borders and keep *them* out, and all I can think is that the *them* being referred to is Hanan.

"And as I feel the world beginning to crumble around me, this wicked, wicked world, I think of Unity. I watch these children of different races and religions playing together, and just enough hope to get through the day presents itself. Every day I spend here, with this community, I accept this hope as the gift it is, and I let it keep me afloat, because if we give in to giving up, the world really will fall apart around us, and in our complicity, we will be just as guilty as everyone else.

"Hanan found her hope here. Unity is the only thing on this earth that sustained her. In the end, she died a horrible death anyway, but I have to believe she found just a little bit of peace before those men murdered her.

"I am sorry if what I am saying is not what you came to hear, but the fact is, it needs to be said, and I plan to say it when I testify in court on her behalf. They found the two men who murdered her *this* morning, of all days, the day of her burial. If there isn't meaning in that, then there isn't meaning in anything.

"I wanted you to know before her story becomes public knowledge, because you were her family."

With that, Lydia steps away from the mic and makes her way outside through one of the side doors. The room is silent.

Somehow, some way, Mr. Luna finds the words to thank and dismiss the crowd, encouraging people to stay and eat, and share their memories of Hanan with one another. When he is through, Aida makes a quick exit from the building, and looks out onto the playground, in the direction she thinks Lydia went.

She sees her friend in the distance, pumping her legs vigorously on one of the swings. Aida walks through the grass in her sandals, and takes a seat in the swing next to her. The two sit there like that in silence, swinging back and forth, back and forth, Hanan's truth now present between them, a truth they will carry with them in the days to come.

⚡ **33** ⚡

Sherry

She is back now, and reality has never been more bitterly real. Being home had been amazing; exactly what she needed as brief respite from everything she didn't want but was doomed to return to. It would have been so easy to stay. Ashraf would have packed her things and mailed them to her, but she wouldn't have just been closing the door on this year of her life, she would be risking slamming it on the next two that she desires more than anything.

Quitting the JVC would mean quitting Unity, and Sherry can't imagine living in Atlanta and going to grad school without still being a part of that community. Unity is synonymous with this city, and she can't have one without the other. She doesn't want it. Ending her year of service at the school prematurely would jeopardize her employment next year, and this is something she is not willing to risk.

To add salt to the wound, as if things for her and her roommates in that forsaken house couldn't get any worse, they did.

While Sherry was spending her blissful week at home with family, she got a call from May. When her phone rang and she saw who was calling, "Fuck!" was the only word worth saying.

"Hey May," Sherry greeted her roommate with fake enthusiasm and ease.

"Hey Sherry. How is it being home?"

"It's great. How are things in Atlanta?"

"Well that's actually why I'm calling," May continued. "Part of the backside of our house caved in."

"What?" Sherry yelped.

"Yeah, the brick just caved in, and the house is still standing, but there is a hole big enough for someone to walk through now, so we had to leave. I thought you might want to know before you came back."

"Wait, so where are you guys staying?"

"We're staying at a hotel, but one of the former JVC volunteers living in East Atlanta is traveling right now and agreed to let us stay in his house for a week or so."

"May, we have more than two months left before the JVC year is technically over!" Sherry said, as if May wasn't painfully aware of that fact already.

"We talked to headquarters, and they're starting to look for a new house this week."

"A new house?" Sherry questioned, not fully grasping May's response.

"Yeah, I mean we can't live there anymore. So the plan is, once they find a new house, we move everything there and that will be the new JVC Atlanta house."

"Got it," Sherry said. The thought of packing all the shit in that house, and moving it to a new one they would be living in for max, a few weeks, made her see red.

"I just thought you should know before you got back here," May said kindly. "Sorry to be the bearer of bad news."

"It's not your fault, May. I really appreciate you calling to tell me."

"Alright, well I'll let you go. Enjoy the rest of your time there, and we'll see you in a few days. I'll text you the address of where we are staying right now."

"Thanks May. Be safe."

With that, Sherry hung up her phone, ran into her mom's room and burst into tears. She already knew she would willingly return to the prison that was her life there, not all of it, but enough to make the proverbial iron bars something she could physically touch. For everything that she loved in that city, Ashraf, Unity, along with her own self-respect, she sucked it up and got on the return flight. While en route, in the air, she actually questioned her own sanity. She could have so easily stayed in California, where things were simple and life was easy, but when the plane landed and she saw Ashraf standing there, waiting for her with a single red rose, she remembered with perfect clarity why she had lasted this long.

The other reason was Hanan. Sherry had returned for her funeral, to say goodbye. There was simply no way she could not be there, and after everything Lydia had divulged, the fuller version of Hanan's life now revealed, Sherry is that much more grateful for the time she and

Ashraf spent with her in the hospital, and for the opportunity to be present when she was laid to rest.

Rest, Sherry mulls the word over in her mind. This is all that she wishes for her friend, that she is finally at peace. The life she led for the last year had to have felt like the greatest cruelty of all. Her family had gone before her, and alone she still found enough bravery within her to remain in this world that had ravaged everything she held dear, taken from her everything that meant anything, and left her with nothing. She had continued on, but now she is with them. Now, she can finally rest.

Today is the first day of Unity Summer School, and Sherry is grateful for the distraction. Living out of a suitcase was already getting old, and it had only been a few days since she returned. She doesn't miss the house itself, but the routine that had been hers for the last ten months is now permanently disrupted.

She stands in front of the empty class, and finds herself missing Ms. Clinton. While Sherry is excited and flattered for the opportunity to be lead teacher, she is anxious and terrified. She will figure it out, just like she has figured everything else out this year, the year that is both the best and worst of her life.

The kids will be here in ten minutes, she tells herself. Taking a quick inventory of the room, and each of the desks, she checks off all of the items every child should have. Everything is ready, so now she will just wait.

With five minutes to go, in walks a pretty young girl, her long blonde hair tied back in a loose braid. Like a light bulb turning on in her mind, Sherry suddenly remembers who she is, having practically forgotten she would be coming in the first place.

"Lejla?" Sherry questions, as she extends her hand to shake the girl's.

"Yes, that's me," she girl replies. Her lips curve up in the shyest of smiles.

"I'm Sherry. Your grandmother and I work together at Unity."

"I know," Lejla says softly, still smiling. "Thank you for letting me volunteer here this summer."

Sherry notices that her gratitude sounds authentic, not forced as she was expecting. The typical tween, forced to spend her summer volunteering in her brother's summer school class, would not be so gracious. Sherry is sure of this. Perhaps Lejla is different from the typical tween after all. Sherry smiles an amused smile at her, and briefs her on what the day will consist of.

While they sit for the next few minutes before the children arrive, Sherry notes that despite looking more like a teen, Lejla is still very much a child herself. Dressed conservatively in her capris khakis and white scoop neck, loose fitting, t-shirt, Sherry can't begin to imagine her in booty shorts and a crop top. The mere thought of it makes her physically uncomfortable. She is just beginning to understand what it must have been like for Aida to see her twelve-year-old granddaughter come home from school in such disturbingly inappropriate attire.

"Do you want to be here?" Sherry asks her, staring gently into the big brown eyes across from her.

"Yes," Lejla confidently replies. "I have been thinking about what I might like to do, like as a career, when I'm older. Teaching seems like a good option."

"I see," Sherry replies, trying to suppress her surprise at Lejla's confidence.

"I've seen how hard my mom and Baka, um, I mean grandma, work to support me and my brother, and the way my grandma talks about Unity..." her voice drops off as she tries to find the right words to express what she wants Sherry to know.

"My grandma was a teacher in Bosnia, before the war. Even though she is a cook here, she has taught me more about who I am than anyone else. Not just who I am, but who I can be, who I want to be.

"She asked me to spend my summer here with you. I said yes, because for her, I want to make her proud, and for me," her voice drops off again. "For me," Lejla continues, "I want to be like her. You can help me with that, right?" she says, not breaking eye contact with Sherry.

Sherry sees another path sprawl out and widen before her, but this time it is not her own. This time, it is a joint path, one walked by two very different and yet similar people. They have stumbled and fallen, gotten up and continued on, sometimes one walked ahead of the other and other times side by side, but always walking the same path, together.

"Lejla," she says, "if your Baka was sitting where I am right now, she would already be proud. When you go home today, you don't have to tell her what you just shared with me, but please tell her, that I just met you, and already know you will do great things in this world, as long as you continue to care as much in the future, as you do right now."

Sherry reaches across the table and gives Lejla's hand a quick squeeze. The voices of the children can be heard, drifting from the hallway into the classroom. As they trickle in, one by one, taking their seats at the little desks, looking up at her with big smiles, the colors of brown, black and white, wearing head scarves and head bands, she is once again stirred. She is once again quickened by the beauty of what is, and the potential of what can be.

⚡ **34** ⚡

Lydia

Sitting in her pajamas and bathrobe wrapped up in a blanket on the couch, Lydia chuckles at Rocky at her feet. He pants and snorts, in the middle of one of his dreams. *Probably chasing another cat*, she thinks.

"Mom," Aimee calls from the top of the stairs. "I need you."

This moment is so reminiscent of twenty years ago, that Lydia can't help but laugh out loud.

"Coming."

She walks up the stairs and stands in the doorway, watching her daughter struggle with closing a suitcase that is bursting at the seams.

"Sweetie, we live twenty minutes from you and Mark. You can make as many trips as you need to."

"I know mom," Aimee says, not bothering to hide her annoyance. "I just want to be done with the whole moving thing as quickly as possible. I'm ready to be back home with my husband."

Lydia reflects on it not being all that long ago, less than a year in fact, that her daughter asked to move back in with them, while she figured herself and her marriage out. *Thank God she did,* Lydia thinks. She never thought she would say it, but she is so glad her daughter is moving out. Living together had been fun at first, but as time went on, it was clear that Lydia and Gary needed their space, and Aimee needed her privacy. On more than one occasion, Gary caught Mark sneaking out of the house in the early hours of the morning. Granted, this was a good thing, what all of them wanted if it was best for Aimee, but it made the house feel like more of a college dorm than she and Gary desired.

"Just sit on it," Aimee demands, and based on her tone, Lydia decides to simply obey.

She sits down, putting all of her weight on the huge suitcase, and clothes spill over the sides.

"Honey, in the same amount of time you are taking to try and close this stupid thing, you could make two trips home and back."

Aimee shoots her a dirty look and Lydia decides to shut up. Aimee pulls the zipper desperately, stuffing the clothes back in as she makes her way around the suitcase.

"There!" she declares victoriously.

"Good work," Lydia compliments her. "What's next?"

"Nothing, that's it. Dad will help me get it down the stairs in the morning. Come sit," Aimee offers, patting the twin-size bed. She sits on the floor, waiting.

Lydia takes a seat and looks at her daughter expectantly. "What's up, sweetie?"

"What's up with you," Aimee shoots back. "Tomorrow is the big day. Are you ready to testify?"

Lydia doesn't really want to talk about it. The trial has been ongoing for the last few weeks, but she hasn't attended. She wants the one and only time that she has to be in the same room as those murderers to be on the day their fate is sealed, by her.

"As ready as a person can be for something like this. I'm ready to say what needs to be said, and know those men will be spending the rest of their pathetic lives in jail."

Aimee looks at her, enamored. "Mom, I am so proud of you. I honestly have never been this proud of anyone. I hope you know how brave you are for doing this."

"Doing what?" Lydia asks, a bit disturbed by her daughter's praise. "All I am doing is the right thing. Since when did that become so admirable?"

"Since the world went to shit mom, that's when. Okay enough, I can tell you don't want to talk about it anymore, so let's call it a night. I just want you to know I love you."

"Thanks, sweetie, I love you too." Lydia gets up from the bed, bends down to kiss her daughter on the top of her head, and walks back down the stairs.

She gently nudges Rocky, who awakes to follow her. The two of them settle in their respective places, she in the king-size bed next to Gary, and Rocky on the floor in his bed, right by her side. Gary snores softly, indicating a deep sleep. Typically Lydia would wake him up to tell him to go put in his night guard, but tonight it doesn't matter. She won't be sleeping anyway.

She lies down, a pile of nerves and anxiety she has reconciled herself to, but only for one more night. *Tomorrow it will be over,* she thinks to herself, in the dark silence of the bedroom. *Once the jury hears what I have to say, about the woman those men beat to a bloody pulp and then threw in front of an oncoming MARTA train, their decision will be made.*

With that dark but consoling thought on her plagued and restless mind, she lies down on her side, reaches over and finds a resting spot for her palm on Rocky's soft, warm belly. She lies like this for what seems like hours, until finally, somewhere between midnight and dawn, sleep ultimately finds her.

* * *

She will be the first character witness on the stand this morning. Gloria, Hanan's Case Manager with Catholic Charities, had gone through the process the first week the case was in court. Afterward, she met Lydia for coffee to tell her what to potentially expect when it was her turn.

"The defense is trying to paint the picture that her murderers were justified to perceive of her as a potential terrorist, and as a threat to national security. Their lawyer is just as xenophobic as the bastards he's defending. Do you want to know their names?"

"Whose names?" Lydia asked, her coffee untouched and cold.

Gloria reached across the table and squeezed her hand. "The men who killed her," she said, looking intently into Lydia's eyes.

"No, no. I have intentionally avoided any personal information about them. It's enough to know I share the same world with people like that. I will have to look them in the eyes my day in court, see their faces, but beyond that..."

"Okay," Gloria had said, smiling gently. She gave Lydia's hand another squeeze before pulling away.

"The defense will be brutal when he cross-examines you. He will try to undermine everything you say, make you question what you already know to be true. He will try and make you doubt your own resolve. Don't be swayed. You don't have to know all the answers. If he asks you to speak to something you don't know all you have to say is exactly that—you don't know. If you say what you said at Unity, after her funeral, the jury will have all of the information they need. The BBC journalist who wrote the original article on Hanan's family, and the one-year follow-up feature, can speak to the facts. You are there to

180

speak to the feelings. The people in that room need to see Hanan the way you do, the only way that does her justice."

They walk up the steps of the courthouse, Lydia's black high heels making a clicking noise each time they hit the pavement. The press is everywhere, surrounding them. She is practically blinded by the lights of the cameras as they snap pictures of her and Gary. Somehow they all seem to know her name, and they shout it again and again over one another, each reporter competing for her attention with the next.

Surrounded by people and blinded by the cameras, she has lost any sense of space and time. Gary is her lifeline. His hand, tightly gripping hers, is the only thing creating a sense of place for her in this moment. Together, they walk up stairs that never seem to end. She feels him tug, pulling her up the last few steps, into his protective embrace. He puts his arm around her, shielding her from the chaos, and she senses the darkness of stepping inside the building as the sunlight fades away behind a closing door.

Gary knows where he is going, and she follows. They take a sharp right, into a room off the main hallway, having reached their final destination. Lydia keeps her eyes trained on the floor, not wanting to know how many people are there, waiting to hear what she has to say. She is devoting all of her mental energy to try and remain calm, avoiding all potential distractions for as long as possible.

Gary guides her to a seat and takes the one next to hers. He helps her remove her coat, and places her bag on the floor beneath him. "You just worry about saying what needs to be said," he had told her in the car this morning. "I'll take care of everything else." And he was.

The judge enters, calling the room to order, and gives the floor to the prosecution. Lydia hears her name called. Deep breath, slow exhale, she gets up and walks toward the witness stand. She takes a seat, keeping her sweaty palms folded tightly together.

Hearing the prosecution approach, she finally looks up and out into the room before her. She searches for her husband first, and trains her eyes on him. He gives her a wink, and a slight nod of the chin. "Go on," he is silently telling her. "Do what you came here to do."

She allows her eyes to leave him, to take in the immensity of this place, its high ceilings, expansive white walls, and row after row of filled seats. *This is good*, Lydia thinks, taken aback by her own reaction. *The more people the better. They need to know who Hanan was. They need to know the countless others she represents, and they* need to know the hatred that exists in the world, the hatred that killed her.

Lydia's eyes look to the jury. Each face is turned toward her own, watching, wondering what she will tell them, awaiting the picture she will paint for them with her truth. And with this, she shifts her eyes to the left of the room, letting them come to their final resting place. This is where her gaze will remain for the rest of her time on the stand. She is not only here to tell the jury Hanan's story, she also came to tell *them*. One pair of blue eyes and one pair of brown stare back at her.

"The first thing you need to know about Hanan," Lydia begins, "is that she was a mother."

Epilogue

The last time she was in this room was when Mr. Luna had told them about Hanan. Lydia shudders, rubbing the goosebumps on her arms, trying to warm herself against the air conditioning that the administration always has on too high. *Yeah, it's only 7 am and already freaking 80 degrees outside, but that doesn't mean it has to be 65 inside. Have they ever heard of a summer cold?* Lydia thinks snidely to herself. *If not, everyone will have one within a week.*

Day one of Orientation Week doesn't officially start until 8 am, but Lydia needs a minute. She needs time in this room, within these walls, with the last memory this space holds for her, alone.

When she told Gary about Mr. Luna's proposal a few weeks ago, she thought he might implode. "Full-time? You just retired, then started volunteering, and look what happened."

That type of reaction was so unlike him that she didn't reply. She just sat there, chewing her crockpot chicken and veggies, watching the precipitation droplets slide down her glass of ice water onto the kitchen table.

When she finally did look up at him, he was staring out the window into the backyard, one hand resting on his napkin, clenching his fork, and the other probably in a tight fist in his lap.

"Is this what you want?" he said, quietly, imploringly.

"Yes," was her simple and apparently sufficient reply, because it didn't come up as something to be debated or argued over again.

Taking a deep breath, Lydia is taken back to the first time she'd walked through Unity's halls, and finds so much comfort in where the unknown can take people if they are willing to go.

There's a soft knock on the open door, and looking up Lydia sees Sherry, and smiles. "Well, there's a sight for sore eyes," she says. She pats the chair next to her and Sherry walks across the room and takes the seat.

"I thought I would hate it," Sherry says, staring blankly ahead at nothing in particular and into the depths of everything all at the same time. She snaps out of her reverie and looks at Lydia. "After everything, I honestly wasn't sure I could be in this room again, but here we are," she says with a small smile.

"I had the same thought," Lydia says, taking Sherry's hand and squeezing it without making eye contact. "But I think it's okay."

"Yeah," Sherry replies, barely above a whisper. "I think so too."

"Enough of this," Lydia says, eagerly brushing off the intensity of the moment. "I guess I just assumed you would be back, but what are the details?"

Sherry takes a deep breath and smiles big this time. "In all the chaos of last spring, I applied for my MA in philosophy at Georgia State and got in, but at the last minute I decided to go for an MA in education instead and was accepted. I want to be a teacher, here, at Unity."

"That's fantastic," Lydia says. "Welcome to the family."

"Yeah," Sherry continues. "It's a condensed year-round program, so in one year I'll get my credential, MA and complete my student teaching, and then hopefully Mr. Luna will hire me on as a full-time teacher."

"Fantastic, and intense," Lydia says smiling. "So, what about this year at Unity?"

"Well, like you said, my MA program is going to be intense, but Mr. Luna said I can work to fill the gaps this year. Essentially, I'll be a floating teaching assistant wherever I'm needed, which is fine, because all I care about is being with the kids. I thought about taking the year off, but honestly, Atlanta is the Unity School for me. I can't not be here," she says, looking around. "So yeah, that's me. What about you?"

"One more question," Lydia continues, the hint of hope in her voice undeniable. "How's Ashraf?"

The mere mention of his name causes Sherry's cheeks to turn a deep red and the smile playing on her lips consumes her whole face.

"Yep," Lydia remarks off-handedly. "That's what I thought, and all I needed to know."

"Okay, okay," Sherry laughs her own intensity off. "Now it's your turn."

"Well, between the trial and my daughter finding out she's pregnant..."

"Oh my god, that's amazing," Sherry interrupts. "Congratulations!"

"Thank you," Lydia says smiling. "We're pretty over the moon about it. But yeah, so with those two things going on I don't even know where the first half of the summer went. And then July was almost gone and Mr. Luna called to offer me a job as a Kindergarten teacher. So, here I am."

Sherry looks at her, shaking her head. "You just never know where things are going, do you?"

Lydia know this is more of a reflection than a question; something that rings fundamentally true for both of them.

Lydia hears a rustling behind her, and turns around to see her friend, Aida, who apparently slipped through the door undetected. "Well, look who it is," she says excitedly, leaning over and holding the woman in a deep, long embrace.

Aida smiles mischievously and holds up two bags of flaming hot Cheetos. "One for you," she says, handing a bag to Lydia. "For being brave enough to come back. And one for you," she says, handing a bag to Sherry. "For showing my granddaughter what she is made of."

"She's all the things she is because of you," Sherry says, winking at Aida knowingly. "Who says you can't have hot Cheetos for breakfast?" The bag pops open and Sherry eats a few before offering it to Aida.

"I ate mine on the way here," Aida says.

"So how about that guilty verdict. Those fuckers are going to jail for life," Lydia blurts out and the other two women stare at her.

"Sometimes the system that calls itself justice actually works," Aida replies, taking one of Lydia's hands and one of Sherry's. "Sometimes."

Discussion Guide

1. In what ways are the characters born and raised in the US (Sherry and Lydia) different from those who came to the states as Refugees (Hanan and Aida)? In what ways are they the same?

2. What is it specifically about the Unity School that unites these four women?

3. Why is Hanan so secretive about her past?

4. Why does Aida bring her granddaughter to the Holocaust Museum?

5. In what ways do we see Hanan evolve throughout the book?

6. Which of the characters can you relate to most and why?

7. What is the message of hope in this novel?

8. What are the "bridges" that these four women build?

9. How does Sherry see the world differently by the end of the book?

10. In your opinion, who is the hero of this story?

11. What are the obstacles Sherry and Ashraf face in their relationship?

12. If you could choose a different ending for the book, what would it be and why?

13. How did this novel change your perspective of refugees?

14. The friendship these women forge with one another is wonderful, and unexpected. Have you ever formed a friendship that both surprised and fulfilled you?

15. Who is your favorite character and why?

16. Do you personally identify with any of the characters and if so, why?

17. Each refugee's experience is unique. How do Hanan and Aida's journeys differ?

18. If you were to become a refugee, what aspects of home would you miss the most and why?

Recipes ≈ A Taste of Home

While food is not a central theme is this novel, it is in life. Food defines each of us on so many levels. A particular smell can immediately transport us mentally and emotionally to another time and place. The tastes of dishes we grew up with are exactly that, a taste of home.

Refugees leave home with what they can carry in their arms, which means their physical homes are always left behind. Recipes however, are carried in the mind and the heart and thus transcend place. They have the power to go wherever we go.

For that reason, food plays an intricate and invaluable role in all of our lives – whether we recognize it or not. For that purpose, each of the characters have shared a taste of what is home to them in the subsequent pages.

Aida

Bosnian Cheese Pie / Pita Sirnica

Ingredients:

- 1 lb. cottage cheese
- 11 oz. mozzarella cheese
- 7 tablespoons melted butter
- 14 oz. phyllo pastry
- 2 Eggs
- 1 teaspoon of salt

Directions:

- Using a large bowl, combine cottage cheese, mozzarella cheese, two eggs, and salt
- Stuff phyllo sheets with filling, then roll them.
- Take one sheet of phyllo pastry and spread it on the table. Using melted butter grease, it and cover with another layer of phyllo.
- Spread the filling over the shorter edge of the dough.
- Begin rolling dough into a long snake-like shape.
- Place finished strips onto baking tray in the shape of a spiral.
- Repeat above steps until you have used all ingredients.
- Using a brush, spread butter over surface of pie.
- Sprinkle on favorite seeds for additional taste and enhanced texture.
- Preheat the oven to 350°F and cook for 35 minutes.

Sherry:

Green Bean Casserole

Ingredients:

- 1 can (10 1/2 ounces), your choice of:
  - Campbell's® Condensed Cream of Mushroom Soup or
  - 98% Fat Free Cream of Mushroom Soup or
  - Condensed Unsalted Cream of Mushroom Soup
- 1/2 cup milk
- 1 teaspoon soy sauce
- 4 cups cooked cut green beans
- 1 1/3 cups French's® French Fried Onions

Directions:

- Heat the oven to 350°F. Stir the soup, milk, soy sauce, beans and **2/3 cup** onions in a 1 1/2-quart casserole. Season the mixture with salt and pepper.
- Bake for 25 minutes or until hot. Stir the bean mixture. Sprinkle with the remaining **2/3 cup** onions.
- Bake for another 5 minutes or until the onions are golden brown.

Hanan:

Knafeh

Ingredients for Syrup:

- 4 cups granulated sugar
- 2 cups water
- 1 tsp lemon juice

Directions for Syrup:

- Mix sugar, water, and lemon juice together.
- Place over medium heat and bring to boil.
- When sugar has dissolved, allow liquid to cool.

Ingredients for Knafeh:

- 4 cups shredded phyllo dough
- 8 cups grated mozzarella cheese
- 1 1/2 cups butter, melted
- 1 cup crushed pistachios

Directions for Knafeh:

- Preheat oven to 375°F.
- Completely thaw shredded phyllo dough prior to dish prep. Place in large bowl and use hands pull strands apart until the dough is completely shredded.
- Pour melted butter over shredded phyllo and mix together completely.
- Using a large round cake pan or a 9x13 baking dish firmly press half the dough into the pan.
- Spread cheese on top of dough.
- Cover cheese with remaining half of dough. Press edges together to ensure cheese doesn't leak during baking process.
- Bake for 15 minutes. Remove from oven and flip over onto a another plate for serving.
- Pour cooled simple syrup over the knafeh. Sprinkle pistachios on top and serve warm.

Lydia

Hashbrown Casserole

Ingredients:

- 1 (30-ounce) bag shredded hash brown potatoes
- 1 yellow onion (chopped)
- 2 cups shredded cheddar cheese (8 ounces)
- 1 can cream of mushroom soup (10 3/4 ounce can)
- 2 cups sour cream (16 ounces)
- salt and pepper as needed

Directions:

- Preheat oven to 375°F.
- Grease a 9 x 13 casserole dish.
- Combine potatoes, onion, cheese, soup, sour cream, salt and pepper, in large bowl and mix sufficiently.
- Pour into greased casserole dish.
- Bake for 30 - 45 or until the top is evenly browned.
- Allow 5-10 minutes to cool, serve warm.

Acknowledgements

While this novel is a work of fiction, it is inspired by real places, people, and events. The Unity School may not exist in name, but it exists in essence in the form of the International Community School in Georgia. Without naming names (you know who you are), I want to thank my Beloved Community of ICS for bravely being in the world, because by doing so, bridges are being built. The refugees that I have come to know and love, that are both my family and friends, are the single-most awe-inspiring group of humans I have had the pleasure of knowing. I wish that everyone might know you as I do – for if not, the loss is theirs and theirs alone. Refugee, you are the hero of your own story, no one else. You are the survivor, the warrior of heart, the one who perseveres.

I want to thank my husband, Rodney, for being such a supportive partner and helping me find the time and space needed to write this book. Without him, it wouldn't have been possible. To my two children, the whole of my heart, everything I do is for you.

Finally, I would like to extend heartfelt thanks to my publisher, Victor Volkman, founder of Modern History Press, and team for giving this book a home. Your experience and wisdom helped guide this work into its complete and finished form.

About the Author

Kacie LeCompte Renfro grew up in the Bay Area, CA. Following undergrad, she moved to Atlanta, GA where she worked for three years at the International Community School – an elementary charter school for Refugee and American children. Through this formative experience she found herself forever changed by the wisdom and love bestowed upon her by refugees from around the world. This school and those years are the inspiration for *The Bridges We Will Build*.

Kacie holds a BA in Philosophy and an MA in Philosophy with an emphasis in Religious studies.

Her professional career has predominantly consisted of working for various nonprofits focused on refugee resettlement and international and domestic education and aid initiatives. She currently resides in Kentucky with her husband and two children, focused on being a mom, writer and human rights advocate.

www.ingramcontent.com/pod-product-compliance
Lightning Source LLC
Chambersburg PA
CBHW071618030726
47598CB00001B/334